THE HOUR
BEFORE DARK

THE HOUR BEFORE DARK

DOUGLAS CLEGG

LEISURE BOOKS  NEW YORK CITY

A LEISURE BOOK®

First edition September 2002

Published by

Dorchester Publishing Co., Inc.
276 Fifth Avenue
New York, NY 10001

ISBN 0-8439-5044-7

The name "Leisure Books" and the stylized "L" with design are trademarks of Dorchester Publishing Co., Inc.

Printed in the United States of America.

1 2 3 4 5 6 7 8 9 10

For Stephen King—
You wrote some kind words to me early in my career, and
they meant a lot to me. Here's a novel for you—a small
token of thanks.

With additional thanks to those who lived through this: Raul
Silva, first and foremost, and Don D'Auria, my editor. Addi-
tionally, thank you to M.J. Rose, Matt Schwartz, Angela and
Richard Hoy, Tommy Dreiling, and Brian Freeman. No novel
of mine would've been out in bookstores in the past five years
if not for Leisure Books, its sales force, and its innovation
within the horror genre. It has been a great five years, thus
far. Hope there are more. Thanks to the booksellers at Mysterious Galaxy, The Book Room on Grove, The Learned Owl,
Dark Delicacies, Stars Our Destination, Adventures in Crime
& Space, Dreamhaven, Joseph Beth Booksellers, The Other
Change of Hobbit, Greene's Books & Beans, Vroman's, and
Borderlands Books—among many other independent bookstores—that have done so much to put my novels in the
hands of readers. Thanks, also, to Montilee Stormer, who was
picked to make a guest appearance in name only in this novel.
And as always, thanks to my readers—I get up every morning
and think about how I can tell a story that will keep you
wanting to turn the page. I hope *The Hour Before Dark* is up
to the task.
   The inspiration for this novel came from several things,
including my absolute love for islands, particularly the ones
along the New England coastline, and those roots of mine that
grew in New England soil. The island and characters in this
novel are entirely fictional.

SPECIAL NOTE FOR READERS: Just for those who pick up
and read *The Hour Before Dark*, there's a special FREE e-book
waiting for you. Just send an e-mail to
DarkGame@DouglasClegg.com to get it.

"Here comes a candle to light you to bed,
And here comes a chopper to chop off your head."
—traditional nursery rhyme

"There are only two ways to live your life.
One is that nothing is a miracle.
The other is as though everything is a miracle."
—Albert Einstein

PROLOGUE

1

A nightmare:

"Do you want to play the Dark Game?"

"No."

"What are you afraid of?" she asks on the other side of the door.

"You," I tell her.

2

The rules for the Dark Game are simple:

First, you need to close your eyes. Do not open them. If necessary, you can use a blindfold. In fact, because kids usually can't keep their eyes closed, blindfolds are recommended.

Second, you need to stay very still for a long time and block out all noise, except for the voice of the chosen master of the Dark Game. You must also block out all smell and all touch, except for the others whose hands you're holding. You have to join hands and form a circle. But block out everything you can.

Except the voice of the master of the Dark Game.

Third, someone has to be in control of where the Dark Game goes. To recite the litany that begins it. To direct your mind into the game.

And lastly, you must never play the Dark Game once it's dark outside.

At night, it becomes too real. You lose control of it. You can't stop it after dark.

You must start the game in the hour before dark, sometimes called the Magic Hour.

You must stop playing when night falls. Because that's when it changes.

Sometimes, you can't get out of the Dark Game once the dark comes.

The stakes heighten after dark.

It becomes real then.

It takes you over.

3

A nightmare:

On the other side of the door, her voice again: "Don't be afraid," she says. "Don't be afraid."

The door swings wide, and from outside, in what seems an

eternal twilight, she enters with arms outstretched, wanting me.

Wanting me.

"I am here," she says.

"I won't play the Dark Game," I tell her.

"Too late," she says. "You can't stop playing it."

4

I've come to believe that absolute evil has a human face.

And absolute innocence is the brother of evil.

I was once innocent, but then I began playing that game.

5

When I was nine, I went wandering on a chilly early evening.

My father owned a vast property called Hawthorn, which included a house, some woods, and a smokehouse, as well as a stream and a duck pond. It seemed like an endless world to me then.

A man found me in the woods—a man whose face I have somehow erased from my memory as part of a feverish week that vanished for me as a child.

He told me that I had blood on my face. He washed it off in an ice-cold stream, splashing it all over my forehead and hands. I felt as if I'd been bitten up by mosquitoes even in the middle of winter.

He walked me through the night-smitten woods until we approached the back of my home.

It was a moment out of time that I could not place within my other memories—why I had wandered, or why I had what might've been blood on my face, or even the face of the man who had washed blood from me.

That was childhood; it ended; I closed its door; I grew up and moved away.

Many years later, when he was in his fifties and I was in my late twenties, my father wandered at twilight, and opened the door to a mystery.

PART ONE

"Oranges and lemons
Say the bells of St. Clemens . . ."
—*traditional*

CHAPTER ONE

1

It attacked with the ferocity of a wild animal.

2

At the point my father, Gordie Raglan, entered the smoke-house, his life was nearly over.

Even if you'd told him that, it probably wouldn't have stopped him.

Knowing my father, he probably had been thinking about the Boston Celtics and if they were going to kick any ass that winter. Or whether he was going to have shepherd's pie without peas for supper when he got back. Or how he was going to repair the half-rotted roof of the cabin down by the duck pond when he knew he should just let the cabin fall apart.

He was a guy who was fairly transparent in his thinking and, though smart, was a simple man. He liked his world to be orderly.

He always looked to me—in photographs and my childhood memories—like a solid structure. A man created for purpose, duty, and care. Even at his worst (he had his terrible days, as all fathers will), he seemed a moral compass within a world spun out of control.

He liked the people around him to be somewhat predictable, which is no doubt why he stayed on Burnley Island most of his life. His main loves were, in fact, the Boston Celtics, what was for supper, home repairs, and his daughter's two dogs, which, by right of whose house they lived in, were his as well. They were rescued greyhounds named for Welsh legend (Mab and Madoc) and might've met terrible fates if he and my sister, Brooke, hadn't gone over to the racetrack in Rhode Island a few years previous to grab two pups that weren't quite right for racing.

Perhaps all he thought about was what was bringing him out in the storm in the first place. There were, at the time, a thousand guesses for this, but none of them got near the mark.

He hadn't called the dogs. This was unusual for him. He might go out to see who was in the driveway or what a certain noise had been, but he nearly always called the greyhounds out when he did that.

Not that he went out often at twilight or most evenings. Not that Mab and Madoc would've gone with him—those dogs dreaded foul weather as much as they did the local veterinarian's office.

But still, he would've called them. If he had, Brooke

would've known he was leaving. She was at the other end of the house—down the boxcar hallways that led like a puzzle from one room to another without end, built that way by some ancient Raglan with a bizarre sense that every room should open on another room. Brooke was down in what was called the second great room, with the dogs at her feet. Reading a mystery novel, halfway falling asleep, having been up most of the previous night.

That afternoon, Gordie Raglan had drunk half a mug of hot cocoa before he left the house. He had a fondness in November for comfort foods—chicken soup, warm cocoa, and shepherd's pie. Cocoa was his favorite. He loved it more laced with a bit of bourbon, but this particular night there was nary a drop in the house.

He no doubt had chewed gum as he headed for the front door—Wrigley's Spearmint or Big Red, either one could be his favorite of the day. He wore his funny red cap—a red wool skullcap that once belonged to one of his sons, but to which he had become attached over the past several years. He drew on a red parka that he'd received as a present the previous Christmas. There were boots by the door, but he chose to wear his scuffed, ten-year-worn Oxfords. It was his storm outfit. No umbrella. Dad didn't believe in umbrellas.

The cap made him look youthful or silly, depending upon who was asked about it. His peppered gray hair no doubt stuck out of the skullcap. My father was generally late with haircuts once November had begun, unless his daughter had been after him about it.

He rarely left the house after three or four P.M. anymore,

unless something needed immediate attention around the grounds of his home.

But something got him outside, during the storm.

3

Barely light out anymore, the fury of the storm brought an early veil of darkness with it.

Something made him put down the mug, slip on his shoes, leaving them untied as he went out the front door of his home. He had a flashlight with him. Around the house, he always kept a flashlight by his side, as much as he kept his spot heater in whichever room he chose to occupy.

Only a man as stubborn as Gordie Raglan would've traipsed out in the worst storm of November to do some mysterious errand in what amounted to a rundown stone shelter that had been locked up for years.

It had been a tempest out at sea, but on the island it was a rough kind of magic—a Nor'easter blowing down across the bogs and ponds and the slips and beaches, through the woods with their sheltering pines, with all the beauty that a terrific storm brings—the overly dramatic light of creation itself swirling through that island.

(I had loved the winter storms when I was a boy. I had gone out into them sometimes and held my arms out—imagine a boy of ten doing that—as if it were my own power that brought the wind and rain.)

But this particular night the rain was incessant.

Maddening.

The lightning, a constant flashbulb in the eyes. Thunder roared overhead like drunken Nordic gods.

He must've been swearing under his breath, given his limp and what he had always called the "old pain," doubly frustrated, for at one point his left shoe went into the mud, deep.

He left it there, a few feet from the entrance to the smokehouse.

The smokehouse itself was hardly much of a shelter. It was a small one-room stone house that had at one time been the place where meat was hung to smoke and dry. It had been kept locked for years.

He had the key with him.

4

He would not have been considered tall by any stretch of the imagination, but there was something in his broad shoulders and barrel chest that indicated a large, imposing figure.

Upon entering the small room, he smelled old smoky odor and the pungent stink of earth in the air. Behind him, the door slid shut—creaking with the wind that howled outside.

He spun around, annoyed.

The rain had been coming down in sheets for nearly an hour. He directed the flashlight's beam to the small, thick square of glass that was the only window. The sky darkened with clouds and a somber grayness. The door banged back and forth briefly, then shut again. Branches scraped the low rooftop.

He glanced back into the darkness, perhaps.

Then up—the ceiling, highest at about six feet, was arched.

He looked back at the door and its window.

The square of light through its glass.

Twilight outside. Rain began hitting the window.

He shot the flashlight beam around the ceiling. He glanced down along the rough stone walls.

He might have heard what would be a clash of metal, like a knife being sharpened on stone.

He heard sound—perhaps someone behind him?

The first slice came down on his shoulder.

He dropped the flashlight.

The next slice caught him on the back of the leg. Something stung the place between his shoulder blades. A cold blade thrust into his back.

After an hour, the flashlight's beam grew feeble.

He was not yet dead.

The door to the small stone structure swung back and forth, and then closed again.

It grew dark outside, from descending night and the storm. Branches of the old hawthorn tree scraped the roof as the rain battered down. Lightning flashed across the gently sloping hills and rocky pastures, followed by a rolling boom of thunder.

The storm, the end of a powerful Nor'easter that had begun off the coast farther south and had ridden up into New England on the jet stream, howled and screamed and groaned through the night.

The lights went out at the farmhouse that stood less than a mile away as the rain turned gradually to sleet and then snow with the falling temperature.

The first snow of the year swept through on the heels of the storm. It frosted the fields and woods.

There was something about the New England woods, and in particular, this island off the Atlantic coast, off Massachusetts, that created a very real isolation within the beauty of a winter storm.

The first snow, a dusting across the pines and oaks, with the last stalks of the balding pasture thrust up through the glittering whiteness.

A pastoral moment: the farmhouse in the distance, the stone smokehouse, the swirls of fine snow, the smell of woodfire in the air from chimneys near and far, and the night, as it descended.

5

This is the story of my family.

Call me Nemo, for that was the name my sister saddled me with when I was a kid. It stuck. Other things stuck from childhood, as well—including the Brain Fart.

The Brain Fart was a week in the memories of my brother, sister, and me that had just disappeared without warning. We imagined it, after a while, as an enormous gassy cloud that had shot out of our ears and floated like mist somewhere above the island before drifting off to sea. By the time I'd turned twenty-eight, that Brain Fart seemed to hover in the air again. None of us knew what had caused the Brain Fart. It had seemed spontaneous, although a certain amount of fever had accompanied it. We had lost a week, which, for children like us, seemed like an entire season.

I suspected even then that the week of the Brain Fart was important, and in the end, I guess it was.

But the beginning was my father, and how he had walked into the smokehouse and set in motion a mystery that drew me back to the island in the first place.

And how my sister, Brooke, had found him.

CHAPTER TWO

1

"What we do in life that determines who we are, we do alone," my father told me when I was much younger and had done something that was no doubt terrible. I can't recall what it was I'd done, but his words had been engraved in my brain since then.

He also was a great proponent of the phrase "Even one person can make a difference in the world. Even the smallest among us."

He was one of those fathers who had those kinds of chats with his children.

2

The current smokehouse was built sometime before 1850. It consisted of one room with a fairly low roof—five feet high for most of it, and just under six feet at its center—that had once been used for smoking fish and meat for my great-great-greats. There had been another smokehouse on the same spot before 1835, but the story was that it had burned down, for it was made of wood. The stones were local, quarried at what was, for most of the twentieth century, a rocky area and a pit full of water, out among the pines just two miles to the north of the property. The newer stone smokehouse had remained intact for more than 150 years. In his lifetime, my father only once had to replace the roof, long before I was born, after a hurricane had hit the island. It had a dirt floor when we'd been children. At some point, my father had set down oak planks, then put another set of pine planks over these as a kind of floor. He'd used pegs and nails to connect the boards, but it had been a very rough, uncouth floor that had warped a bit over the years.

It was always cold in the smokehouse, no matter what the season.

When I was very little, my siblings and I used the smoke-house as something of a hideaway to play games in; then, when it became the place of all punishment for us (spankings, lessons-to-be-learned-from-our-misdeeds, and the Time Out room), the place lost its enchantment. I mainly remembered it for being nasty and chilly, and for making me feel as if I were going to be trapped inside it forever and no one would ever come get me.

Years later, my father put a deadbolt on it because he said that he found two summer people making out in it (I suspect now that they were doing more than making out). The smoke-house became mainly just another object of quaintness on our

property, of equal interest as the duck pond and the old pump
out back.

3

A reconstruction of the crime scene:

The door battering, the flashlight on the wood slat floor,
the way his body was positioned when he'd be found, and the
approximate time of the electricity going out at the house.

His shoe, in the thick mud.

His hands, severed at the wrists.

The blood, which had made the first policeman on the
scene think that the floor and walls had been painted a messy
red.

Joe Grogan, the local police chief of the very small police
force on the island, knew better.

The smokehouse door was locked, always. There were no
windows but the one in the door, and that was too small for
anyone to fit through. It had not been broken or removed.

My father had let himself into the smokehouse.

He had unlocked the door.

He may have even let the murderer in as well.

4

No one alive really knew what had happened in the smokehouse that night. All anyone knew, it turned out, was that
something must have drawn him there.

Here, the theories seemed to scatter to the winds: He knew
whom he was going to meet, or he guided them there, or they

jumped him, or . . . well, it was pretty wild, the variety of theories. It might've been a stranger, or a group of thugs. Getting on and off the island would have been difficult.

And the modus operandi of the killing? To imagine that one human being could inflict this on another seemed beyond the reach of all sanity. It had been a curved blade of some sort (none was found). Whoever had done this—in mid-November, when there was only one ferry a day out to the island—had somehow eluded authorities and gone off-island without anyone seeing them. How could that have happened?

But the basics were that my father had left the house a bit earlier, with a parka on and a flashlight in his hand.

Brooke had been reading in her bedroom, she told the police, and was rarely aware of her father's comings and goings at night. The house was large. The floor plan, which twisted like a snake along the grounds, allowed for various ways of leaving and entering. One room opened on the other. There were no hallways—just one boxy room after another, upstairs and down.

With the doors between the rooms closed, as they were, it was hard to hear one sound from the other end of the house. Even the dogs didn't hear beyond one or two rooms, at best.

Brooke had once gone a week without ever seeing her father, so completely independent was her life within the house where she'd been raised.

I got the details later, but by then it had already been called the worst murder in the history of eastern Massachusetts. I'm fairly sure that wasn't entirely true. There were other terrible murders—all the time, I suppose—but they'd been forgotten in the fickle memory of those who did the recording of recent history. The Brain Farts of the media.

Surely, there were murders daily on the mainland, in the crackhouses and dens of vice that existed there, but those deaths were seen as somehow less interesting than my father's—a war hero, a survivor of torture and deprivation, a family man who raised three children nearly by himself, cut down at the last by some psycho with a sharp blade on a resort island after the resorts had all closed for the winter. It was news, as they say. It would keep some young reporters in line for a promotion if they made enough of the murder.

Sure, Burnley was no Martha's Vineyard, no Nantucket— we had no celebrities to speak of, and the rich didn't flock to the island as much as the wannabe rich did. But it still sounded cool, no doubt, to turn in a story to a newspaper editor that had in it the words: *resort, island, murder,* and *war hero.*

It certainly was the worst murder that Burnley Island had ever known, and the worst to ever take place near Hawthorn, the house where I had grown up.

"Life is full of casualties," my father told me when I asked him why Granny had to die when I was young. He was one of those wonderful fathers who brought life's lessons out of any situation. "We look away until we have no choice. Then we examine them, remember them, and look away again, as if we're not meant to think too much about them, but to live. Just live and forget."

Brooke found my father dead in the smokehouse, but apparently could not look away.

He had been dead since seven or eight the previous night.

5

The storm's howling had kept her up most of the night.

She had argued with Dad the day before. She had avoided him, which was fairly easy to do at Hawthorn. She was very sad about something, but told me that none of it mattered once Dad died.

She said later: "I had the worst night of my life. Let's leave it at that. I had a big fire going in the back bedroom, and even with that, the place was freezing. I could not get it warm enough. I went to take a hot bath, but that didn't work. I just wanted to go to sleep. I couldn't. Hadn't eaten. It was the barometric pressure. It always does that to me when winter comes on. It plummets and my mood just goes. I feel like I want to bury myself alive or just lie in bed or walk through the rooms, back and forth all night, until the headache goes away. The dogs even stay away from me. They sense it. All I could think about was what was wrong with the world."

Brooke had slept late—'til two.

She hadn't even thought about where our father had gone. It was not unusual for him to be inspecting parts of the property or running his errands in town in the afternoon. She had made some eggs, toast, and coffee, but would not eat them because she said she had an upset stomach from the night before. She left a plate of eggs and toast out on the kitchen table, thinking that her father might be back at any moment from his errands and would want a snack.

She thought it unusual that he had not already made a pot of coffee earlier in the day.

Even so, he might've gone to have coffee at Croder-Sharp-Callahan, where he could talk women and weather with Percy Shaw and Reg Miller, both of whom spent their lives at that lunch counter having what Brooke called their Old Salt conversations. She had warned her father several times that if he hung out with them, he would grow old before his time and then no woman would have him.

Brooke took the dogs out for a walk down to the woods.

She guided them back up to the dirt road that ran from the back of the property up to the main road. She saw Paulette Doone and her husband, Ike, in their truck on the way to get groceries in the village. Paulette had mentioned that the lights were out in half the island because of the storm. "Won't be back on 'til six. Maybe eight," Paulette said.

"Maybe ten," Ike said.

Brooke had mentioned that her lights came back up sometime after midnight.

The Doones lived in the Cape Cod house set back from the road. Paulette asked if the Captain (although my father had been anything but a captain, he was known as the Captain or Cap by the villagers since he'd been a boy) needed his favorite kind of candy from the store, or a prescription from Hempstead Apothecary (because she knew he'd had a bad cold all week). Brooke had asked if they could pick up some Halls Mentho-lyptus and maybe some kind of over-the-counter inhaler, something to help his sinuses. Brooke mentioned the barometric pressure and was generally furious that the cabin by the pond had flooded. Paulette mentioned Jesus and God and being saved, which is something that she never seemed to tire of bringing up, no matter how rude Brooke got in return. Paulette felt that Brooke was agitated (as she informed the police chief when asked). Paulette even called her "heated" later to her husband, but Ike privately thought that Brooke had seemed radiant, as if she were in love, with a rosy complexion and bright eyes. Paulette had interpreted this as something bad, because she felt that Brooke was a dangerous woman to the married women on the island—and Paulette elbowed her husband whenever he glanced at their attractive neighbor for too long.

Brooke told Paulette that she thought her father might be in the village, at the lunch counter talking storms and boats and the upcoming winter festivities in the village.

"I wouldn't mind a movie," Brooke added.

Paulette had glanced at Ike, and then nodded. "Sure, we can go by the video store. Any particular one?"

Brooke had asked for one with Matt Damon or the Harry Potter movie if it was in. Paulette had blanched at the mention of "that movie that promotes witches" but felt that there might be an old-fashioned movie like *The Ten Commandments* or *Ben-Hur* that Brooke might enjoy more.

"If we see the Captain, we'll drag him home," Paulette had told her.

"If you see him, tell him we're having chili tonight," Brooke had said. "Hormel's. And corn bread if I can find any corn flour. Can you pick me up some in town? I might be out. Chili's always better with corn bread. Or spoon bread. Something with corn. He wants shepherd's pie, but I won't make it three nights in a row. He can cook his own supper if he wants what he wants."

"Ike is like that, too," Paulette said. Her burly and often-sullen husband gave a grunt at that. Paulette mentioned to Joe Grogan later on that Brooke had seemed preoccupied, as if speaking to them had been a disturbance for her.

"I thought she was very sad. She looked like she hadn't slept in days," Paulette had mentioned, giving Joe Grogan something that was as close to the Evil Eye as he had ever in his life witnessed. "But *you* know, Joe, women like *that*. Well, they don't sleep much. Do they? I'd say more, but I'm a Christian woman, and I don't like to speak like that."

6

Because our father often hiked the mile to the village and got rides home with neighbors or anyone he could talk into giving him a lift, this was just another ordinary day.

Brooke had her own inner turmoil.

She told others that she had been anxious and somewhat depressed. She talked to Dr. Connelly in the village a week earlier about perhaps getting a change in prescription for her sleeping medicine. "Are you depressed?" he'd asked.

"Not depressed," she said. "Just not quite feeling like myself."

He had asked her if she might want to see a therapist on the mainland—he knew a good one in Falmouth. She told him she'd consider it, but she didn't think talking out her problems would be the answer.

She fought the urge to be impatient with Mab and Madoc. They'd run off to the woods chasing squirrels or rabbits, and returned a long while later, covered head to foot with mud. She went and checked on the cabin—the damage to the roof was extensive. She made a mental note to talk to her father about just tearing it down before it turned into some kind of eyesore.

The snow melted where the sun hit it. In the shade, the duck pond had a thin scum of ice on its surface that had not hardened.

At four, she noticed that one of the trees near the smokehouse had been split in two by lightning. She said she had been standing in the greenhouse, with the windows steamed over, and feeling the warmth of the place.

"I was looking at something—I thought it was mist coming in from the road. It was nearly beautiful. It was twilight—dark came early—and this romantic, soft mist just slowly poured along the road. Remember how Granny used to say you could see angels in the fog? I remembered her saying it, and I almost saw an angel in the mist," she said of it. "And then, I noticed the half-fallen tree."

One of the hawthorns in particular, but also the young oak that had not quite grown to adulthood yet.

Lightning, she assumed, had ripped across the trees. She was thankful there hadn't been a fire.

She went to see if there was any other damage.

Her feet crunched in the glaze of snow that hadn't quite melted in the shadow of the smokehouse.

She saw his shoe, his brown Oxford, stuck in mud—now frozen, she found, as she tried to pull it out. She ended up leaving it where it was, mired.

She glanced first up to the road, perhaps hoping that Paulette and Ike would still be there.

Then to the fields and the pasture—and beyond it, the woods. Mab and Madoc were running down into the duck pond, splashing around.

She glanced up at the sky with its overcast gloom.

Then she went to the low door of the smokehouse and touched it. Something told her not to—she told me later that it was an electric shock of memory—of never liking the smokehouse since before she could remember. Of remembering my screams as Dad spanked me there, or of remembering Bruno crying there for no reason at all when he was six or seven, sobbing and telling her that the smokehouse gave him nightmares.

When she touched the door, it moved a bit.

She grasped the latched handle, expecting the deadbolt that had been applied years ago to keep it shut, and surprise, surprise, it opened outward.

And that's when she found him.

(She told me later, "I wasn't sure whether it was him or not for a second. It was something I'd never seen before in my life. It was as if something had exploded, but had been reconstructed again. Something about it was like a dream—or a nightmare—something I'd visited before. As if I'd had some premonition of this. And my brain just short circuited. It just seemed to fade, and I couldn't think. I went somewhere else in my mind, I suppose. Somewhere safe.")

She sat and stared at him for hours before contacting anyone. I don't want to even imagine how she could've sat there on the cold floor, blood everywhere.

My father.

And Brooke sat there in the icy stench of death.
She called someone just after ten that night.
Her older brother.
Me.

CHAPTER THREE

1

I had a nightmare for all those years, and it repeated itself in a never-ending loop, now and again, at my most anxious times:

In it, we played the Dark Game and could not stop. It was as if the Dark Game had kept playing in some compartment of our minds even as we each grew up.

2

Brooke left no message for me other than to say "Nemo" on my answering machine.

It was a name I hadn't heard since I was about fourteen or fifteen. Even then, it was mocking.

My real name, Fergus, was redubbed Nemo in my ninth year when Brooke discovered Jules Verne—or at least the

Disney version of Jules Verne's *Twenty Thousand Leagues Under the Sea*. She decided that because of my interest in sailing craft and my willingness to eat fried squid in a dare with Harry Withers, I must be kin to the infamous captain. Since I preferred Nemo to my real name, which just didn't fit for me, I had taken it on while on the island. After I left Burnley, once in college, I reverted to Gus, a diminutive of Fergus that didn't annoy me too much. But the islanders knew me as Nemo Raglan. As did my sister. "Nemo, Nemo," she repeated.

After saying it, she hung up.

I listened to it twice, then erased it. I called her back. The phone rang several times. I heard the familiar clicks and that strange wind tunnel-like noise that I always heard whenever I called the island. Finally, the message machine picked up.

"Brooke? It's Nemo. Good to hear from you. What's up? Call me back."

Later, I got a nervous call from my younger brother, Bruno.

3

"Brooke said she called you," my brother said. "You've been out."

It was nearly one A.M. I was half-asleep. Beth, whom I'd been out with that night, lay beside me and turned over, clutching a pillow.

" 'Lo? Who's—asleep. Bruno? That you?" I asked.

Beth made some small noise that was part-snore and part-groan. I reached over and stroked her back lightly. She made my bed smell of lavender and something murkily sexual, a musk, an odor of femaleness that I enjoyed. I loved her scent. I pulled the sheet up around her shoulders to keep her warm. I wanted to kiss her again, just on the back of the neck. She turned over, annoyed even in sleep.

"Someone's with you," Bruno said, his voice not quite as Yankee as it had once been. It was gentler.

"What's up?" I repeated, annoyed that I could not cuddle up with Beth and drift to sleep. "I tried calling Brooke back, but there was no answer."

"You need to come home now. Tomorrow. A lot's going on."

"Like?"

"Dad's dead."

We both were silent for what seemed like minutes.

I gasped a word or two, meaningless. I felt as if someone had knocked the wind out of me. I leaned back on the pillows. I looked up at the shadows that the bedroom windows cast on the ceiling, with the curtains moving slowly back and forth from the slight draft. I closed my eyes and fought back a stupid anguished cry that wanted to come out of my body.

"Call me tomorrow," Bruno said. "We can talk then. To-night's bad. There's more to it. Fly in tomorrow. I'll pick you up in Boston."

Then he hung up. No more details. Bruno was like that. Sometimes he spoke in telegrams, as if he were being charged by the word.

I called him back several times, but there was no answer.

4

I spent a sleepless night, made worse by not knowing how exactly my father had died. When I did close my eyes—for what felt like a few minutes—a dream came abruptly with the ferocity of a nightmare. I watched outside myself (in the dream) as twilight descended on Hawthorn. The trees seemed to list to the side as my consciousness broke through them. I saw three children, standing in a circle, holding hands. It was me as a little boy, my sister, and my brother. Walking slowly to the left and then the right in the summer grass. Then, with the swiftness and brute force that can accompany shifts in a dream, I stood in the darkness, somewhere, and I heard my little brother Bruno say the words, "Here comes a candle to light you to bed."

In the dream, the phone began ringing, and I let go (for I held my brother's small hand in my left, and my sister's in my right) and cried out, "Someone get the phone! The phone's ringing! Get the phone!"

Someone asked, "What are you afraid of?"

Then I awoke. Covered in sweat. Breathing hard.

I gave up on sleep for the night.

It was maddening. I tried to call my brother back every few minutes until dawn. I left message after message. Finally his answering system must have been full and stopped taking my messages. I could only stare at the walls. I went in the bathroom and curled up on the floor, just to feel its coldness and to be in a small space. For some reason, small, dark spaces often made me feel protected. I felt like a child. I didn't want to think. I didn't want to imagine my father's face. I fought to pretend that somehow this wasn't the whole story, that perhaps my father had a stroke and Bruno had gotten it wrong. Or perhaps he was in a coma—as much as that doesn't sound better than death, it is. It would give me hope. I wanted to hope badly. I hadn't seen my father in years, and I had loved him, but I had hoped that in a few months, I'd go back and see him and we'd have a good conversation and he'd tell me that I'd turned into a good man.

It was never going to happen. Nothing worse than lying on a cold bathroom floor at four in the morning and looking at the bottom of the white wooden door and wishing that the world could somehow change, magically, to suit your own needs.

I returned to bed, snuggling against Beth, as if I could just plow into her flesh and disappear, along with everything pounding in my head.

Beth left well before sunrise, annoyed by my pacing and turning in bed. It was hard not to want her. She was one of those women who seemed to know that she was headed for great things in life, and she had a great body and cute face to accompany her vision of the future, and even a first-rate mind in many ways—how could I not want her? She was a prize. I knew well why she wouldn't want me. I'd been laid off a few days earlier. I wasn't headed, apparently, for great things in life. I could predict the most ordinary life ahead of me, and somehow, I knew I'd muddle through it. I burned for more, but in my twenty-eight years my only extraordinary contribution to the world was that I'd written a novel that apparently no one had read. Younger, I'd wanted to change the world. But by that morning, I was just hoping that I could rise above the usual storms of life and get through it.

I suspect that I was looking for a woman to rescue me and

make love the extra ingredient, and perhaps not even love, but some kind of great sex that passed for love in a city like Washington, D.C.

I had lowered expectations for all that life had to offer.

When we kissed goodbye, it was brief and forgettable. Our lips barely touched. I got the sad feeling one gets at the end of a misbegotten affair: as if it reminds us that we're merely animals, enjoying mating for mysterious reasons in order to pass time until something else comes along.

"My dad died last night," I said.

"I'm sorry," she whispered. She kissed my cheek. "That's terrible." Silently, she telegraphed without moving her lips once: *I need to get to the office.*

"I need to go up there. I guess. I'm going to need to go up for a while," I said. I didn't expect her to say too much else at that point. It was over between us. I was the one feeling discarded. I was the revenge in life for all men who treated women badly—I was the lightning rod of the wrath of women whose loves had walked away from them. I didn't really give a damn. I just wanted to pretend for a minute with her. And for her to play along. I wanted her to embrace me and emanate human warmth. To experience the smallest spark of sexual fire between us so that I'd feel that there was something else in the world other than the ice that had crept into my blood during the night.

She looked at me as if she were worried for a minute that I might fall apart on her—and that she might have to deal with it, when all she wanted was to be out of my life.

"Look," she said. "You—"

"No, it's all right," I said.

"What I mean is, what you need isn't here. So don't feel bad about leaving."

"What do I need?" I asked, a somber puppy staring at her.

"Something you left behind somewhere," she said. "I don't know what it is. I just know it's not here. You'll find it." She kissed me on the forehead like I was a little boy. "You're the kind who finds what he's after."

She meant these as words of comfort, but something in her tone gave me a slight chill. It created a slim dread within me—as if I knew that something was scratching at my window in the middle of some endless twilight. As if her words echoed something I felt, but not something that was good within me. Something about the home I'd grown up in that had never felt right to me.

And I was after it. I would find what it was.

5

I watched her dress, knowing it would be the last time. In my head, the words "Death and the Maiden." My father's voice. Sometimes his voice was in my head, in times of crisis. My imagining of his voice comforted me. His voice soothed the nicks and scars of life. In the years since I last saw him, last set foot in his house, I had internalized him.

What we do in life that determines who we are, we do alone.

6

I had already drunk a pot of coffee by eight thirty.

I made reservations for a flight to Logan Airport, charging

it on a credit card I should not have even had let alone used. Somewhere in there, I called my father's house more than ten times without an answer. I had a minor-league migraine by nine A.M. Black circles under my eyes, a feeling of drymouth and that wound-up tightness in my gut of caffeine overflow. Showered in less than five minutes, and dressed carelessly in whatever was not lying on the floor of the closet. Packing involved me throwing everything in three suitcases, and when that was done, it seemed I had left nothing of value in my apartment. I looked at the suitcases: None was huge. *My life, in three suitcases.*

I finally got hold of my brother. "Hello?" I asked. "Bruno?"

"Nemo, Nemo," he said as if grasping the name for the first time. "So, can you get a flight?"

"Cost me a fortune. You tell the airlines it's an emergency, and they triple the charge. I get in at one."

"Okay. I'll be at Logan."

"What the hell happened?" I asked.

"Somebody killed him," he said. "It's terrible. Look, we can talk when I pick you up at the airport."

"Are you crazy? Someone killed him? What?"

But Bruno had already hung up the phone.

Imagined my dad's face.

Fury coursed through my blood.

I wanted to destroy my father's killer. A front-row seat to an execution. I wanted someone to hurt for what they'd done.

CHAPTER FOUR

1

On the plane, midflight, I closed my eyes as I sat in my seat near the window.

I felt numb, tired, and far older than I was.

Soon, a mix of dream and memory came upon me. I was a boy, back on the island, again. It was dark, and I stood in dirt, my hands tied behind my back—some childhood game. Something pressed against my eyes, but in the dark I couldn't tell what it was. I heard someone tell me—was it my father?—that I needed to keep my hands to myself. I heard my sister, somewhere nearby, recite a nursery rhyme. I heard Bruno breathing—his four-year-old self with his slightly deviated septum breathing through his nostrils, like a light wind through creaky boards. I felt a strange comfort there, as if we were being held tight again by both our parents, snuggling against my mother's bosom, or pressed against my father's arms, falling down into sleep as if it were a cool, dark place.

I opened my eyes, to the airplane, to the gray clouds outside the window.

All I had ever wanted as a boy was to leave the island. I wasn't even sure what I wanted as an adult. I had nothing but confusion in my life.

Now this.

2

At Logan Airport, Bruno met me with anxiety on his brow in the form of lines I wouldn't have thought a twenty-three-year-old would've had, and dark circles beneath his eyes. Yet he had managed to pull himself together enough to brighten a bit when he saw me. He waved, and then came over to give me a shoulder squeeze. It passed for a hug between us, although it felt like an obligation fulfilled.

"How was the flight?"

"Terrorist free," I said.

"That's bad luck," he said. "Saying things like that."

"How bad can it get?"

"Pretty damn bad, you ask me," he said. "You're always trying to be funny." Then he cracked a bit of a smile, shaking his head. " 'Terrorist free,' he says."

"You gonna tell me some more about all this?" I asked. "Who did it? Who killed him?"

"Nobody knows," Bruno said.

"What the hell does that mean?"

"It means nobody knows," he said.

3

My younger brother, at twenty-three, was strapping and mus-
cular without seeming affected—he had a dollop of physical
grace, which was in direct conflict with the generally messy
way he had been screwing up his life. He was a natural athlete,
had been since he was six or seven and staged swimming races
at the beach or impromptu soccer games in the pasture. He
had only just slipped into his prime—no longer the scrawny
kid, he had taken on the look of an island tourist—tanned,
even at the outset of winter, sandy-blond hair; and that peculiar Yankee quality of having thin lips; and a slender, sharp
nose; smallish eyes made larger by round spectacles that softened his sharp features; and basic handsomeness. I possessed
none of these qualities. He and Brooke got the handsome and
beautiful genes—my mother's. They both had her coloring
and her lankiness. People often looked at them as if detecting
an attractive scent. I was more like my father, although tall. I
was dark, and the only compelling feature to me (since women
had mentioned it) were my blue eyes. Black Irish had somehow snuck into the Welsh gene pool of the Raglans.

He was dressed as well as you could ask a recent college
grad to be dressed—jeans, a scruffy old cotton shirt with a
dominant coffee stain where his heart would be, and a brown
leather jacket. And he still looked like the terse and generally
quiet kid brother I used to regularly have to defend in ele-

mentary school from the bullies when he was still small and scrawny.

I nearly hugged him, but he drew back. I noticed then that his eyes were as bloodshot as mine, and there was a surface tension to his expression.

4

He slipped on a pair of ill-fitting sunglasses and shook my hand, formally. He picked up one of my bags. "I'd say it's great to see you, but under the circumstances . . ." he said.

"I was trying to call all night. Drove me nuts."

"Brooke turned the phones off," he said. "It was constant. A barrage."

"Jesus," I said, stopping in the middle of the crowded ramp at Logan Airport. "What exactly . . . what happened?"

"Reporters. What a crappy job they got. Calling all trage-dies and milking them," he said. Avoiding my question. He didn't want to veer to the topic of the murder. "It's funny none of them called you. I mean, not even Grogan?"

I shook my head slightly. Shrugged. "Nobody remembers I exist."

"Ha. Some remember."

"I'm sure they'll get hold of me soon enough."

"Your old friend's been asking about you."

"Which one?"

He looked at me funny. Like I was fishing for something. "You think I'm going to say Pola."

"No," I said.

"I saw her on Monday," Bruno said. He didn't add: *She*

asked about you. Perhaps Pola Croder, who had been my high school sweetheart, hadn't thought about me in years. "She looks good. She's a remarkable woman, I think."

"So who's asking about me?"

"Withers."

I shrugged. "He's got my cell phone number."

"I know. He told me. He's waiting for you to get here. He's the only reporter we let in the house last night."

"He's still there?"

"No, he went home. I thought he was your old best friend."

"Yeah, I guess he is. Sorry," I said. "I feel like crap. You look like crap. Must be hell out there. Burnley must be buzzing with this one."

"None of it means shit," he said. His usual understatement. "Look, we've got a special boat—borrowed just for you. I brought an extra coat in the back. It's pretty damn cold out there right now."

"I hate winter," I said. "Dead trees. Dead everything. Dead dead dead." Then I added, "Sorry, that was a weak attempt at humor."

Bruno made some noise in the back of his throat that was both muffled cough and disapproval. "Breaking the tension is good, I guess," he said. "Me, I got Jumblies."

"Jumblies" was Raglan-speak for mixed-up feelings. Granny used the word, and after she died, I made up stories for my little sister and brother about creatures called Jumblies that hopped in peoples' mouths and made them confused.

I guess I had Jumblies in me at that moment, too.

Ten minutes later, in the car, we drove onto the highway.

5

"Who do they think did it?" I asked, as a blur of wintry Boston sped around us.

"Like I know. They haven't quite figured it out. Who does that . . . kind of thing? Psychos? Maniacs?"

"God," I said, covering my face with my hands. "I don't even want to think of Dad like that. I can't believe it. I just can't. Brooke okay?"

"Guess," Bruno said. Then he added, "No, I mean. *No.* How can she be? I'm not okay. Christ, he was red. He was red. It was that bad. I wouldn't have known it was him. If Brooke hadn't told me."

"You saw the body?"

He glanced at me, sidelong. I felt some sort of repressed fury, as if he never wanted to think about seeing our father's corpse again for as long as he lived.

We didn't talk again until we were nearly to the coastline.

I watched the speedometer, cringed when the back end of the little car slid on a patch of ice or rattled across a pothole, and just hoped we'd make it at all.

"You wouldn't believe last night," Bruno said.

Then he told me.

6

Bruno had been with a buddy of his, having a beer at the local pub in the village, when Brooke called him on his cell phone.

He ran out of the pub and down to the police station—a few blocks away. When he got there, he saw Brooke shivering, covered with a blanket. Her hair wet. It was the blood. She'd lain down in the blood, next to our father and just gone catatonic or something. She was covered with blood, only he said it looked brownish and not red at all (as he had expected). She didn't recall the hours that had passed. Then she'd gotten up and left the smokehouse, dragging herself back inside, called me. Then she had called Joe Grogan.

There were already unfamiliar faces at Grogan's office—it was just about midnight, and cops had begun arriving. Some of the neighbors were there, as well. Brooke had been screaming in the house afterward, just standing in the living room screaming. The Doones had called over because they heard the noise, and Brooke picked up the phone but had hung it up again before saying anything. Paulette Doone then called the police. Paulette had told them she thought she'd seen someone over by the smokehouse earlier, and with the screaming she heard later, she was afraid something awful had happened.

By two or three A.M., other cops had arrived, including an investigative detective and her team.

Helicopters came over from the Cape, bringing reporters, landing out at the Point as a helipad. Bruno had no idea that so many people would suddenly appear out of nowhere.

Bruno was up most of the night, answering questions, sitting with Brooke, who began talking incoherently until she had exhausted herself and fallen asleep by five.

Bruno managed two hours of sleep at that point, having

been smart enough to unplug the phone and switch his cell phone off. The news vans were outside when he left to go to the mainland.

His biggest fear was that Brooke would feel scared when he left, but she had told him that she was going to bed and would wear earplugs and maybe even take a pill to calm her nerves.

7

"And now, that's what we're coming back to," he said. "I saw a report on the morning news about it. I was just waking up on the couch, and I flicked it on, and there we were. Well, there was the mention of it. It sounded almost interesting, the way they talked about it on the news. Seven A.M., it already reached the Cape."

"What about the killer?" I asked.

"No word."

"Brooke must be so upset. I'm glad you've been here."

"Yeah, I know," Bruno said. "She's really freaked. She walked around all last night, room to room, with a candle, like some kind of gothic heroine. She thinks that the killer's waiting for her in the dark. We had men go through the house just to make sure no one was hiding. She's paranoid."

"Can't blame her."

"Maybe more than paranoid. She's been doing funny things."

"How funny?"

He breathed hard through his nose. It was a technique

he'd had as a kid when he didn't want to talk about something. Then, "I found her out in the rain four nights ago. Nearly freezing rain. She was completely naked. She . . . didn't recognize me. And she did some things." He blushed. "Well, she was sleepwalking, I think. But it really bothered me. She was . . . *Okay,* look, she was sort of playing with herself."

I took a deep breath. "God." My mind went blank at the thought. I didn't want to imagine my sister like that.

"I know. But she wasn't herself. She was asleep the whole time. It shocked the hell out of me. I had a friend with me, and we got her into the house, wrapped her up, and she just slept on the sofa that night in front of the fire. I don't even think she remembers it. I didn't tell Dad, but by then Dad and I weren't exactly talking to each other."

"Hoo boy," I said. "Jesus."

"Yeah," Bruno said.

We let that subject cool a bit with some much-needed silence.

"They search the house?" I asked finally.

He nodded. "One of the off-island cops told me that he'd never seen such a wacky house—the way the rooms are laid out. The way you can't hear anything from the back of the house to the front. The front door doesn't even lock right. They scoured the woods in back. Who knows? Who would've thought this would've happened there? I mean, Boston or New York, sure. Or even the Cape. But way the hell out on the island?"

"I still can't believe this," I said.

"Me, neither. Grogan said he thinks the killer already left.

Brooke was driving me nuts all night long. She kept talking about hearing things, and that made me freak out even more. It's a mess. She's a mess."

"As well she should be," I said. "You must be exhausted."

"Maybe it's adrenaline," Bruno said, "but I couldn't fall asleep right now if you paid me. My head keeps replaying what he must've gone through. His last moments. Nightmares. Brooke's not helping. She's convinced herself that she saw a ghost."

CHAPTER FIVE

1

"Blood. All over," Bruno said, accepting an offered cigarette. He reached into his pocket and drew out a lighter. Flicked it up, lit his cigarette, and then passed it back to me. "You don't want to hear it."

"Yeah. I do."

"No," he said. "You don't."

We arrived at the dock down at Buzzard's Bay sooner than I'd expected.

Across the water, our destination.

So distant it was invisible.

2

The sky turned a bit dark for noon, even for Massachusetts in November, and this heralded more snow. Deeper snow, perhaps. I didn't love snow. If I could've, I would've lived in Aruba or even Hell, rather than in the snowy climes.

The sky smelled of that peculiar freshness of a change of weather. From cold to frigid.

Bruno parked the car in the long-term area. "Brooke was going to drop the truck off at Burnley Bay," he said, naming the docks where the ferries and smaller craft launched and landed. "We'll pick my car up when you go home."

"I may not go home for a bit," I said, unsure about any future that existed for me beyond the moment.

"That's okay," he said. "I sort of hope so, since I'm going to be here 'til at least . . . well, 'til at least I figure out what next."

"It looks like Pompeii out there," I said.

Snowflakes had just begun falling from a gray wash of sky. A handful, as if they were white petals of a flower falling at the end of summer. The grayness had overtaken the morning. It was a thick sea mist. You could not even distinguish the sea—it all looked like a wall of ash, and the horizon line barely divided water from sky.

Beyond it, my Pompeii.

My Burnley.

3

"Embrace what beats you down," my father told me after I'd had a terrible time in junior high with bullies and a particularly sadistic soccer coach. "If you fight it, it will fight back better than you ever could. You must learn to make friends with the enemy. You must learn from your enemy because there's something of the enemy already in you, and that's who you're really fighting against."

When I was growing up, I sometimes felt that the island was my enemy.

Sometimes my father, as wonderful as he could be, was my enemy as well.

He was the most wonderful person I knew.

He was the most irrational person I'd ever met.

He could beat me up with a look, or reward me with a wink and a smile.

Now that he was dead, I knew that I had never really known him. Not in the fundamental way you're supposed to know your father.

He used to say something that cracked me up everytime.

"The sun shines on a dog's ass now and again." He'd say it to me when I was low and felt everyone else had the good life. Always made me laugh.

I missed him.

4

I froze my ass off on the boat ride over.

Our boatman, Cary Conklin, was a guy just out of college who had no idea what to do with his life, very much like my brother. He was a little goofy, and shot what I'd call "knowing looks" at my brother when I spoke to him. I hadn't known him from my years on the island, although I knew his oldest brother (of five), Chip. Cary looked a lot like his brother, particularly in the strong chin and lazy eyelids that seemed to run in the Conklin clan. I briefly asked about Chip. We made the kind of small talk you make on long, freezing boat rides when you don't want to talk about the vicious murder of your father, I guess.

Somewhere in there, Cary mumbled something meant to be comforting about my father.

We could've been crossing over from the world of the living to the world of the unknown. Cary was our Charon, taking us over the River Styx—or in this case, the Sound.

I didn't want to keep messing my mind into the death metaphors that came far too easily to me—but I had begun seeing mythological significance to this journey, to my father's death, and to God. I went from watching the last of the shore with its rows of Cape houses and rocky beach and the smoke from chimneys in towns and villages along the coastline, to looking into the haze of gray and white ahead. My mother, what I remember of her, was depressed whenever the fog rolled in on the island. And roll it did, far too often. She hated it. She had no love for the place. I guess in that respect, I was like her. The fog, the cold, the isolation from the mainland all had gotten to me.

It all seemed like a shroud. The dullish clank of ship's bells and the intermittent cries of seagulls that had not yet gone inland. The stormfronts that were the norm for that time of year reminded me of my youth and days and nights spent out on the island. Burnley Island was both beautiful and horrible, idyllic and monstrous, calm and turbulent. It was like the weather itself: unpredictable. You live on an island, you live the year from one extreme to another.

I looked out onto the unnaturally calm sea and watched the light snow come down, and for just a minute, just a hair of a minute, I saw some beauty in the world. I sipped from a mug of coffee. I closed my eyes and wished my father would be there, alive, to meet us at the harbor on the island.

It didn't seem fair that he should miss a beautiful snowy day and a cup of coffee, and I felt a little guilty that I was alive and he was not.

Something cut through my mind like a scalpel, trying to remove memories I wished I didn't have.

The good memories.

The memories of how loving my father could be, even at my worst times.

5

What seemed like hours later, my limbs frozen and my ears red, Bruno leaned into me. "Okay look, I'll tell you some stuff. You're going to find out anyway. Last night, when the storm hit, he apparently went out to the smokehouse."

"Jesus," I said. "Why the hell would he go in there?"

"I don't know," Bruno said.

I closed my eyes. My father's face: his off-kilter jaw that was both square and mildly dimpled. His thin lips barking out orders for us kids to never play in the smokehouse. I felt nauseated. I hated the smokehouse. It was an awful place—always freezing cold, even in summer, with that lingering smoke practically plastered into the stone walls from years before I came into the world. I'd always felt dread whenever I went into it—often, it was because my dad was going to punish me for some familial misdemeanor.

I opened my eyes. My brother had been talking, but I'd managed to block most of it out. I heard the tail end of a sentence: ". . . couldn't function. I got her dressed. But it was pulling teeth to get her to talk to the police."

"How bad was it?" I asked.

Then he told me how bad it was. How it was more than just "Dad died" or "someone killed Dad" or "a murder." It was one of those crimes that sounds impossible to have happened. As if another human being could not possibly *physically* do to a person what had been done to my father.

Unbridled savagery. Perhaps even sexual sadism. "The floor?" Bruno said. "In the smokehouse? *Soaked* with blood. The cops called it the 'red room'—it was that bad. I have to tell you," he whispered, glancing at our boatman in the stern. Bruno practically put his mouth to my ear. His breath was steamy and felt good on my frozen earlobe. "It was like a wild animal did it. Or six men."

"Jesus."

"There's something else," Bruno said. His voice dropped

a bit, as if he were trying to gulp back the words. "I just . . .
I just don't know . . . how to say it. Out loud."

"That's okay. If you can't, that's okay," I said.

"No, not about him. But it got me thinking last night. I
tried talking to Brooke about it, but she wouldn't listen. But,
Nemo, it was like . . . when . . . it's hard to even say the
words."

Something within me seemed to clutch as he fumbled with
his words.

"I mean, I'm not completely stupid," Bruno said. "But I
keep thinking about it. You know how you get those things
in your head and you can't stop thinking? They keep you up
all night? It's like that. It's something that just keeps playing
in my head over and over again. Know what I'm talking
about?"

6

I didn't reply. Could not. My head felt as if the granddaddy
of all headaches was coming on. I wanted to shut down.

Then I began to feel an uneasy dread. Not of returning to
the island. Not of dealing with my father's death. Not of the
monstrosity of the murder.

But a dread about whatever words were about to spill out
of my little brother's mouth.

Bruno took a deep breath. "You know how when I was
little, I had those nightmares? I mean, all of us did?"

The words formed in my mind, a whisper from the past:
Here comes a candle to light you to bed.

When he said this, I had to catch my breath. My lungs

felt frozen from the air. But now my heart froze, too. "Bruno, that was nothing . . . no . . . that was a long time ago."

"All around the Brain Fart," he said. The two words together sounded pretty funny: Brain and Fart. But they filled me with dread. We had been playing in the smokehouse, and suddenly, all three of us lost our memories for a week. We didn't tell our dad. We didn't tell anyone other than each other. We thought maybe we'd just woken up on Monday of the following week and perhaps nothing had happened the week before. But somehow, we doubted that. When we asked our father, he told us we'd had fevers that week that had scared him. High fevers that had him putting us in ice baths and pressing boxes of frozen Bird's Eye peas behind our necks to bring the fever down. Had it been scarlet fever? He wasn't sure. Equine encephalitis? That sometimes happened when the mosquitoes from the backwoods got too plentiful in early summer or early autumn and swarmed the low fields. But no, it was none of those things. He told us Dr. Connelly had come by briefly, and just told him to let us get rest and stay cool whenever the fever spiked. But it had been something more— the Brain Fart had affected us almost like a bodily injury, but we couldn't remember what had started it.

"It's some twisted, sick individual who did this to Dad, Bruno," I said. "Get that other stuff out of your head."

He looked at me with a half-cocked grin. I remembered how golden his hair was when he was a little boy. How he'd wake up singing. How he used to dance with Brooke out by the duck pond on summer nights while I chased dogs around in the mud. How I used to thank God every single day that I had a baby brother like Bruno, and that he looked up to me, and that I protected him in every way I could from the thorns and burrs of the little world we occupied. He had once been such a happy little boy.

Somehow I wanted to bring that back in him after this tragedy.

What I got from him, his twenty-three-year-old self, was anger.

"Don't sit there and pretend," he said. "I am so sick of people in this family pretending everything's all right when it's not. Never has been."

I cursed under my breath, closing my eyes again. I wanted to just block out everything in the world and have a moment of private oblivion. "Okay, let's not talk about it right now. This is going to be awful for all of us for a while, I guess."

"It's the Dark Game," he said.

"No, it's not. It is not." .

7

I had grown to hate the Dark Game as a boy.

The more you played it, the more power you felt.

And then, one time a few weeks after the Brain Fart, Brooke had decided to be the master of the Dark Game, speaking with someone else's voice.

But we had been children then. And we'd broken one of the rules of the game: We let it go beyond twilight.

We'd spent hours in the smokehouse, playing the game, all of us with blindfolds on, rags torn from old clothes.

We had overactive imaginations. Perhaps this was the reason our father eventually locked it up.

We had imagined that the smokehouse had become a red

room, and that someone lay at the center of the room, between the three of us. That someone lay there, and spoke to us—

Oranges and lemons, say the bells of St. Clemons.

In the Dark Game. Not in the real world.

You owe me five farthings, say the bells of St. Martins.

The real world changed when we played it. It had different rules.

When will you pay me? say the bells of Old Bailey.

Dark had come too fast, and we'd kept playing, as if we couldn't stop it.

When I am rich, say the bells of Shoreditch.

The problem with the Dark Game: It had always seemed to have been there waiting for us.

When we closed our eyes.

When will that be? say the bells of Stepney.

When we were together.

I do not know, says the great bell of Bowe.

In the hour before dark.

It had become an addiction when we were children.

Here comes a candle to light you to bed—

And here comes a chopper to chop off your head.

CHAPTER SIX

1

Bruno drew back from me in the boat.

He reached for the coffee thermos. "More?" he asked.

I shook my head. "Look, it was just a game."

"I know," he said. "But it was like that. It's going to be all over the papers—the details—pretty soon. One of the local news crews from the Cape came out, so it'll be on TV tonight. They talked to Minnie Wooten. She told 'em that we were all no good." We both laughed a little at the mention of the name, despite the gruesomeness of the crime. Minnie was nearly a hundred years old and as weathered as the gray, bowed planks on her front porch. She had been known as one of the Women Whom God Forgot—there were four of them on Burnley Island, each more ancient than the other. Somehow, despite the nasty winters and the isolation, some people seemed to grow old well on Burnley.

"I bet Minnie's famous all over now. She'll probably get her own talk show," I said, managing to laugh, even when something in my mind had begun to shut down. I tried not to imagine my father or what had happened the night before.

I didn't know that *we* would become famous on the island for all the wrong reasons from that moment on.

2

The Raglans had what might be called a spotty history of both the good and the bad.

I had been a bad kid in the way that kids who aren't quite demonic are bad, and if you were to ask me, I could not tell you what drove me to badness. I suspect that being born in New England, being Catholic, and being a Raglan, I was triply blessed with a sense of Sin with a capital S, GUILT with all capital letters, and atonement, expiation, and possibly re-demption all following thereafter. I was bad in the only ways I knew how: I did the things I ought not have done. Harry and I snuck into the movie theater when we were broke at the age of ten. At eleven, we kidnapped the Croder's Maine Coon cat (at Pola Croder's request, I might add, although she denied this later). We took Monster (as we called him, for he attacked and scratched up many a kid—the demon cat's real name was Scooby) to St. Bartholemew's to baptize him in the name of the Holy Ghost because we were sure that animal would go to Hell one day or another. We brought the cat back, but it was soaked and furious, and its talons were wrapped in bits of white sheet so it wouldn't scratch Harry or me when we dipped it into the baptismal font. Mrs. Croder called the local cop on us and we had a stern talking to and a half hour in the holding cell behind the police station.

Then my misdemeanors increased: borrowed my dad's truck to drive my friends out to Palmerton one night and go skinny dipping with the Evangelical Christian kids, all of whom taught us a thing or two, at fourteen, about human anatomy. Harry and I, altar boys, drank the wine reserved for communion at fifteen, and that was the worst of my church-related crimes. Luckily, the wine had not been blessed, and while my father took me home to be punished, the worst of it was throwing up in the back of the truck on the way home.

I didn't hurt anyone. At least, not directly. I wasn't a bully. I just tended to be in trouble with whatever trouble could be had. If there was a store to be broken into on a weekday night for no reason other than to have someplace to go, I was part of the crew. We never stole anything, nor did we break locks or windows (in the fall, winter, and spring, nobody on Burnley locked doors). If there was a car to be borrowed from Harry's uncle without him knowing about it, you can be sure Harry and I were probably doing the borrowing. If the horses from the stables in The Oaks had been let out to run wild on a soft, summer night, somehow my name was linked to the deed.

I was your basic screwup, and not cool enough to even be a good one. Always, I was in the wrong place at the wrong time, and for some reason I never had a good excuse for being there. I always got caught, and being the good Catholics we were, my father would drag me down to St. Bartholemew's and toss me at the confessional, before dragging me back home. I can guarantee you that being a six-foot-tall sixteen-year-old, it was shameful to have my five-foot-two bull of a father practically pulling me by the ear along the streets in the village. At home, he might use a belt, until I reached high school, and then he just used denial of privileges—no television, no phone, no dinner, and no books, the worst for me. He'd removed every single book from my bedroom once he discovered that I loved reading so much it was really no punishment to just go to my room. I'd sometimes yell those absurd things that teens do, how he didn't understand me, he didn't love me, he was no kind of father, that he wasn't even trying to be what Mom would be and if I were her, I'd have moved to Brazil, too—and the ugly heads of Sin and GUILT would rise up in me afterward, and I'd meekly apologize and tell him that he was right to punish me and I was rotten to the core.

(I wished I could go back and change those moments. I wish I could go back and tell him how much I loved him and how much he meant to me.)

I respected my father enough to let him punish me. It seemed just. He was never more harsh on me than I was on myself. The parish priest ended up being kind toward me in these transgressive periods of my childhood as time went on, and although it was rare for me to see the inside of a church once I went away to college, I had nothing but warm memories of Father Ronnie and St. Bart's church.

Despite what happened with my mother when I was nine, we were not mired in some sense of sorrow. All our Christmases were brightly lit confections; all our summers were adventures and dares.

Our early history as a family on the island was actually quite good. My great-great-great-everyone were stalwarts. Welshmen, Irishmen, Scots, and some English, a mix of Anglicans, Presbyterians, and Catholics that married out of the island over the years, until my father and his younger brother were the heirs. Then his brother died in the same war in which my father nearly died—but managed, through "the grace of God and a pack of Wrigley's," to survive. The story went that he had exactly one pack of Wrigley's gum with him when he was captured.

He used it as a psychological tool to resist the brainwashing that was done to him over the two years he was held prisoner.

"I chewed that gum over and over again, and each time imagined that the flavor was something I loved and missed from America. The taste of coffee. The sweetness of honey and lemon. Chocolate. Peppermint. It allowed me to get away in my mind to another place. To not listen to the brainwashing. To not be discouraged by the sensory deprivation they put me through. It was my own kind of brainwashing. I could chew the gum and close my eyes and just go somewhere else. Believe something else. And gum was easy to hide, virtually invisible."

It became such a famous story that for a while gum companies put it in their advertising. All of that was long before any of us were born, but the stories were legendary.

My mother's mystery and my father's heroism and the house itself: Hawthorn—all had stories attached to them.

Named for the thorny trees that grew wild near the house (although Minnie Wooten was quick to point out whenever she could that in fact they weren't "true hawthorns," whatever that meant), Hawthorn was a rambling old structure—a farmhouse that had grown with a few generation of Raglans, a poor Welsh family turned rich then poor again with my father's generation. Two stories high and simple in one way—for it was as plain as a New England farmhouse could be—it was also eccentric in many ways. It seemed of no particular age or time, for it had elements of various incarnations—from its humble early eighteenth-century beginnings as a stone house of one room right through the creation of its many rooms, and its serpentine curving along the rocky acreage where it grew. The last addition had been the greenhouse, which was under construction for most of my life and still remained unfinished to some extent. It had been intended for my mother.

Then Hawthorn had begun to fall apart, on bad pastureland that had lain fallow for decades, edging deep New England woods, beyond which lay the village of Burnley, known more for what it didn't have than what it did, and beyond this, the sea.

My father's favorite things about the old house, he told us, were the lessons it taught him. "Never let your roof get too leaky, never let the gutters fill with leaves, and always check the gas before you light the pilot." He had once, accidentally, nearly blown up the house because he had not checked the gas first. "Life is like a house. You have to do routine maintenance constantly or else it all just goes down the tubes at once." My main memories of him at home generally were about repairing and fixing things. Or putting up drywall when the old wall near the front staircase had rotted out—I wasn't much help, even though I tried my best to pitch in. My dad had a temper when he worked on the old house. He'd cuss a blue streak if I so much as held a hammer the wrong way or wasn't sure how to change a drill bit. He worked on the plumbing himself, allowing no one to come in and "rob us blind just for changing a washer and unscrewing a bolt." He had an ongoing project of tearing down walls, putting in new insulation, putting the walls back up—as if it were his main occupation. About the only thing he allowed me to do was install locks (I could handle this by the time I was fourteen or so) and carry his toolkit for him. He loved that house, and had worked on the ceiling and floors and walls as if he treasured the place.

I had left Hawthorn and hoped to never spend more than a weekend there ever again. Not because of terrificly unhappy memories, or because of something stupid that I took part in just before I headed off for college, but because of something I did that had cut me off from knowing any peace on the island.

I fell in love with a girl who would not love me back.

Between that event—when I was eighteen—and my mother's abandonment of us when I was a little boy, and yes, the arguments with my father, which never seemed to end, I just had no reason to return.

I always told anyone who asked—outside of the village—that my mother had died when I was nine.

3

I'd make up a story about her awful lingering illness, and how we gathered 'round her bedside, with my sister weeping to bring the angels and my father kissing my mother on the hand. I cribbed the emotion of the scene from the death of Little Nell in Dickens's *The Old Curiosity Shop*, and part from the death of Little Eva from Stowe's *Uncle Tom's Cabin*. These were deaths of absolute purity and saintliness, as befitted a beloved family member. There was an intensity to the innocence of those deaths. I wanted to believe it happened that way, too, with Mother beneath a snow-white comforter, her golden hair falling across the tear-stained pillow, the scent of lavender and bitter herbs in the air, a small red rose of color in her otherwise pale cheek, and a last clasp of her hand as she gave me motherly wisdom and departed to Heaven with one final and wistful sigh.

But that was a lie.

Everyone in Burnley knew the truth. Anyone could tell you—in broad daylight on a Wednesday afternoon, you could walk into what might roughly approximate a village and ask any of the children who had just gotten off the school bus. I'm betting they'd know about the Raglans' mother. How she had abandoned her husband and family, and was probably very much alive and enjoying a different family somewhere in Sao Paulo, Brazil. My mother was, after all, the most exotic creature that Burnley Island had ever seen after the summer was over.

She ordered perfume from London, from a perfumerie that her grandmother had once run, that her great-grandfather had founded in the South of France, and from which she had been disinherited when she purportedly stole several thousands of dollars from my grandmother's bank account. (How many times had I been told by people as I grew up that she was a

Bad Woman? That I might turn out just like she had, somehow tainted with her blood?) She had been raised in London, Switzerland, and Majorca, gone to college at Columbia. She had met my father in Burnleyside one summer when visiting a college friend's family there, dropped out of college, and went slumming with him until she ended up pregnant and in love. Her family never spoke to her again. And she never spoke to them. They never spoke to us, the grandchildren, either. They lived in other countries, and were mythological to me—real but not truly to be believed.

My father had his own share of fame, but without the wealth, so he was her equal in many ways, despite his rough-and-tumble upbringing, as opposed to her refined boarding school years. She had been, without question, the most beautiful woman on the island (Brooke and Bruno both got her looks, while I got the more Irish-Welsh looks of my father's side). I remember her looking like a fairy princess—slender, ethereal, with almond-shaped eyes, and a sloping but elegant nose. She had golden hair—not blond or yellow, but a rich autumn gold that might look sandy blond on her worst days, like creamy toffee on others, and spun gold at her best. She always smelled of vanilla and lime and lavender, for she daily dropped the essences of all in her bath water. I would sit with her while she bathed, and she would tell me tales from the Arabian nights or of how she had stowed away once with a friend on a tramp steamer and had gone to Brazil, her favorite country in the entire world. "I was sixteen and running away," she said, "but it was just for the summer. A wonderful summer of romantic suspense," she added, without explaining any details. My mother had many talents: She played music, sketched on long summer afternoons, read from books, and tried her hand at poetry briefly. I remember her mainly surrounded by candlelight—she was a romantic at heart, and I suppose it's what changed her, that romantic yearning.

She had mischief in her as well. I discovered this early and was charmed by it—by her misadventures in finding ways of getting to Boston faster than anyone could get there, the way she'd spend money cautiously one minute and then as if nothing were more important than something whimsical she'd just seen—and had to have at any cost. My father adored her, and adored the attention men gave her—he told me that he was proud that his wife was such a prize and yet had chosen him.

It all ended one night, years ago. December 19th. A red-letter day.

My mother walked out the door when I was nine years old and told my father that if he loved his kids so much, he could have them. The details: She wore her reddest dress (as small-town minds like to recall), she had one of my father's guns for protection in case he tried to force her to stay, and it was four A.M. The story went that my father sobbed quietly, gave her his blessing, and told her he would be there with the kids when she got tired of this new man in her life.

My father was a good man, so said people in Burnley and everyone who had ever heard of him. He told us that our mother loved us very much and left us only because something inside her head had control of her—but he promised he would be there, to take care of us and keep us safe.

He kept that promise, in his own way.

He even told us he'd take her back, if she wished to return.

"But to stand in the way of someone's happiness," he told me once, "is the cruelest of impulses. It's as cruel as killing them, in my opinion. Real love sometimes means letting love fly."

I had a dream soon after my mother left us. When I spoke about it to my brother and sister, when we were young, they told me they had dreams like it, too. In the dream, our mother came home and took each of us up in her arms, embracing and kissing us all over. In the dream, our father hugged us as well. It's only natural for children to want to see their parents reunited, even if those same children know that it's like wishing there were an Easter Bunny, or that birthday candles release some magic when they're blown out. I sometimes wonder if we don't long for precisely what we know in truth we can never have.

I dreamed about a silver crescent, too, like the moon. Like a crown that our mother would wear when she returned to us from the man she'd run off with so many years ago. The shadow man we'd never known, but who had come into our mother's life and stolen her from us.

My father had been taken by a different kind of shadow man.

Viciously.

"A peculiar ferocity," wrote Harry Withers, who reported for the *Burnley Gazette*, but whom I knew primarily from the playground of my childhood. "One does not associate this sort of crime with the peaceful island of Burnley, Massachusetts, known primarily for its plover shelter in the wetlands and its role in the Revolutionary War. The bogs and woods and meadows no longer seem benign. The hunt is on for the person or persons who committed this heinous act upon a war hero, upon a father, upon a man who stood for everything that was good in Burnley."

The first I knew that my father had been tortured in a war was in second grade when that boy I had only just met named Harry Withers taunted me with, "Your daddy's got only one ball! The other got cut off and fed to snakes! Your daddy's a freak!"

4

It never occurred to me at that age that just because my father had always been missing two fingers on his right hand, he might have had something happen to him that caused it. Or that other parts of him might be missing as well. Since I was only dimly aware of what balls were at the age of six and a half, I wasn't sure if it mattered how many my father possessed.

Harry Withers seemed to think it mattered a hell of a lot. There was something in the nature of both challenge and humiliation for him to say it out on the blacktop during recess.

I ended up in a fistfight, which got me to the principal's office, then to the nurse's office, and then a note to my parents about how I'd nearly bitten Harry's ear off.

I had barely snipped at his ear with my teeth, but it did bleed a lot. I was afraid I'd mutilated Harry, that I'd be thrown in jail for having done it, and that poor one-eared Harry would haunt me forever. As it turned out, Harry's ear would heal within days. Not so my troubled heart. Why did my father have only one ball and eight fingers?

I went home nearly in tears and angry enough to cuss. I asked my mother what this was all about, after she'd given me the disappointed treatment from reading the principal's note.

Modest though she was, she had no problem setting me straight on my father's testicular health. This was followed by a bit of birds-and-bees, and how loving, legally wed people lay very close together and then nearly a year later, a baby would be born. Even with my father's condition, apparently he had no problem fathering three children.

My father, she told me, did indeed have one "testicle, and yes, some bad things happened to him over there," and she took me in the library of our home—a dusty room that had always seemed misshapen to me, packed with shelves and books—and brought down a photo album. She went through my father's childhood, his parents, the war, his capture, the news clippings, and finally said to me, "So two of his fingers are gone, and yes, his testicle was also taken, but it doesn't make him less of a man. You just remember that. There are many men who walk around in life with no balls whatsoever."

I learned most of what I knew of my father's heroics by the time I was nine.

He had fought in a war before I was born. He'd been taken captive for twenty months, had tried to escape from his captors twice, had lost two fingers on his left hand for reasons of which he never spoke, had been decorated a hero, and had returned to the plow as it were—or in his case, returned to his own father's farm, married, and started a family.

My mother retrieved the articles for me. She substituted them for the comic books I loved to look at. She would show me the old home movies. Daddy getting a medal. Daddy standing beside a helicopter. Daddy meeting some news anchorman. Daddy standing in line with others to meet the president. Daddy and Mommy on their wedding day, with swords and guns and soldiers standing in a halo around them. The glow of heroism surrounded him in all these photographs. I felt better about my father. I loved him even more for being not just a hero to me, but to the world.

Sometimes, an old-timer from town would see me at the playground in the park and call me over and tell me that I looked just like my father did when he was my age. "Your grandfather wasn't much good, but he made himself a good man in your daddy," someone might say; once I heard the librarian, Mrs. Pollock, tell me that my father had been the most famous man to ever come out of Burnley, and that no one had expected he'd come back to run Hawthorn again or even try and get along when the money ran out.

"He could've been president or at least a senator, once upon a time," she told me. "That's how famous he was after the war. Not famous like movie stars or rock and roll people. Not that vulgar thing. And not rich. I mean to say famous in the ways that count. And just like you, he got in trouble as a boy sometimes. So don't think that it's the end of the world for you. You can be a hero, just like your father."

Or I'd hear the story of how my father had managed to save seven men from certain death, or how my father had piloted a helicopter "without knowing nothin' about helicopters but that they spin. And he bombed the hell out of them. He just dropped it all back down on them. And he got his men out."

My father would rarely speak of the past that existed before meeting my mother, other than to hide the medals of valor in places where my brother and I could not find them. He'd scoff at the idea that he had ever been a hero at all. After my mother ran off, he lived under a terrible burden. He expressed little that wasn't dour or dutiful after that. He gave lessons or lectured; he rarely spoke to me and even more rarely listened. I suppose my mother's abandonment affected all of us, and may have been part of the fog that kept me confused about life and my place in it as I grew into an adult.

I grew up under the burden of his heroism, and I became less than a model son because I knew I was no hero. My impulses were never heroic ones. I began smoking by the time I was twelve, and when I was seventeen, I'd done all the things teenagers do that they will regret in merely a few years, scarred by such foolishness and disregard for any rule in life. I was the embarrassment of the family when I left it.

Yet, I could look back on the love and affection of the household; on the way my father would tell me—even at my worst—that he'd done just such a thing when he'd been my age, and it was wrong, but it was not wicked, merely childish.

His words had the effect of arms around me—it was his way of embracing.

I took his wise words to heart and knew that despite my missteps in life, my father had gone through many more difficulties than I could dream up, and still, he had done good.

My mother had been a slightly different story.

5

After she left, my father told us that she sometimes called, late at night.

No matter how much he begged, she would not come back to us. He told us that she wanted to see us. He promised that one day she would come for us, would collect us, but that "now" wasn't the time.

She sent letters and postcards, as well, but none of them mentioned our names. Notes like: "I want to keep in touch, but the past is so difficult to mull over. Please don't let's keep in touch. I don't want to cause you more pain." She sent a few of these that I saw.

I assumed my father had been writing her late at night, posting his mail without our knowing, begging her to return.

"She's got a new life," my father would say at times, and begin to brood. "I would love to tell the three of you that she doesn't love you, but I know she does. This is the hardest thing I've ever said. Even in war, nothing was this hard, but I will say it regardless. You must each overcome this. I can't force your mother to come home. I can't go chase her down if she is with this other man and she claims that this brings her happiness. You've been crying since she left, and you haven't eaten enough, and you all have to stop it now. She is not the woman I married. She's not the mother who brought each of you into this world. She changed. Perhaps she'll change back. But the best we can do is hang tough and get through this. And each of you needs to pitch in and do your share. Accept this, somehow. Accept it now. Life is its own kind of war. You've got to fight it and win it."

As he spoke, I saw his eyes become glassy and distant. I couldn't look at the sadness in his face, but glanced down at my shoes. Somehow, I felt all of us were to blame. I felt that if I had just been nicer to my mother, she would've stayed. If

I hadn't gotten into any trouble, she would've stayed. If I'd said my prayers every morning and night, she probably would still have been with us. I have no doubt that Brooke and Bruno felt the same way.

"None of you deserves this," he said. "Not one of you."

And that was all he really spoke about it.

6

Now and then, one of us would ask about her. He'd tell us to write a letter and he'd send it. None of us ever wrote a letter, although I started a few, but put them aside. I suppose we accepted the finality on some deep level, regardless of our wants and needs on the surface of things.

Once she wrote to us all and mentioned a new child. She had a new child. A boy. His name was Steven. That's all she said about him. My father tore the letter up after reading it aloud, tears in his eyes, and held us close. At other times, he went into horrible rages and locked himself in his room for an entire day, screaming, as if at the walls of the house itself.

All this to begin to tell you: Our father was both loved and hated within his own family, he was a hero to the world and to each of us, even though he had his dark periods.

When my father died—was killed—none of it mattered.

CHAPTER SEVEN

1

My father was butchered.
Sliced up.
In pieces.

2

"Man, I'm angry," Bruno said. "Sucker punched. Dazed. That's how I've felt since finding out. I was just talking to him the other day. And now . . ." This was the most open I'd ever heard my brother be. He never talked about his inner life or feelings that I knew of. He was a mystery to my sister and me in that respect. "Brooke's had the worst of it. She's been depressed this fall. I don't know why. I know she hasn't been sleeping right since before this. Now, who knows?" He said this with an appealing meekness, as if he needed something from me. Some reassurance about the good in the world.

I did something I've never done before, but I suppose you don't do what you're used to doing until a nasty tragedy has stomped you and your family. I reached over and hugged him to my side. Like the little brother he was to me. He put his head on my shoulder and cried for a little bit. I felt like I was ten and he was five again, after having a bully at school say something mean to him about our mom running off, or about his glasses, or how he couldn't play softball as well as the others.

"They'll get whoever did it," I said, without much confidence. I meant it. If they didn't, I'd make it the quest of my life to hunt down the madman.

I would not stop until the guy was caught.

When we got to the docks, Bruno walked ahead of me, lugging one of my suitcases, while I had the other two. We loaded the back of Brooke's truck and headed out onto the road away from the sea.

The sky, slate gray; the woods, like broomsticks; the air, salt, snow, and that memory-scent of winters past.

3

Bruno turned down Goose Creek Road with its overhang of gloomy trees.

In the distance, I saw the beginning of the woods that would guide the narrowest of roads up to the house where I'd been born and raised, and where Raglans had lived ever since they'd been in America. We turned up Dunstable Road, and

Hawthorn came into view just over the ridge. There were police cars along the road, and three news vans from the television studios, nearly blocking the driveway. We passed the
smokehouse to the left, and I didn't want to look at it, but I
couldn't not look. It was surrounded by what looked like a
makeshift wire fence, with orange police tape up around it.

"Christ," I said.

"Feeling some Jumblies?"

"Definitely," I said.

"Can I tell you something?"

"Of course."

"I've never really told anyone this. It makes me feel guilty.
Right now. Promise not to hold it against me?"

"Okay."

"I hated him," Bruno said. "I hated Dad. He didn't like
me much either. But I hated him. He drove our mother away.
He drove you away. As far as I'm concerned . . ." Then he
stopped himself. A bit more evenly, he added, "It's terrible
this happened. I feel this awful guilt. As if it's my fault."

I wasn't sure how to reply to this. "Bruno," I said, and
thought, *what the hell do I tell him? It's okay to hate the guy who
was just butchered? It's okay to hate the guy who raised and clothed
and fed you? That yes, he drove me away, when in fact I did a
damn good job of just driving myself away? That he could not have
driven our mother away any faster than she had run herself, out
the door with her red dress and her suitcase and all the money she
took, and the secret lover she had when she should've kept her love
for her young children and her devoted husband?* Bruno had,
within him, a little of what we all felt—an undercurrent of

anger, directed at our father, but really meant for our mother, who had left us when we were nearly too young to remember. Somehow, we had all blamed the one who had remained behind to some extent.

Now that he'd been murdered, guilt followed these feelings.

"Don't tell Brooke," he said. "Promise me. She idolized him. She'd hate me. Now, I guess, more than ever."

"All right," I said. It was our family sickness, I guess: *Don't tell someone else in the family how you really feel. Hide it. Bury it. Make it go away.* It had been ingrained in us from an early age. Its origins were as hard to pin down as the fog that surrounded Hawthorn for half the year: *Who had made us feel that way? Was it something within ourselves? Some organic sense of burying, the way dogs bury bones?*

Part of me felt like lashing out at him for being so cold-hearted as to talk like this within two days of our father's death. Part of me wanted to understand him as I never had before.

And I hated to admit it, but part of me agreed with Bruno. I couldn't understand it—why had I disliked my father so much? Had I blamed him for things? Had I made him too responsible for the confusion I so often felt?

He had been rough on us, that was the bottom line. And we had rebelled.

That big GUILT I generally felt was going into hyperdrive in me.

I was not looking forward to any aspect of this homecoming.

4

The old house, on the outside, was still haggard-looking, as it had been ten years before. It was a grandfather of a house. It had even turned a bit gray in the intervening years.

Slowly maneuvering around the vans and cars, Bruno turned down the drive. The gate was closed, of course. I got out of the car, feeling the blast of icy air again, and ran to open it.

Bruno drove through, and I shut the gate to the driveway again. I glanced up at the road. There were people in jackets and trenchcoats up on the roadside, watching.

5

"Brooke," I said, when my sister met me at the front door. I did everything I could not to imagine her naked in a storm, her fingers reaching down below her flat belly. I regretted Bruno had ever told me that story.

Too late to move out of the way, I was jumped by her two enormous greyhounds, Mab and Madoc, and I went backward onto the porch. A pain in my butt told me I'd landed on part of the flagstone walk. Dog licks covered my face. Despite the pain, I began laughing and shoving the dogs away.

Brooke stood over me, doing her best to pull the dogs away by the collar, but they were out of control.

Then she offered me her hand, helping me up.

6

My sister Brooke: an unkempt beauty.

Her hair, darker than I'd remembered it, hung down and around her shoulders, somehow framing her face so that her eyes seemed owl-like. She wore no make-up, looked as if she had just rolled out of bed. She wore a stretched-out gray wool sweater that came down to the ends of her fingers and fell nearly to her knees, baggy khakis. Barefoot on the porch. Oddly, there was the smell of turpentine about her—I noticed what might've been paint on her sleeve. Had she been painting something?

Somehow, she still managed to radiate beauty. Some women have organic beauty—their bodies are formed as if meant to be looked at by men and appreciated. This is simply nature, and no doubt many have had it who were undeserving. Some women have magical beauty—where their features aren't symmetrical, or their face looks slightly off-beat, but they have an aura about them that creates beauty around them. My sister had a bit of both. She had the same beauty our mother had possessed, when I could remember our mother's face. Brooke did whatever she could to hide her looks in sweaters and sweats and a general sloppiness. But it was still there: that touch of our mother.

7

First thing Brooke did was whisper so softly that I was afraid I wouldn't hear her. "Do I look scared, Nemo?"

She had an air of the bittersweet about her—pale and rosy and golden at the same time, her lips bitten and her eyes lost. Botticelli hair falling around her woolen shoulders—the perfect result of the blending of my mother's Northern European fairness and my father's Welsh darkness. "Do I? I feel scared. But I don't want them to see it. I don't want the world to see it." She pointed to the news van out on the road. "Goddamn buzzards," she said, her voice rising to its normal tone. "Come on in, Nemo. Good you made it. Carson greet you?" Her New Englandese turned the perv's name into "Cahsehn," and I had to admit I liked hearing it. Carson was known for seducing island sheep and for masturbating from the front seat of his small yellow pickup truck at the harbor as a kind of welcome wagon.

"Nope," I said. "No miraculous vibrating truck."

"Dad called it the 'Burnley Hello,' " she said. "He said it just a week ago. Better than what most men do with those things, I suppose." Then the bravado left her face, a sudden retreat. She whispered, "I don't want them to see me upset. I feel like I'm being watched all the time."

She clapped her hands, and the dogs went running back into the house ahead of us. A loud crash—Brooke swore a blue streak—and when we got to the kitchen, the dogs had already knocked over a small chair by the glass table. Brooke shouted, "Kennels!"

The dogs, finally obedient, ran to their respective, enormous wire crates that edged the living room.

In personality, Brooke was solidly Yankee in a way that neither Bruno nor I had remained. She had the strongest accent, which was vaguely masculine despite her petite softness.

She was a category of woman who lived on Yankee islands, just as there was a category of men who did as well, who had thick hair that always needed cutting, and ruddy complexions from constant movement in the cold, a nearly downcast expression as she spoke, as if gravity were her only make-up; she used profanity as insecure gourmets used spices: as if no sentence were complete without at least a "fuck" or a "goddamn." In this way, she was unlike any of us. She was as Yankee as the low stone walls that had surrounded Hawthorn for more than two centuries. She was like a weathervane on the roof, or the shingles themselves: part of the way things looked in New England, part of its charm, but also part of its expectation. Few on the island could out-island my sister. She had an old soul for the place, as if she were the reincarnation of my great-grandma Cery (pronounced Cherry) Raglan, a salty bitter woman of enormous bosom and the iron will of a mule.

As I held her for a moment, I smelled our mother's scent—particularly the essence of lime—and for a moment, I was truly happy. Happy to be with my sister. Happy to be home again. Happy that at least the three of us would be here for the time being.

Even if for all the wrong reasons.

8

When I entered Hawthorn again, I felt enveloped in its plain New England arms, its brick and wood and white walls and smell of earth and coffee and winter spice.

Its length seemed less like a serpentine pattern and more like a series of Christmas boxes waiting to be opened.

Why had I hated this place so much?

Why had I left it behind and done everything I could to let work and life get in the way of coming back?

Now it was late in the game. My father, gone. I'd thought I'd have some time later in life to sort out our problems. Maybe in my forties. After I'd somehow established my own territory in the world. Sometime in the future, when he was older and softer and I was wiser and more understanding of my own nature. I had made a huge mistake by running away from my problems.

Despite the length of the house, it wasn't that wide, nor were the ceilings high. It was built for Welshmen and women—my great-greats, none of whom were tall. It wasn't until my father married my mother and produced two sons who had some Norwegian and German in them, that the house seemed smaller and less grand to my dad. He told me that no one should really be taller than five-foot-six anyway.

I could practically feel my father still alive in the entry-way—and yes, though my mother was long gone, I felt her there, too, and saw her in my sister's face. I looked for the penknife notchings in the doorframe—and there they were. The notch that was me at four, then at six, then at twelve; and Brooke and Bruno's notches, as well, all of us lined up against the doorframe every few years to check our progress.

I went to hug my sister, and she whispered in my ear, "Good to see you again."

My sister and brother and I had seen each other in the years I'd been gone—but not more than once or twice. I hadn't seen her in nearly six years, though, and we'd been so close growing up, that I felt my eyes tearing up just to be there, in the house, with both her and Bruno. It was enough for the time being.

Brooke loved the island more than she loved life itself, and Hawthorn was the heart of her love. She had told me as a child that she wanted to grow up to either be a fisherman, or a fisherman's wife, and she had danced along the edge of the shoreline on many summer twilights, stretching her arms up to the pink sky, while her friends gathered around a bonfire that had just been set for the night—but she was separate from them, a nature spirit on the island.

Some heaviness had come into her—not in terms of weight, but an aura, as if remaining on the island had tugged away at her vitality, her ability to dance on the shore or love the smell of the fishing boats as they came into the harbor.

I suspected that, whether she ever married or not, she would always remain in that house, always caring for it and tinkering with its upkeep, and making sure that someone remained to remember the Raglan history. It was as if the doors were not open for her.

9

Brooke went to flick on the kitchen light, and when her back was turned, Bruno whispered to me, "Sedatives."

"Yes," Brooke said, turning to face him. She shot him a poisonous look. It nearly scared me, because it didn't seem like the soft gentleness I'd remembered her having. "You drink, and I get a pill now and then."

"I didn't mean it as—" Bruno began, but shut up. "Sorry."

Brooke's face smoothed out. Then to me: "Pola and her

little boy came by. Just paying respects. It seems early for it. I didn't run her off, but I have a hard time with the idea of people just popping over the day after this. Harry came by this morning, too, and it's making me angry that everyone has to say something to me. As if it's required." The sorrow in her face nearly astonished me. She needed sleep badly. Sleep and peace. "Just make yourself at home. Your room should be okay. Mab and Madoc seem to like sleeping there some nights. If they bother you, just shut them out. Don't put up with any crap from them. There's a spot heater in the den you can have if it gets too cold. I'm not sleeping at night. Don't bother me 'til after seven tonight. I just want to sleep right now. As long as I can." She whistled for her dogs, and they leapt nearly across the living room and ran to her.

And then my sister went down through the living room, out the door that led to the dining room. I heard a series of doors open and shut as she went through twelve rooms, upstairs, to her own room, near the back of the house.

"She's was on edge before this," Bruno said. "Either quiet or like a cyclone. She and Dad were fighting all week. Mainly about money."

10

Within an hour of being home, I got a call from the local police chief.

CHAPTER EIGHT

1

"Nemo?"

"Joe," I said. I had always known him as Joe rather than Officer Grogan. The island was like that. We had been tight-knit. Too tight. First thing I asked him, "You catch the killer yet?"

A pause on the line.

"First, I'm sorry for all this." He said it in a low, quiet voice. It reminded me of my father a little, when he was trying to tell me something bad.

"I just got in," I said. But I wanted to just sink into a soft sadness and not deal with anything.

"Well, I want you to know we've been scouring the island for this killer. Everyone is cooperating."

"Thank you," I said, unsure how to respond. I still wasn't

certain how I was supposed to continue in life, thinking about this murder. I wonder if anyone who has been touched by a murder really knows how to react to it or to how people treat you afterward. It was as if you somehow came out of another dimension, as if you lost your pact with the rest of the human race, and then you were either a wounded victim or simply a foreigner in the land of normalcy.

"We'll need to ask you some questions, soon," he said.

"Of course," I said.

"Good. How's Brooke?"

"She seems to be . . . well, holding up."

"Hang tough," he said, before hanging up.

I glanced at Bruno. Hung up the phone. "Grogan," I said.

"He's calling too much," Bruno said. "Means he doesn't have anything. He really wants to talk to Brooke. I think he's scared of her."

2

The first week was a blur of reporters, who didn't bother us as much as I thought they might, but generally were around if one of us left the house and actually ventured to the village. (I stayed home with Brooke unless a trip to town was absolutely necessary, and then I just went to buy eggs or coffee or milk at the QuickMart, where I knew no one.)

The reporters from the mainland seemed a little scared of us—or were ashamed to have to circle around us. Brooke hated having her picture taken, so when she went outside, she always gave the photographers and cameramen the finger just to keep her picture out of the paper.

Harry Withers, running the *Burnley Gazette*, was not among them, despite my brother's promise that he had been camping out somewhere nearby. I guess I should add a word or two about Harry here. Harry Withers, my best friend when I was growing up, was a bit of a nut case. As a kid, he'd been into being a complete geek, which was cool in its own way—he read books on improving brain power, and he knew what NASA was working on, and he was completely convinced that Earth would eventually be contacted by aliens. He used to even try to hypnotize my brother, sister, and me as kids after seeing a guy on television make a bunch of people quack like a duck. He was the son of the owner of the *Burnley Gazette*, an island rag that tended toward gossip and tourist promotions and the odd story about how pennies were getting scarce on the island. When we had been kids, he was like my brother— more so than Bruno in some respects, because Harry and I were the same age, and got into nearly the same trouble. He slept over at Hawthorn a lot as a kid, too, so my family knew him well—his parents had troubles that I won't get into here other than to say they were mismatched. His father died of emphysema when he was fourteen, and then he turned bad in a way that was destructive.

I was nearly thankful that Harry hadn't come by Hawthorn yet. I just didn't want to see him if I could help it. Not with all the other crap going on. Not with the shroud of gloom and confusion that hung over the house.

He did call once, though. He wouldn't say much other than that we needed to get together soon, and that he knew "something about the smokehouse."

"You calling as a reporter or a friend?" I asked.

"Both, I guess," he said, and added, "But I'm a friend first."

"It's hell here," I whispered into the phone.

"Yeah," he said.

A pause on the line.

"I guess I can't say anything pleasant in the face of this," he said.

"Nope."

"I'm just sorry it happened. The way I used to hang out over there with you, I always felt like one of the family."

"You were," I said. "I know Dad considered you an honorary Raglan."

"Sorry we've been out of touch."

"Feels like I just left the place yesterday," I told him. "Like I just saw you the day before yesterday."

But despite the warmth of this last part of our conversation, I felt distant from Harry and distant from everyone I'd grown up with.

I still wasn't sure why I'd created that distance.

3

I didn't see Harry that first week at all, but Joe Grogan came by Hawthorn more than once.

He was the only policeman of note on the island in the winter, under whom was a very unused police force of three. During high tourist season, from Memorial Day to Labor Day, this increased to ten, most of whom were at The Oaks rather than in Burnleyside. Joe and his gang of three were eager to take part in this most interesting of local crimes, even though the police from the mainland flocked, briefly, to Burnley once the story got out. Like seagulls to a trash heap.

Joe Grogan had aged quite a bit—my guess was he was about forty-eight, but he looked a lot older with wrinkles and white hair and a general hangdog expression.

He had the look of a man whose life had worn him down to the nub.

"It goes like this," he said. "First, we secured the area around the crime scene. Not difficult for this time of year, but you never know who will decide to tromp through there. We're keeping the smokehouse locked up, though. Investigators have been going through, trying to examine everything they can."

Brooke turned cold, briefly. "How many men went through there?" she asked.

"Six or seven. At the most."

"He would've hated that," she said. "Tweezers out to pick up hair samples. Blotting blood trying to find evidence. I can't imagine all the gory details."

"It's procedure," Joe said, glancing at me with a slightly bewildered expression. "Unfortunately, the weather hasn't helped any of this. The police tape has blown away twice already, and between the snow falling and melting, I'm not sure we're going to have much luck. Finding anything in the perimeter beyond the building, is, well . . ." He splayed his hands, a gesture of futility. "Pretty soon, we'll just have some additional informal interviews with neighbors, and each of you, of course."

"Interviews?" Bruno asked. "That's it?"

"There's a lead investigator, and she's got to find out if anyone saw anything. Anything at all."

"I don't feel very safe," Brooke said.

"The killer—or killers—may well have already left the island," Joe said. He took his time saying this—he was being careful with his words. He seemed to watch Brooke's face equally carefully. "This person is on the move."

"He could have easily killed me," Brooke said. "The doors weren't locked. If he wanted something, he would've come and taken it. He just wanted to murder someone. That's my guess. He's some insane sociopath."

Joe seemed about to say something, but then held back.

Bruno nodded gravely, looking at the tattered Persian rug on the floor instead of at our sister. "Brooke, it could even be someone here. Someone who lives here. Maybe someone who didn't like Dad."

"Do you think so, Joe?" Brooke asked, fixing what I'd term a sharp and terrible look on Joe Grogan, as if he had failed her just by being there. "You think Carson did it? Or Ike Doone?" Her voice rose a bit. "Or me? Do you think I killed him and sat in his blood for hours, thinking about my hideous act?"

When Bruno next spoke, his voice seemed small, like a child's who has been scolded. "I didn't mean that. I didn't."

Joe glanced at me, then at Bruno, but averted his gaze from my sister. He was overpowered by her. I had an inkling of why. *They'd had an affair.* I could smell it at ten paces. They had some broken chemistry between them. It was as if they were talking about one thing, but meaning another. It felt like it. Like they had too much intimacy. *Joe and Brooke.* The way they both seemed uncomfortable in each other's presence. I didn't know this for sure, but something about the chief of police sitting there in the chair. *He sat in that chair before. He has been in Hawthorn more than a few times.* Holding the cup of coffee in the saucer. Nearly relaxed, but a strange underlying tension. It all seemed too familiar. Brooke seemed too hostile toward him.

"The investigators have gathered what evidence they could," he said. "But it's still too soon to not keep going over every detail."

"What about DNA?" I said, not really knowing what I asked.

"Samples already went down to some labs in Connecticut. It may take some time to determine anything. But we'll get whoever did this. Don't worry."

"I feel unsafe," Brooke said. Her eyes filled with glassy tears. She reached for a tissue in a dispenser near her elbow. Blew her nose.

"Do you have any ideas?" I asked. "It takes a while to go on- and off-island. There's the coast guard. How hard is it to—"

Joe's face turned grim as he cut me off. "Every cop from here to Boston is formulating theories. They'll keep scraping for evidence they might've missed. Your father didn't seem to have enemies. There haven't been reports of strangers on the island since before the end of October. Even the logs on the ferry for the past three weeks—all accounted for. This is a tough one. We'll crack it. Maybe if we're lucky, the killer had his own boat and drowned during the storm."

As bloodthirsty as it may have seemed, I hoped in my heart that was true.

Brooke wiped her eyes, then her nose, with the tissue. "You think it's me."

"Don't be ridiculous," Joe Grogan said. "No one thinks that. It's just . . . just the damnedest thing." It must have been his favorite phrase.

"I sat there, in that blood," Brooke said. Then she covered her face with her hands. I went to her and sat on the edge of the large leather chair she was in. I stroked her back lightly.

"I don't want any of you tromping around by the smoke-house," Joe said to me when I walked him to the front door. "And watch out for Ike Doone. I've caught him twice trying to get close to it, and he and that wife of his are all caught up with America's Most Wanted, so I don't want him grabbing souvenirs. Chase him off if you see him out there."

4

The moment Joe's car had pulled out of the driveway, Brooke went to the front window and stared out at the road. "Fuck!" she shouted.

Bruno and I just sat and watched her.

"She's going through Hell," I said.

I really meant it. You grow up Catholic, and there's some inkling that Hell is always right around the corner. It's the place you accidentally step into when you least expect it. I asked my dad, when I was a kid, if he thought he was going to Heaven, and he told me no. He wouldn't explain why, and it was the saddest thing he ever said about himself. I guessed, as I got older, that if you lived long enough, you spent time in Hell as you went through life.

I figured we'd all just bought a little bit of real estate there, with this murder. We knew something about life that many people get to skim over in the papers or on the nightly news.

Brooke had sat in Hell for hours, staring in its face.

She had the right to her obscenities.

5

We could not have a funeral yet because my father's body was needed for forensics evidence. It was unpleasant to contemplate. I had the idea of a funeral at St. Bart's, with Father Ronnie, now nearly seventy, giving mass. Bruno shook his head to shush me up, but Brooke told me, "We had a falling out with Father Ronnie. Dad didn't like him in the end. I didn't like him. For a priest, he had no sense of Christian forgiveness. To him, I'm Jezebel or something. He called me a harlot once. I called him a drunk. We parted ways." She said this last part with a bit of acid in her voice.

"What's that all about?" I asked. "He actually called you a harlot?"

"You'll hear about it soon enough," she said. "Joe Grogan and I had a fling. Well, more than that. For nearly a year. Do *not* give me that Nemo look."

" 'Nemo look'?" I nearly laughed. It felt good to feel a little light.

"That 'I knew you were up to something' look," she said without a trace of humor. "Don't judge me. I will not be judged by you or anyone. His wife has had affairs with men up at The Oaks every summer since they've been married. He needed a little happiness. I did, too. It ended badly. Dad was furious, but kept a lid on it. He felt I was . . . I don't know . . . devaluing myself, I guess. He told me I'd never find a husband, and I guess I pissed him off by spitting back at him that I could find any husband I wanted, so long as the wife was away. Father Ronnie scolded Dad for allowing a woman like me to live in his house. Dad told him to fuck off. So, no absolution for us. We're headed for limbo. Or worse."

"True," I said. "I'm not sure you can ever come back from telling a priest to fuck off."

"He didn't quite say it that way."

"It's a relief to know we all won't be excommunicated for your sins," I said cheerily.

"Always the funny one," she said in a way that was not funny at all. It was the Yankee in her. "I never liked church. Sunday should be a day to sleep in. Ronnie's mass went on too long. I could always smell whiskey on his breath in the confessional."

6

When I was out piling up cords of firewood that Carson Mc-Kinley brought (yes, he had a good delivery business with his truck, despite his predilictions for sheep), I saw Joe Grogan's police car up on the roadside.

Joe stood over by the smokehouse, just on the edge of the last of the police tape that hadn't quite blown away. He peered around it, as if he didn't want to step into some sacred circle.

I waved to him and called out. He glanced in my direction, then crouched down just outside the building. He picked at something with his fingers.

There was a kind of silent barrier to winter on the island, and he may have even called out to me, but I didn't hear it. The wind had picked up.

When I got over to him, he stood, a grim expression on his face.

"I have to tell you, Nemo. And I hate doing it."

I remained stonily silent, my heart sinking a bit.

"We got nothin'."

We shared a smoke, because it was cold and he had a pack on him, and then he said, "It keeps me up nights. Thinking about this. About how someone could do it and get away. How they could do it and not leave some print. Hair. Footprint in the blood. Some small thing. The blade was some kind of small scythe, best I can figure. Hasn't been found. Nothing's been found. All those mainland people are beginning to leave it alone. They don't like this kind of thing. Where a suspect isn't apprehended fast. They like to either close the book or move on. They're gonna pin this on some guy who's been killing people down in Jersey, but I don't know how. There's nothing here. You and I know Brooke didn't do it. She's no Lizzie Borden." He took a long drag on his cigarette, and then looked at me as if I were not really there and he'd just been talking to himself all along.

We both stood there awhile in the cold, a cord of wood at my feet. The wind picked up.

He said, "It's the damnedest thing."

That was it. He walked back up to the roadside, dusk coming on.

After he started his car, I took up the wood and went into the house to make a fire.

PART TWO

"Vision is the art of seeing things invisible."
—*Jonathan Swift*

CHAPTER NINE

1

The weather forecast storms. That's pretty much all we got out there in the Atlantic in winter. Freezing cold, storms, snow, sleet, gray or even blackened skies. It had depressed me as a boy, but now it didn't bother me much. I had a constant fire going in the living room fireplace, which made it all toasty when I wanted to sit and read or just dwell on things. I'd glance at the sky in the morning and try to predict when the snow would come, and by noon, if I'd been accurate, I would go outside just to feel the cleanness of it on my face.

2

Paulette Doone, from across the way, stopped by that night with what she called a "care package." It consisted of a paperback Bible, a copy of a book called *Give Your Troubles to the Lord and Watch Them Disappear*, as well as raisin-oatmeal cookies, gingerbread men, and some apples she'd bought at one of the local markets. What she really wanted to do was snoop and pronounce some judgment on us.

Paulette looked grim when I brought her into the house. She glanced left to right as if she were taking inventory. ("That's a lovely vase," she said, pointing. "And the piano. Your mother used to play it all the time. Is it still in tune?") But when we got right down to it, she came over to tell me one thing and one thing only: that we needed to get to the Lord, and fast.

"I want you to know that no one ever blamed you kids for the trouble you got up to," she said. She patted my hand as we sat next to each other. She kept the grim expression— Bruno later called it a "death's head rictus"—as she recounted her memories of our father. And then she said, "I thought I saw someone that day. Earlier. Might've been seven or so in the morning. It was a woman. She was walking in the fog."

I began to feel as grim as Paulette looked. "Did you tell Joe?"

She nodded. "She scared me, that woman. She seemed out of place. She wasn't from around here." When she said this last part, I had a horrible feeling in my gut that I'd made a big mistake by returning home at all. She reminded me of what I truly had hated on the island: the bigotry and prejudice against anything "foreign," and by foreign, this meant anyone who was not from the island in the first place. Anyone who had not lived there for two generations or more. "Wasn't from around here" was a popular way of saying, "outsider." Outsiders were considered somehow tainted, somehow worth less than insiders. The provincialism of the place was appalling. Worse, with Paulette, was the fact that she was rabidly religious and believed the Devil was everywhere and angels fought for our souls.

And it was embodied for me, for that moment, in Paulette Doone, with her grimness and her fears and her made-up world of demons and angels.

My contrary nature got the best of me.

"It must be terrifying," I said.

Her eyes lit up as if she loved terror as much as she did the hint of scandal.

"To live across from our home. To know that whoever did this . . . this horrible thing . . . might be somewhere nearby," I said. I felt petty and mean, but something in her story of "wasn't from around here" reminded me of why I'd set off stink bombs in her yard in the first place—she had shouted at me more than once that year that I was going to turn out just like my mother. My mother had been, after all, the ultimate island outsider. She quite literally was not from around there. She had the audacity to have married and carried children with the local hero, the prize, the man who had put Burnley Island on the map with his heroic deeds. And then she had run off like a scoundrel in the night, with a lover, no less, leaving the man broken and raising children alone.

Paulette nodded as I spoke of the lingering terrors of living near the murder site. I felt like a rat for doing it to her—for scaring her more. But she'd come over to just say something bad about someone, and I was sick of her within five minutes.

"I've stayed up the last two nights and wondered about it. I read mystery novels, and Ike says I'm always trying to solve crimes. I listen to the satellite radio—Ike has it in his garage—so I can hear what goes on off-island, what criminals are doing. And I don't think this was out of the blue. I think your father was murdered a certain way . . . well, it was like a ritual, don't you think? Do you believe in God?"

That was it for me. She was going to try to save us. Using the opportunity of our father's murder.

"Get out of our house," I said.

3

Sometime after the Revelation of Brooke as a Scarlet Woman, Bruno brought up the possibility of a memorial service.

"Did Dad ever talk about how he'd want it?" I asked.

She squinted at me, as if she didn't quite believe I'd asked that. "He was only fifty-eight. He didn't talk much about dying. I don't think he anticipated this." Her sarcasm nearly bit me. I had never been able to read her moods.

"I guess he wanted to be buried down in the old cemetery," she said, as if I needed reminding. "Among all the Raglans. All of us should be buried there."

"Granny was buried in Falmouth," I reminded her.

"She was only a Raglan by marriage," my sister said. "That was her sister's doing. Dad wanted her here, but he didn't like to stand up to the aunts from that part of the family. They were harpies." Then she nearly brightened. "There must be a way to get in touch with Mom. I know there is. I wrote six months ago to the address I found in Dad's file cabinets, but I got it back unopened. Someone else lives there now. There's got to be a way to find her."

"Why?"

"Why not? How many years has it been?" Brooke asked. "She's our mother. She may be married and living on a coffee plantation or something, I don't care. I want to find her. Don't you?"

"I don't know," I said.

"I want her to know," Brooke said. "And I want that door to be open for her."

"If she won't find us," I said, "I'm not sure we can find her."

4

Brooke once turned on the TV, only to be faced with the six o'clock news out of Boston. It had a mention of the trial of some priest, and how some vandals had destroyed some of the trees on Boston Common, and a mention of Dad's murder and the suspicion that it might be a serial killer who had been responsible for the death of a New Jersey couple from the previous summer.

"Joe said they'd do that," I told Brooke. "That the detectives would link it to other murders. He doesn't think it's true."

She didn't reply, but when I looked over at her, her hands covered her face as if she were weeping, but she made no sound.

5

Bruno used music as anger therapy.

Even as a kid, he had played the piano like it was his angst expeller.

He tried to play our mother's piano in the living room, but all I heard was a flat tinkling of the keys, as if he could not remember a single composition from the three years of piano lessons he had taken.

He could not even muster *Moonlight Sonata*, which was a tune he had banged out for a solid year, it had seemed, when he had been twelve and seemed to show signs of musical prodigy.

6

Me, I drowned the noise in my mind with Sam Adams Ale with Bruno down at the local pub.

Bruno had become far too familiar with brands of beer (he could distinguish between Alsatian and French and German with his eyes closed; he knew the brewing techniques of Rolling Rock and Coors and how they differed from an upstate New York beer of which he was fond called Genesee). During one of these bouts of beering, Bruno said to me, "I saw something spooky last night."

"It was Brooke. She's walking all night. Even the dogs won't get up for her."

"Oh yeah, I noticed. Those pills she takes don't seem to help her sleep much." He waited a beat and took a sip of beer.

"No, it was outside my window," he said. "It was someone outside my window."

I shrugged, grabbing the pitcher and pouring out a bit of Guiness into my glass mug. "Brooke."

"On the second floor," he said. "Jesus, do you ever listen? I saw someone outside, like they were in the oak tree."

7

Some hours of the day, I found myself glancing out at the smokehouse. Thinking of the cops. Of Joe Grogan. Of damnedest things. Of my father.

His last moments.

8

The smokehouse was surrounded with dead yellow stalks of weed and grass poking through the snow and what seemed like a never-ending mist, as if a translucent veil of white-gray covered the world.

It had been both a playhouse and the place of punishment for me as a child. My father had been stern when something truly bad had happened. I tended to be the troublemaker. I think he wept sometimes when he drew off his belt to spank me there. He had been punished horribly as a child (so horribly I did not even understand the stories he used to tell me about a whipping post and a riding crop or a cat o' nine tails that my grandfather hung over the inside of the front door when my father had been a boy).

My own punishments had never lasted long—usually one

or two whacks on the butt, and then I had to sit on the dirty
floor of that smelly place for an hour and think about what I
had done.

My father was afraid I would become a delinquent, as his
oldest brother had, and end badly. He worried, I'm guessing,
that he was more lenient than his own father and that I might
turn out to be a terrible human being.

He believed that there was bad blood in the family from
the Irish and Scot sides, some kind of madness and bullhead-
edness, and that it had landed in his brother, and might have
entered me at conception as well.

He may have been right, since I seemed to always get in
trouble or have unexplainable mishaps happen around me that
seemed to only point in my direction.

It had all been centered around the smokehouse, those
punishments I got as a kid.

And the games we used to play as well.

I circled around the building and adjusted the strip of
police tape, even though I knew it was futile.

The wind would blow the tape away again.

Didn't matter. The investigators had found nothing. There
was nothing to find. Only Brooke's prints and her hair, and
my father.

The smokehouse seemed consecrated now.

Consecrated by my father's blood.

9

One time, I was trying to clear out the gutters of the house,
since they'd been neglected since the fall and were full of

leaves and muck. I saw Ike Doone out by the smokehouse, and I could not get down the ladder fast enough to go chase him off.

Other curiosity seekers drove by, slowing on the road as they got near the crime scene.

10

At night, after I'd been drinking with Bruno, I'd lay in bed and look at the ceiling believing that the world was somehow an unfair and tragic proposition, and life was a joke.

One night, I dreamed my father and I were out in a boat together.

11

The dream: It was a dinghy, and the sea was calm as a mirror. In the sky, an enormous silver crescent moon, but it was barely dark yet.

My father was turned with his back to me. He had on the tan baseball cap that he often wore when he went fishing. He had no shirt on—his back was bare and pale white. He had a fishing line out in the water. When I looked in the bottom of the boat, near my bare feet, it seemed alive with wriggling fat eels and freshwater trout, their tails flipping as they tried to get out of the boat.

He turned to face me, and his eyes were no longer there, but blood poured from the empty holes.

Seagulls flew in the sky above, crying out, and somehow I knew they had taken his eyes.

Then his eyes were intact, and he got that jolly twinkle in them like he did whenever he was about to tell a funny story. "Don't be afraid," he said. "Just close your eyes. Don't touch anything."

I glanced down at the eels in the boat. "Them?"

"Just stay still here. Keep your eyes closed. Don't lean. No talking. Ignore the noise," he said. "Listen to what I'm about to say. Listen very carefully. Each word I say is important. Each word is like a key to a door. I want you to imagine a small red light, so small you can barely see it. Everything about it is completely pitch dark, but the light is red like a tiny, tiny fire. I want you to follow me with that fire, follow me as I take you somewhere else."

I watched an eel with a mouth like a python as it devoured one of the fish. I nodded, not wanting to say anything to him.

When I looked up again, the moon had grown larger, as if our boat had moved closer to it. My father hooked a long pike with a wood handle and a sharp barbed tip into one of the eels and was holding it over the boat. The eel wriggled in slow motion against the crescent moon. The moon seemed to have barbed tips, also, and for some reason looked like it was made out of metal.

One of the seagulls shrieked louder than the rest, and its cry seemed to grow with the echoes of it.

"She went away," my father said, returning his gaze to the ever-growing moon as the seagull's shriek became a scream. "But someday, she'll be back."

"Pola?" I asked.

CHAPTER TEN

1

I awoke and, strangely, felt calm from the dream.
As if my mind was somehow giving me permission to say goodbye to him. As if, despite the savagery of the crime, he was all right, somewhere, on some glassy sea, fishing.

The only part of the dream that disturbed me was somehow knowing my father knew I was still in love with Pola.

As I always did whenever I had a strange dream that seemed significant to me, I got up and got a spiral notebook I'd had for years and wrote down the details I could remember in it:

Moon, fishing, eels and trout, fingernail crescent moon, seagulls, eyes missing, eyes returned to normal, tan baseball cap, calm water. Pola.

2

For the first time in daylight, I went to the village.

The village was only about a half-mile walk from the eastern edge of Hawthorn. The day was overcast and the woods to the south sent a piney scent up to me as I trudged through the crunchy bits of snow. It had snowed off and on since I arrived, but generally melted by late afternoon down to a manageable slush. I could've borrowed Brooke's truck, but she was sleeping and had the keys somewhere in her room. I didn't want to disturb her.

The road to town was slick and wet, and I enjoyed the freshness of the day as I went. Part of me wanted to jog the whole way in, to feel my lungs working, but instead, I opted for a lit cigarette out the side of my mouth. My self-destruction would be slow and take as long as cigarettes could take.

Everything about Burnleyside was unappealing in winter.

It seemed Main Street had no color after summer—the peeling paint of the white clapboard two-stories all ran together in a jumble of storefronts and thin slivers of small Cape houses. The locals called it the Shambles—the way the stores seemed to pile on top and over each other on Main Street. It always seemed overcrowded in summer, and like a mess of poor architectural planning in the winter. The Oaks, up island, was more picturesque owing to the money poured into the houses and few convenience stores at the end of the island. In the summer, there was a Baskin-Robbins there, and even a McDonald's, all of which closed down for the winter as of October 20th. On Main Street in Burnleyside, I saw MontiLee

Stormer with her swanky new hairdo. "Just like Julia Roberts," she said, and at first I wanted to smirk and chuckle at the provincialism of Burnleyside, but when I looked twice at her, it did give her an ingenue sort of look. MontiLee was the woman who women kept their husbands away from because she seemed to be catnip for the men in the village, even if she had never strayed from her own husband. She had the look of a woman who might stray, and no matter how she protested, there were those who thought she'd spent her life in dalliances. MontiLee quizzed me about what it had been like living in the South (as she thought of Washington, D.C.) and asked if the senators and congressmen were as corrupt as they seemed. She talked politics a bit—first national, wondering what the president was up to and why he didn't respond to the letters she'd sent him about what she considered were the growing concerns of the nation. Then she switched to local news.

"I know I shouldn't be mentioning this," she said. "But any news?"

"On?"

"*The murder,*" she whispered, and glanced about the street as if others might hear her. As if it were a big secret. "We're absolutely terrified to go out at night."

"They think it's a killer from the mainland. Who's back on the mainland," I said, fairly sure that it was a lie. I had to admit it: "I really don't know. I don't even understand what the cops are doing about it."

"I watch all the Discovery Channel shows on forensics, and it's fascinating. How they can even see how blood sprays a certain way, and—" but she must've seen the look of revulsion in my face, because she stopped. "Our hearts go out to you, dear," she said, and placed a hand on my chest, right above where my heart would be. For just a second, I thought she might be flirting with me, which was less annoying than uncalled for. I will grant that it gave me a tingle, partly because MontiLee was so attractive; I was not immune to her charms. "And you know," she said, keeping her voice low, "You look like you're holding up."

"Thanks. Ah . . ." I said, fumbling with words. The only thing I could think to say was Joe Grogan's "It's the damnedest thing."

"I keep meaning to come by and pay my respects," she said, next touching my wrist, lightly. "But with Christmas coming up, and the business—well, my time is never my own."

After we did the small talk of small towns, MontiLee turned away. She sashayed to the other side of the street, heading toward her realty office. The row of shopfronts seemed dead now. Christmas lights were strung up, blinking even in daylight. At the end of Main Street, the small memorial park, with the one great fir tree, lit up.

Christmas was around the corner.

The year was nearly over.

I stood there, watching her go, remembering all those things I ought not to have shoved from my brain: a woman's touch. It made me think of another woman. The woman I just could not forget. *Pola Croder.*

All women I found attractive had made me think of Pola. I was beginning to suspect that even Beth, back in Washington, knew that my interest in her might've had something to do with her vague resemblance to Pola. No wonder she had distanced herself from me so easily; I had not been much of a prospect.

I walked by Croder-Sharp-Callahan, and casually looked through the glass, but could not bring myself to go inside. I wanted to see Pola, but I did not know what I would say to her if I saw her. My pulse quickened a bit, thinking of her, and I knew I was doomed: to replay the goodness and richness of a high school romance in my head until the end of my days.

Still, she had come by the house after my father's death.

She still cared, and I still cared, and I kept hoping that one of my father's famous quotes, stolen no doubt from others, would be true: that the universe rewards belief.

I still believed that love couldn't die. Down in my toes I believed it. Even with the bad things in life, even with murder and sorrow, I believed that love just couldn't die if it was real between two people.

And I knew I was a doomed fool to believe it.

After picking up some eggs and bread at the local grocer's, where, thankfully, no one talked to me, I went by the old store my father had run.

The storefront was smaller than I'd remembered. The CLOSED FOR THE HOLIDAYS sign was in the window, and when I peered through the windows, it looked as if nothing had changed since I'd been eighteen.

3

Back home an hour or so later, I caught Bruno peeling back some old wallpaper in the dining room that was never used.

"Look at this," he said. "Three layers of wallpaper under here. This must've been Great-Grandma Raglan's pattern." He pointed out a dulled rose pattern. "About 1905," he said. "Or 1904. Boston. I'm willing to bet it cost a pretty penny then."

"Brooke's gonna shit when she sees you tearing at the wallpaper," I said.

"It's amazing how old this house is. Think of all the things. Our rooms have been painted over so much," he said. "I scratched at my bedroom door and—get this—it's really made of glass."

"Glass? It's wood."

"No," he chuckled. "People have been painting over it so much, the center of that door is a thick oval of glass. And it's etched. I bet there are little treasures around here like that. I had no idea. Good for the *Antiques Roadshow*."

"If it ever comes to Burnley."

"It comes to Boston, I think," he said. "You never know what's around here. Last night I was going through the shelves at the back of my old closet, and I found a small pantry behind it."

"Full of treasures?"

"No," he said. "Nothing, really. A couple of little ceramic salt and pepper shakers and a naked doll with its head cracked. Probably Granny's."

Bruno apparently had taken to picking at parts of the house—looking through cabinets, finding the old secret staircase—a narrow child-sized staircase that led from the laundry room—through a cabinet door—down to one of the kitchen cabinets on the first floor. As kids, we used to play hide and seek in it, and our father would raise unholy hell when we leapt out of the kitchen cabinet while he was cooking supper. Bruno found several items that had been missing for years: his old teddy bear, a dustmop after a nineteen-year disappearance; he also discovered that there was a way to reach between the walls in his old bedroom, by way of removing a thin board in his closet.

He found his old sketchbook there, which he had forgotten that he'd hidden away at twelve and kept private from the rest of us. He showed some of them to me. They were scenes from the Ice Queen stories—and how the goblins ended up torturing the Queen eternally for her crimes. The Ice Queen was poorly drawn, but could be identified by the crescent moon in her hand and her hair, which was straw-yellow and flowing. It was pretty vivid stuff for a little kid, and I suspect that Bruno had been getting some of his frustrations out on paper. "You made up the stories," he reminded me. "I was just using crayons to illustrate your books."

"Only you never showed me," I said.

"I'm showing you now. I'm not the artist that Brooke is. But I tried."

"It's pretty violent," I said, ever the observer.

"So were the stories. I wonder why we liked them so much," he said, flipping through the sketchbook. "Dad would've had a fit if he'd seen these. He'd think there was something wrong with me."

"There *is* something wrong with you," I said, grinning. "You're a Raglan."

"We were a pretty creative bunch."

"Not a lot to do in the winter."

"Remember the words we made up?"

I nodded. "Jumblies."

"Gran made that one up. I mean like the Greasels."

"The result of Weasel and Groundhog mating," I said with some authority. "And the Eyestopper."

"Oh, yeah," he said. "That was a bad one. The evil poison that turns children blind when they see the sun."

"And the goblinfire," he said. "Look." He showed me a page in the sketchbook of a boy who might've been me, but with pointed elf ears, and a blackness of night all around him. In the middle of the blackness was a smudge of fiery yellow and orange.

We looked through some more of the sketches, pointing out what we remembered. The little ogre-girl who gobbled up people who said no to her; the boy whose skin was made out of bubblegum and blew up in a big pink bubble when he wanted to fly.

The most unusual one had me, Bruno, and Brooke all standing in a row with our mouths open in screams, and the tops of our heads were exploding.

Underneath this, Bruno had written in purple crayon: BRAIN FARTS!!!

And then there was the picture that was of us playing the Dark Game.

I barely glanced at it.

In a circle, holding hands.

Three children.

Bruno, Brooke, Nemo.

Blindfolds over their eyes.

"I wasn't much of an artist," Bruno said, and quickly closed his sketchbook.

4

I awoke the next morning, with Bruno standing over my bed.

He had on what looked like long underwear. Something about the way he looked, his hair all scruffy in his face, and something of an excited expression on his face, reminded me of him as a kid. "Get up! Nemo, you gotta see this!"

CHAPTER ELEVEN

1

After I'd rolled onto the floor, sleepily trying to find my bathrobe, Bruno dragged me from room to room until we came to my father's bedroom. It was exactly as I remembered it: the king-sized bed with my grandmother's quilt thrown over it and one goosedown pillow at the head.

A small black-and-white television on a metal stand by the window.

A lamp by the bed, with a small round table beneath it, on which my father kept the TV guide and his nail clippers. Above the bed, a photo of him and my mother on their wedding day.

"Look at this, look," Bruno said. He opened the doors to the wardrobe, the very one we had all squeezed into as children. It had wide doors, and when he drew them back, they revealed my father's clothes, hanging. Bruno parted these. There was no back to the wardrobe. It was open and went to the wall. The wallpaper had been scraped back around a hole about four feet tall.

"What the hell?"

"Yeah and it gets better," Bruno said. He crouched down, stepping into the wardrobe, and withdrew a stack of papers and magazines. "Haven't completely gone through these, but want to see what Dad was up to in here all by his lonesome?"

He passed me the magazine on the top.

Slaves of Lust was the title. On the cover, a not-so-beautiful model with large, sloppy breasts covered from head to foot in rubber, only her face showing through a zipper. Others in the pile included: *Master and Harem, Love Torture*, and *Punish the Naughty Lady*.

"He was an S&M porn hound," Bruno said.

2

I didn't expect my father not to have a private sex life that involved his hand (this somehow kept him purer for all of us, who had hoped he'd remain true to our mother, a fantasy in its own way for kids whose mothers have run off), but when Bruno dumped the magazines on the bed, they were plainly the kinds of pornography I'd never seen before. I mean, I'd watched porn in college when someone had videotapes, and I'd flipped through the odd *Penthouse* and the other assorted girlie magazines.

But they'd seemed tame in comparison to what my dad had been stashing away.

The kind that made me flinch a little and not think well of people who were pornographers. (Porn is a funny thing. When you see the mainstream pornography, what Granny used to call "marriage manuals," it all seems full of happy, willing participants. There's an element to human beauty and fantasy in it. But when you see this kind, it looks as ugly as anything that is human can look. Call me puritan. But watching people being whipped or tied up wasn't my idea of eroticism. Not to say it's not someone else's. To each his or her own. Obviously, it was my dad's idea of a turn on. Call me prude, but the last thing I wanted to find was my dad's porn stash.)

"You think it was 'cause Granddad used to beat him?" Bruno asked.

"What?"

He shrugged. "I don't know. If a guy is into this, doesn't that just mean he had a lot of punishment as a kid and it became eroticized? I've known a few guys who liked this kind of stuff, and they all seemed to have this whole discipline thing going on. Granddad had that bullwhip or whatever that he kept above the door. It must've had some effect on Dad."

"You're talking about *Dad*. Christ. Gives me the willies."

"Yeah. I guess it's freaky. Who knew?"

"Let's just throw it out," I said.

"It's not the porn that I care about," Bruno said. He got down on his hands and knees and crawled into the hole, groaning a bit where he scraped his back. He back-crawled out, and brought with him a stack of letters. "Lots of this stuff. I put some in my room, too. Look," he said. "All this stuff. And two thousand cash." He pointed to the dresser. I went over to it, and touched the top of what turned out to be three stacks of hundred-dollar bills, wrapped in baggies, and bound with rubber bands.

"His bank account?"

"Mad money," Bruno said. "And these, too."

He came over to me, and passed me the letters he'd found.

At first, I thought they were letters from my mother to him. Love letters from when they were young.

I picked one of them up. Turned it over.

3

Dear Mia,

Please come back to us. The children miss you more than you can imagine, and I am going crazy without you. I didn't know loneliness until you left. Please fulfill my greatest wish, that you love me again, that you love your children again. Nemo is nearly fourteen, and is going to be a man soon. But he needs his mother. He doesn't always make correct judgments, and I'm just not good at understanding why he's different than I was as a boy. But you were so good with him. Brookie is as beautiful as you, and as bright. You must see her. And Bruno still cries for you at night, even thought he barely remembers what you look like.

Please come home, Mia. Please. I love you and I wish

that night had never happened between us. I will always love you and always keep a light on at Hawthorn for you. If you ever think for a moment that I have lost all love for you, or that I hate you, know in your heart that you are mistaken. You are the only one for me. You are the love of my life. You are my only light.

I beg of you, on my knees, and to God, and to everything holy and sacred in the world: Come home and be a mother to your children, and if you feel even an ounce of kindness and pity for me, come home. Come home and take care of them, be their mother, hold them close. I am so sorry for what I did to you.

Love always,
Gordie

4

The letters were dusty and written on various kinds of paper—parchment, typing paper, notepad paper, as well as elegant stationery. The envelopes, from which my father had torn the letters before stacking them all together, had a single address on them: a house in Sao Paulo, Brazil. My mother's name: Mia Raglan.

It gave me a lonely feeling to read through them, between the porn, like a parade of the sacred and the profane.

I went and sat on his bed, and then lay back and put my head on the pillow.

I read letter after letter.

5

We ended up tossing the porn in the garbage without telling Brooke, since she was a bit judgmental about anything to do with pictures of naked women.

But the letters I passed to Brooke.

We also gave her the money that was found, although Bruno really wanted to keep some of it (he had debts, he said, and I told him I had bigger debts, but it still should be for Brooke since there were bills to pay at home).

On the sofa in the living room, while Bruno played something on the piano that sounded vaguely like a classical lullaby, Brooke flipped through the letters the way she might look over legal documents—with a kind of spirited disinterest. "He wrote these all the time."

"He didn't send them," I said. "I don't know why."

"He may have. They might've been returned. He said that some came back undeliverable."

"Look at the dates," I said.

She glanced at the top righthand corners of some of the letters. "Every week," she said, nodding. "That makes sense. He always went to the post office on Monday morning. Sometimes there was nothing to mail, and he still went. I saw him writing to her once. He told me he did it because he had to keep the faith."

"He really loved her."

"I suppose he did," she said. "I was never sure of it. I'd guess he was angry at her. For leaving. I always wondered if they really loved each other at any time. He told me she had mental breakdowns more than once. Sometimes I wonder if he wasn't just a caretaker for her. But I guess he still wanted her to come home. All these letters. Sent back. She must've hated all of us."

I didn't jump on her comment, which seemed cold. It had been a rough time for all of us.

Bruno, playing the piano, stopped. He said, "He never sent them. Check the envelopes again."

Brooke held up one of the envelopes. "Oh. We missed it." She passed it to me. "Bruno's right. No postmark. He must've just written these and held on to them."

"Poor guy," I said.

Bruno turned around on the piano bench. "He used to hit her," he said, that Brunoesque anger rising in his voice as if he could go from "calm" to "storm" in seconds flat.

"He did not," I said.

"Sure he did. I saw him. She came and got me. I was maybe three. I just remember he hit her. He was yelling at her, and he hit her, and I was there, and she picked me up and took me up to her room. She snuggled up to me in the bed, crying. He tore her dress, and he made her cry, and he hit her. It's a vivid memory. That's the first time I remember not liking him at all."

"You might be remembering wrong," Brooke said. "You always remember things a little twisted and negative."

"Not damn likely," Bruno said.

"From the age of three?" Brooke let out a mocking laugh. "Even if he hit her—and I still don't believe it—maybe it was just once. And a bad time."

"You believe that?" Bruno asked. "You think it's okay for

a guy to hit his wife under any circumstances, Brooke? You think he took us out to that smokehouse and used the belt on us, and he didn't use it on her at some point?"

"We were kids," she said, her own piss-and-vinegar rising. "He was spanking us. It's not the same."

"I watched him spank Nemo one time," Bruno said. "I stood in the corner of that freezing cold place, and I saw blood on Nemo's rear end. He wasn't just spanking us."

"Shut up," Brooke said. "Just shut up. He's dead now. Let it go. Jesus, you'd think he never did anything for you. You'd think because he spanked us a couple of times—"

"It wasn't just spanking," Bruno said, disgust rising in his voice. "Spanking a kid is different. What I saw him do to Nemo was whip him."

As he said the words, I tried to remember a time when I felt as if my father had whipped me, but I could not. It was a great blank spot for me. I remembered hating the place of punishment and Dad's anger, but I could not for the life of me ever really remember feeling that he'd gone overboard.

Bruno turned back around and began banging something out on that upright piano that sounded like nothing but noise at first.

Brooke shot me a glance that seemed to be full of curiosity.

Then we recognized the tune—it was *Jesu, Joy of Man's Desiring.*

We had all heard it as little children, from our mother's music box.

6

The cloud that hung low, the mystery and depression and trauma we'd all sustained from this shocking murder of our father, remained, but as the days rolled out I began to realize that we were all that was left of us. We still could remake ourselves, grow back together a bit, get along.

My heart felt a bit heavy with the knowledge that somewhere out there, my father's killer was wandering free.

I didn't trust the universe enough to think they'd get him anytime soon.

7

Bruno confided in me that there wasn't much money left, perhaps ten thousand dollars after some debts Dad had accrued, plus the two thousand Bruno had found upstairs. Twelve thousand sounded like a lot to the two of us, but we knew that it wasn't much of a savings. Brooke would need it for her own life as much as Bruno and I wanted to paw at it ourselves. Brooke had to run the business and Hawthorn. I didn't really want Hawthorn, and neither did Bruno. We saw our futures off-island.

"What kind of debts? He was cheap."

Bruno shrugged. "He spent money like anyone else. There's some company in New York he'd buy books or something from." He shook his head. "Maybe that was the porn. Who knows? I found receipts for other stuff."

"But the business," I said. "It was running okay?"

The business was the store my dad had in the village, the one that Brooke ran. A small sundries store, it was a direct competitor for the larger Croder-Sharp-Callahan Store, which always turned a profit. Apparently, my dad's store had been losing money. It ran itself, it paid Brooke's meager salary, which allowed Hawthorn to keep up appearances, but it didn't run into profit, even during the abundant summertime.

"I guess you didn't know some money was missing," Bruno said.

"Grogan told me something about money problems. But I didn't think it was anything other than Dad having no financial sense."

Bruno snorted. "Well, it was his life. And his money. I guess given that he always did things his way, it's fine, right?" He had challenge in his eyes, but I was not up for an argument over Dad's corpse.

"Maybe it's time we sold off some of Hawthorn," I suggested. "Not the house. I mean, maybe the woods, or over by the creek. There's a lot of unused acreage. It's worth something. We could keep five acres around the house and sell the rest."

"Brooke wouldn't let it happen," Bruno said.

I glanced at him with some curiosity. "You need money, don't you?"

"I don't give a damn about the money," he said. "I just give a damn about what Brooke's gonna need now. She's stuck here."

"Well, when things are better, we'll all sit down and figure this out," I said. "If Brooke needs money to stay here, we'll figure it out. She's closing the store for a couple of weeks. I like the idea of helping her out a little. I just wish I weren't the official fuck-up that I am."

"I'm officially the fuck-up," Bruno said. "I'm the one who hated Dad. I'm the one who thinks bad about everything. I drink too much. Just right now. I think I need to stop drinking."

"No, no," I said. "We both drink too much. Actually, I watched you. You had three beers last night. To some people, that's barely drinking."

"To others, it's alcoholism," he said.

"I wasn't fond of Dad either," I admitted. "I can't for the life of me figure out why. He wasn't mean to me. I insist: I *am* the family fuck-up."

"Nope," Bruno said. "I'm the family fuck-up. Nemo, you don't even want to know."

I shook my head, enjoying this. "You're in the minor leagues. I'm the major league fuck-up. Who else got run out of town at eighteen? Who else can't hold a job for a year at a time? Who else—"

"You wrote a book."

It was true. I'd written a fantasy novel a few years previous. It was published. No one bought or read it. It had been my dream to be a writer, but by twenty-eight that dream had eroded.

"Lots of fuck-ups write books," I said. "Libraries are full of the evidence. You're the athlete with the good grades and the charm who everyone loves. You can play the piano. I lose a girlfriend every time I say I like her. I lose a job when they discover how incompetent I am."

"Okay," Bruno sighed. "I've got a trump card. I'm gay."

I sat there in silence. The word hadn't quite registered. *Bruno? Gay? My little brother?* "Wow. Wow. Bruno. Wow. That's news to me."

"Yeah," he said. "To you. Dad knew. That's why he didn't love having me staying in the house. Dad was a homophobe. You know what? I think he hated me, too. Since I was born. He told me he thought I was doing it to get back at him for something. Don't tell Paulette Doone. She'll do an exorcism." Then he added, "You shocked?"

8

"You knew he was gay?" I asked Brooke as soon as we had a minute alone. She was pulling clothes out of the dryer, while trying to keep the two dogs from getting into the laundry room.

"Of course," she said. "Here, help fold."

"Not good at this," I said, as she passed me some warm towels.

"Folding? Or getting used to having a gay brother?"

"Folding. I don't care that he's gay."

"Yes, you do," she said. "I knew it when he was twelve. He told me when he was sixteen."

"Told you?"

"What, you were around for him to talk to?" she asked, and it stopped me cold. "He wanted to tell you, but apparently you didn't want to stay on the phone with him long enough to talk about it. Bruno has a lot of anger about Dad, and I think some of it is directed at you. He assumed, from some comment you made to him once, that you'd be like Dad about it."

"I would not ever—damn it," I said. "Damn it." She was right. I vaguely remembered a long phone call, very late at night, when Bruno had been sad over something that had happened—I assume he had broken up with a girl in college—and he never quite got to the point. But it had been mostly me, not wanting him to get to the point. Not really even listening the one time Bruno had seemed to open up to me as an adult. I had never been there for him at all, past the age of twelve. Even then, I was too preoccupied with my girlfriend and buddies and getting up to no good. Bruno must've felt a little lost not having someone to talk to about it. I felt terrible. GUILT rose up within me. I had been an awful older brother.

"Oh," Brooke said. She waited a beat before speaking again. "He has a boyfriend. Cary Conklin. Try not to be too shocked."

"This family will never cease to amaze me," I said. "Good for him."

She dropped the sheets she'd bunched up in a pile on the floor. She squeezed my arm. "I'm glad you're home, even under the circumstances. You should stay a little longer this time."

"Yeah," I said. And meant it. "It always amazes me what I don't know about stuff around here. Do you realize that none of us really knows each other?"

"You mean, you don't know us very well anymore," she said.

"Busted," I said, nodding.

"What drove you from this house?" she asked, as if it were the weightiest question in the universe.

I didn't even need to think about it. "I always felt something was rotten here," I said. "And I never knew why. But maybe I was just so messed up then. It's like it was a different life, not the one I have now."

"It's because Mom left," she said. "Dad always said that. He said you took off because you'd been abandoned more than any of us. He said you cried and cried the night she left and begged her to stay, and then you blamed him."

I tried to remember this, but none of it came. "I guess I buried it all."

"I did that, too," she said. "Bruno seems to be the only one who doesn't bury stuff. He just throws it all out there on the wall. Sometimes too much."

"I know so little about Bruno," I said. "Is there anything about you I need to know?"

She gave me a curious stare, as if she were about to surprise me with something. "Nothing you don't already know," she said. "I gave up on love this fall. That kind of love—the kind that's about two souls binding together. And so on. It seems a little empty to even think about it after what happened, the whole idea of dating. It seems trivial. Anything I want to do seems trivial. After that." That's what she'd called our father's murder. She swore she could not even remember sitting in the smokehouse with his body, or what it looked like, or how she felt. It had been that bad of a shock. All she could say was "after what happened," "after that," or simply, "after." I wondered how many years needed to go by before all of us would somehow get better from this. "I refuse to go out on any more dates with local men until I know that they're not just here because they have no place else to go."

"That's what I feel like. I have no place else to go," I said.

"You always have Hawthorn. By the rights of the firstborn,

the house is probably yours." She said this seriously, as if she believed it.

"Spoken like someone who doesn't give a damn. Well, it's yours. It has been since we were kids."

"I'm not sure I love it anymore," she said. "Not like I did then. Sometimes it's like a prison. It's like a place with too many doors. And none of them lead outside. Even before. Sometimes it's like a splinter inside me that won't come out. Someone said something to me a while ago that's been bugging me. Someone said that he thought we were too incestuous."

"You and Dad?"

She shot me a look that was half-grimace and half-mocking. "God, no. All of us. He told me that I'd never find a mate because I was too caught up in this family. Which is ridiculous, isn't it? We're a half-assed family now. Mom's gone, Dad's dead. Bruno hated Dad. I think he doesn't like me too much anymore. You both have lives elsewhere. How can we be incestuous?"

"Who said it?"

"Joe Grogan," she said. "But do you think we are? This whole Raglan thing? How we keep too separate from everyone here? How Dad didn't like our friends, and how we had those games we all played and kept other kids away? Was it unhealthy?"

"We played with Harry when we were kids."

"I meant *in general*," she said, somewhat testily.

"What's bothering you?" I asked.

"Nothing," she said.

"Joe said that just to hurt you."

"You know what?" she said. "I think all three of us aren't meant to be happy. Maybe we *were* too close here. I always felt like I was betraying him to have a life outside Hawthorn. I felt like if I did, it would be like Mom leaving, or you or Bruno taking off. Can I ask you something? Something I don't want to be judged on?"

"Of course."

"Do you believe in ghosts?"

CHAPTER TWELVE

1

Before I could answer, Brooke jumped in with, "Not ghosts as in dead people. I mean, the idea of someone haunting someone. The idea that inside a person, there can be another person."

"You mean, *psychologically?*"

"Maybe. That might be it. It's Dad I'm thinking of. He always told me that someone haunted him. He didn't start talking about it 'til last year, when we were fighting. He started drinking again, and we . . . well, we got into it. Yelling at each other. I'm not proud of it, but it happened. And he told me that he thought he was losing his mind because he felt like someone was haunting him. Do you think there are such things as hauntings?"

"No."

"I think I do," she said. "I think I believe there's one here. I think Dad was haunted. And I think I am, too."

2

That night, as I lay in bed, I had the disturbing feeling that there was a woman in the room.

Standing near my bed.

Please don't let it be Brooke naked, sleepwalking, her fingers running all over her body.

I opened my eyes in the dark, expecting to see Brooke, but no one was there.

Yet each time I closed my eyes, I had the distinct impression: a woman.

Not a figure, and not a man. If I opened my eyes, she would be gone. Once I closed them again, she'd still be there, a phantom.

And not only standing there, but angry.

I had this sense, it was crawling around in my brain and body, as if I could detect her aura. Anger and madness. It pissed me off that it took me so long to fall asleep. I could picture nothing about her, but it was like a negative image behind my eyes when I closed them. It was all that ghost and haunting talk that Brooke had been going on about. It influenced me too much in the late night. It frightened me a little, as well, because it reminded me of the madness our father had told us that our mother possessed. I wondered if we each would go mad someday—some biological imperative, some little signal sent out from an obscured part of the brain. That we'd somehow begin to show signs of mental breakdown. I wondered if Brooke had already been experiencing this. I wondered if it was the reason we had ever played that awful game as children, where our minds seemed to work differently afterward.

I felt my inner life was unquiet. Restless. Constant thought, constant debating over family and my father's death and what I sensed versus what I didn't—my brain didn't seem to stop at night at all. I tossed and turned, and wrapped myself in the comforter and blankets, and then threw them off the bed and rolled up in the top sheet.

I don't know when sleep finally came, but soon after, I awoke to hear Brooke screaming.

Three bloodcurdling shrieks, the like of which I'd never heard before. I stumbled out of bed and called to her.

All the doors were closed, so I had to open the five doors that separated my room from Brooke's—Bruno had come running as well.

As I went, I could see the first morning sunlight out the windows.

When we got to Brooke's room, she was sound asleep in her bed.

On her dresser, at her bedside table, even on the windowsill: small votive candles, all nursing small flames.

Bruno and I stared at each other for a second. Bruno whispered, "That's *fucked*."

I figured he meant having heard the scream, or even the burning candles, but he pointed to the big window over her bed, the shades up, the curtains drawn back.

3

It was as if just seconds before we'd gotten there, Brooke had taken her finger and rubbed words across the condensation on her bedroom window, then had breathed heavily on it so they'd show up.

The words were written largely enough to be read from across the room:

HERE COMES A CANDLE TO LIGHT YOU TO BED

CHAPTER THIRTEEN

1

All right, let me put it all down here: When we were little kids, we'd played that damned game as if it were real, and we broke the main rule about not playing it after dark.

We played it when we weren't supposed to, and I suspected that it screwed with our heads, only I wasn't sure how to talk about it. It had an accompanying dose of shame with it, and a decent bit of fear. (And it was fun.)

It turned bad when we couldn't stop playing it. When we'd sneak away, and put on the blindfolds and start going into the Dark Game.

Start going where it went.

Brooke had been most affected by the Dark Game, and by the Brain Fart.

She had been the one who had nearly died at the age of eight, afterward.

Her heart had nearly stopped, at least that's what it had seemed like to me. I practically got hysterical and kept telling our father that she needed to go to a hospital, but he told me it wasn't that bad.

"She's had a fright," he said. First he brought her temperature down with an ice bath. He made me his assistant, and he had me running all over the house for the thermometer, the ear drops, the nose drops, and the Vicks VapoRub to help her breathe better.

Dad kept her in warm blankets for two weeks after that, and spoon-fed her, and wouldn't let her so much as go to the bathroom by herself until he was sure she was better.

After that, he took me by the hand down to the duck pond, and he told me that if I ever played the Dark Game again, he would make sure that I lived to regret it.

I lied to him and told him I never would play it again.

But my fingers were crossed, so it didn't count. Or so I thought.

As I grew up, I lived to regret pretty much everything.

2

"Locks," Brooke said. "I want new locks on every door."

I stood in the doorway, having just come back from a hike with the dogs down through the woods. It was two in the afternoon—the earliest I had seen Brooke get up in a few days. "How many?"

"Seven," she said. "For the outside doors. I want at least two for the inside."

"All right," I said.

"Deadbolts. All of them," she said.

"Not for the inside," I said.

"Inside and out," she said. "I'm sorry. I just haven't felt safe. We can call a locksmith if you want."

"No, I can do it. Dad's tools still around?"

She nodded and went to show me where the tool kit was—under our father's desk in his den on the first floor. The desk was piled high with folders and papers. "He was doing some genealogical research," she said.

I flipped through some of the papers, but have to admit that I began feeling very numb doing it. I felt as if I were picking over his bones.

"It's the Raglans going back to before William the Conqueror," she said with some wistfulness in her voice. "He spent too much time on it. But sometimes it was the only thing he did at night."

I pulled the tool kit out—a large metal suitcase that my father had loved dearly. I crouched down and opened it.

"Seven deadbolts," Brooke repeated, as she stood over me. "Might as well be the same key for all of them. Can you do that?"

I glanced up at her. "Sure. It's just a key assembly."

"Good," she said.

"Why inside?"

"I don't feel safe," she said. "I want the doors to the upstairs hall to lock. Both ends of the hall."

"That's not practical. If there's a fire and it's locked and we can't get the key . . ."

She thought a moment, and then lifted her hands as if weighing options. "Get enough keys so that they can be on the inside of each door."

I murmured something that might've had the words "fire code" in them.

"Mumblespeak?" she asked.

"What?"

"You're mumbling."

"I'm just not sure if the fire department would like that. If someone needed to get out, during a fire, they might not have their key. And you have those candles going in your room at night." I thought of the candles she kept burning in her room at night. There must have been at least ten or twelve of them. The last thing I wanted to worry about in Hawthorn was a fire.

"I don't care," she said. "I wouldn't mind a deadbolt for my bedroom, but since it already locks from the inside, I'll be fine with it. There's a killer somewhere. I want to feel safe. I can't sleep at night. Every little noise frightens me." She said this as if it were obvious, even though I'd never really seen her be afraid of anything. "I wish we could get better locks for the windows. When I can, I want to replace them."

"We can get an alarm system."

"I already ordered one," she said. "But it won't be here for another week."

"I don't blame you," I said.

"I don't want anyone coming near us," she said.

"Are you all right?" I asked.

"I'm just being sensible. We need to keep this place locked up. It's not safe here anymore."

"This morning, early, you cried out. You were asleep."

"I was probably dreaming," she said. As she passed me on her way out the door, she added, "Would you mind doing the locks today?"

"Fine," I said. "Are you painting or cleaning something?"

She glanced back at me from the doorway. "What?"

"I keep smelling turpentine."

"Oh," she said. "I paint sometimes. At night."

3

"She paints?" I asked Bruno, stopping him during one of his great concertos at the piano that had been giving me a bit of a headache. I wasn't about to complain. I figured if he was getting creative like that, it probably was healthy. It's how he had released rage as a kid, and I knew he had built up a lot of it over the past several years. Just as it might be healthy that Brooke was painting again, as she had as a young child.

"Does anyone in this family ever ask a question directly to the person that it's about?" he responded, with a somewhat bemused expression.

"God, I can tell you've been shrunk. That sounds like therapy-speak. Brooke's too sensitive about her drawings," I said. "Since she was little."

"Well, yeah, she paints," he said. "She set up the back of the greenhouse like a studio. She's pretty good. Hey, you using the tub by Dad's room?"

"No," I said. "His stuff's still in there. I feel weird about it. I'm using the downstairs shower."

"Maybe Brooke's using it. Something's leaking downstairs. I thought it might be the caulking in the tub," he said. "Check the ceiling in the dining room. There's a water spot over toward the window. It grows by leaps and bounds. Daily."

"Shit," I said. "I bet the same pipes are in here that were there in 1895."

"At least," Bruno said. "I wish I knew a little about house maintenance. Other than from watching *This Old House*. I mainly just know how to tear walls down."

"Hawthorn is the original *This Old House*," I said. "Call a plumber."

He shook his head, laughing. " 'Call a plumber,' he says."

Then he pressed his fingers to the piano keys and began playing again.

4

While Brooke was asleep, early in the day, I walked back through the rooms to get to the very end of the house. The greenhouse door was open, and I went through it.

Past the empty pots and stacks of gardening tools, stood an easel that was low to the floor. On it a half-finished canvas. Brooke had been painting the woods out back, and using some kind of gray wash for a background that seemed to heighten the color of fire—for she painted a fire in the woods. It was not half bad.

Behind this, several jars of water full of thin painbrushes, a can of turpentine, and small gray cloths. Crushed tubes of oil paints—nine or ten of them—lay beside the easel as well. Four or five canvases leaned against the glass wall beyond all this.

I crouched down and lifted one up.

It was medium-sized, and at first I wasn't sure what it was of—three indistinct figures standing in what looked like a dimly lit room.

Then I realized the figures were us as children. Their faces were gray and unfinished, but there was no mistaking Bruno in his little red T-shirt, with his yellow hair, at the age of four. Brooke, with her hair straight and long; and me, scrawny and wearing my jeans that were torn at the knees. We held hands, standing in a circle.

It was the Dark Game. We were playing.

I was impressed with her memory—to have been able to paint these images, remembering the clothes we had worn at one time. Remembering how our bodies looked. Even if she couldn't quite remember our faces then.

I set this canvas back down and reached for the one behind it.

In this painting, it was our father's face, but young. Younger than I could remember, so I assumed it might've been from an old photograph. He had a smile, and she had managed to capture a peculiar brightness in his eyes. Something was too flat about it, as if she hadn't quite mastered perspective or even the interplay of light and dark. But it looked so much like him in its details. I pressed my thumb against my forehead to ward off a headache. *I can't believe he's gone. I can't believe it.*

I set this one down, carefully, behind the first.

Then I pulled up the third canvas.

This one I found disturbing.

It was a painting of Brooke herself. At least, I believe it was Brooke.

She stood on the front porch of Hawthorn. She was naked. There was rain.

She had painted her breasts and stomach and thighs completely red, as if smeared with blood.

CHAPTER FOURTEEN

1

I put the canvases back in place.

I managed to spend the rest of the day, from morning 'til night, putting deadbolts on each of the doors to the outside. The front door, back door, the door from the kitchen that went down to the brick walkway out to what had once been my mother's garden, the door to the fenced-in area at the east side of the house, where the dogs could be let out to wrestle and gambol all day. And the door that came off the greenhouse, to the side and back of the house.

The doors to the front and back hallways seemed problematic to me. I really worried about the possibility of a fire. One had broken out once, many years before my birth, but had been contained to the kitchen and front room. I really wondered what would happen if there were a fire on the stairs, and we had two locked doors. So, instead of deadbolts, I put on ordinary locks such that each door could be unlocked without a key from the inside.

2

Several days in, I got a call from Joe Grogan, asking me to come in for a few more questions. I borrowed Brooke's truck and went to the station at about three in the afternoon. Joe's office was very much as it had been when I was a boy. I'd been hauled in once or twice when it was suspected I'd broken in with a gang of my friends to one of the summer people's places. Not only had I never done this, but I had no gang of friends. Other than Harry Withers, and later Pola Croder, I hadn't really made many close friends—let alone a gang.

I felt like a boy again, walking in there.

Joe was not alone. A woman of at least thirty, short-cropped red hair, looking severe and somewhat like a pigeon (gray clothes and a sort of beak for a nose), stood, leaning a bit against his desk.

"Nemo Raglan, this is Homicide Detective Raleigh."

"From Hyannis," she said, clipping her words as if small talk were an annoyance for her. She stepped toward me to shake my hand.

"She just needs to ask a few questions," Joe said.

"Take a seat, Mr. Raglan," the detective said. She had a stony look on her face. "I don't want to waste your time. This will be brief."

"Sounds good," I said, feeling somewhat nervous.

"You arrived the day after the body was discovered," she said.

"Yes."

"Your sister called you the previous night. Do you recall precisely when?"

"No. It was sometime before midnight. I was out that night with a friend."

"Does your answering machine log the time?"

I shrugged. "Yes. But I erased the tape. I always do. Once . . . I've heard the messages."

"But you can guess that at the earliest, she might've called when?"

"Well, she told me she called around nine."

"But she might've called earlier."

"I hadn't been home since morning. I went to work, then went out after work."

"You left Burnley when you were eighteen?"

I glanced at Joe. Then back at the investigator. "Yes."

I glanced at Joe again. "Is this something I need a lawyer for?"

Raleigh smiled. "Let me tell you, we're having a tough time with this one, Mr. Raglan. For various reasons. It would be helpful if we could at least learn more about your father's relationship within his own family."

"Well, it was a good one. I was a bad kid, basically. I don't know why. There was just something here that made me want to get away. I hated this village, and this island. I felt stuck. I was also stupid. I just wanted to get away, so I did. I haven't been that close to my sister or brother or father since then. Well, 'til now."

"Did you know about your sister's mental state?" she asked.

"What?"

"Detective," Grogan said.

She continued. "She'd been depressed. Neighbors mentioned to us that she sometimes wandered at night—since late November. She was seen once out on the road in front of the house, completely naked. Your brother mentioned finding her in such a state, sleepwalking. She's even contemplated suicide."

"Brooke? I don't believe that." I stood up, pushing the chair back. "I'm sorry, Joe, but it sounds like you're looking to scapegoat Brooke."

"She told us," Raleigh said. "She didn't hide it. She showed us scars on her arms. Have you seen them?"

3

"It wasn't exactly a suicide attempt," Bruno snapped when I told him. "She said that she'd fallen asleep. She'd been taking a bath, and she has the little plastic pillow that floats—in the tub—and she fell asleep. She almost drowned. But it wasn't an attempted suicide."

"I don't think it was about the bathtub," I told him.

We were at yet another of our favorite watering holes in the village that night, having one beer too many. "This investigator said there were scars. On her arms."

"It was the upstairs bathroom," Bruno said, testiness in his voice. "With the sliding glass door for the shower. Dad's.

When she woke up, she panicked, coming up from the water, and smashed it. She cut her arms a bit, but nothing much. Nothing deep. It freaked her out. She was embarrassed. She said she tracked blood into her room and had to wash it all up that night."

"Were you there?"

"No. But I know Brooke. If she'd tried to kill herself, she'd have done the job right."

4

Out of curiosity, I went upstairs and down the long hallway of rooms to my sister's bathroom one morning when she was sound asleep. The glass doors to the bathtub were gone, although the frame around them remained.

It definitely broke. I left it at that.

For the time being.

I grew restless. I began to feel as if Hawthorn had become a prison. We certainly were too incestuous, too much in each other's business, too much on top of each other's lives. I felt like hopping the first ferry off the island, just to be away from both of them: Bruno and Brooke, brother and sister.

And that house.

And that smokehouse with its residue of murder.

At twilight, I took a walk into the village, wrapped in a big overcoat and gloves and hat—feeling as if I just wanted to freeze a little, just feel the cleanness of air and the freshness of the sea breeze.

5

As I walked along the road, snow fell so lightly that it was barely perceptible at first.

By the time I reached the village, it was pitch black with very little moon shining through the overhang of clouds. The streetlamps of Main Street were well lit, but the block I strolled along was completely empty. Half the shops were boarded up for the winter; the other half, on the north side of the street, were open. A few had just closed for the night.

I stood for a few minutes and watched the faint beginnings of snow spin downward, and I watched some of the shop-keepers lock up their stores.

Croder-Sharp-Callahan was still open.

It was a longish building with Victorian flourishes along its rooftop and a wraparound porch. It probably had begun its life in the village as a great spread of a house. When the store had taken over, it had worked hard to retain that charm of the the turn of the nineteenth to the twentieth century, as had many of the shops on Main Street. The lights were on inside, and I could see the rows of food and household supplies.

And then I saw her there. Through the slightly blurry window of the store.

Pola Croder.

It was as if I were not standing across the street, with a car or two passing between me and the store. It was as if I were right there, next to her, looking at her.

She stood behind the old lunch counter, an apron wrapped around her broad and lovely hips, her blond hair pulled back. She had gained a little weight since high school, but I had to admit, it looked damn good on her and gave curves to her formerly angular body.

Work up the nerve, you mouse, I told myself. I wished I could've downed a beer just to give myself that warm, false courage of hops and foam. *You've spent your life running from her. You have to make it right. Somehow. You have to at least let her close the door on you. Again.*

6

I went into Croder-Sharp-Callahan, its front door practically slapping me on the ass as I stepped over its threshold.

Inside, the lights were bright and flat. I saw a few faces I recognized. You can't grow up in a town that small and not know everyone. Even if you move away for several years, you come back and you still know everyone. Truth is, time truly does stop there and only begins again upon your return. "Neem," they said, and I said "Hey" to each of them and they said "Hey" back, and then we all got down to the business of ordering what might be the worst Chinese food on the planet, but the only kind available on the island.

"Pola," I said.

I wasn't sure if she would ever look my way.

CHAPTER FIFTEEN

1

In her teens, her hair had been white-blond, and she had glossy red lipstick and let cigarettes hang out of her mouth as if she wanted a guy to flick them out and kiss her. She was the closest thing to glamorous we had in Burnleyside.

Pola. That name came from her Russian father, but it had been an unfortunate one in our childhood. We had called her Pola Bear on the playground, and because she had the usual amount of baby fat straight up until her teen years, this nickname no doubt hurt.

All right, I had never called her Pola Bear. I was an outcast even then, and I felt a great deal of sympathy for anyone who was bullied or called names. The fact that we all had funny names (with the exception of the few Bills, Daves, Annes, and Debbies among us) didn't seem to stop any of the kids from picking out someone to ridicule for name alone. As Nemo, I was often called "Feebo" (you figure out how it got from one to the other, and you will have discovered the secret of childhood cruelty).

But there was Pola, at Croder-Sharp-Callahan. She was no longer the pointy-chinned little weirdo from childhood, the girl with a dirty face and a dirty dress. By high school, I had found her completely irrestistible, and we'd fallen in love fast and stayed that way until about the end of my senior year. I had adored every inch of her, the smell of her, the brain of her, the laugh of her.

She finally turned and said her "Hey," and took my order of chicken chow mein and egg drop soup. I wasn't sure if she recognized me at all. My heart seemed to beat too fast. I felt my throat dry up a bit, but soothed it with some warm tea.

Seeing her again, I will admit, I felt that lust hunger that wasn't as awful as I suspect women think it is.

I wanted to hold her, and kiss her, and somehow be with her again.

I figured it would never happen.

I felt five times the loser for even wanting it.

2

The chicken chow mein was as smooth as ever, and the soup, though tepid, satisfied. It was difficult to even notice the taste because Pola was nearby. I kept glancing at her, out of the corners of my eyes. Had she recognized me at all while I slurped at the cup? While I wiped at my chin? Pola didn't seemed to have noticed me beyond the way she might notice any other local entering the place. Certainly others said their "heys" with more marked enthusiasm, and with questions about my travels to the outer edges of the universe. Here's what I can recall of Pola, standing behind the counter with her smudge-stained white apron, her breasts so noticeable as to be an entirely separate creature parasitically attached to her chest, her hair shiny in the fluorescent lights that hummed above us: She was a beauty, and not just on the small-town Burnley Island scale, but she would've been a beauty any-where, and it was not her bra size, or the blondness, but it was her eyes and her rather direct use of them when happy, sad, annoyed, or disturbed.

She looked as if she had lived her life once with some recklessness, and now relived it with wisdom and understand-ing and a certain amount of unpleasant resignation.

And so, there was I; there was Pola; and between us, a metal counter, an apron, and my understanding that there would be no time to again make out beneath the school bleachers, or to dance beneath icy moonlight on the edge of a clear and frozen lake while my father's car idled at the road-side, nor would there be another second of stealing a kiss and feeling like a thief. Whether it came at thirty, or at forty, or at fifty, it didn't matter. I had already begun to long for what was past and what could not be grasped again.

And then the little miracle began.

She came over to me and drew a chair back across the table.

"It's terrible what happened," she said. "Your father was a good man."

"Yeah," I said. I wanted to say: *I tried to call.* But that sounded so lame. I wanted to say: *I've thought about you for the past ten years.* I just wasn't sure what that really meant.

Instead, we got to talking families and pasts and presents, but always with some kind of unanswered question about where love goes. How does it ever really change? You can tell me that when you were truly in love with someone, and it ended, that you no longer love that person, but I won't be the one to believe you. Anyone I had ever loved—in my heart, not just in my flesh or in my mind, I still loved. They had remained with me in some way that was maddeningly difficult to pinpoint.

Pola seemed to have set her expression in stone: neither smile nor flatline, her lips were slightly parted as if she were about to whistle. Then, "Well, it's good to see you here, anyway. You should come around and meet my son."

"Ah." That was all I said. Mention of her son reminded me of all the reasons I'd left Burnley Island behind. She and I were in love. I was in love with her. She was in love, but not with me. She had fooled me for a time into believing she adored me. But she had already moved on—she was pregnant at eighteen, and she told me, tears in her eyes, that it was another boy, a few years older. She was going to marry him. She wept on my sleeve, and I held her on a long summer's night. She had kept saying to me how right it was that we should break up, that she wanted to stay her whole life on the island, that she loved it there, and that I was going to get out in the world and would've hated her more for trying to keep me there. The whole time she'd told me this, when we were both eighteen, I had hated her. Hated her in the only way that a lover could. It seemed careless of her—to me— that I should give her the purity of my love and be willing to dedicate my life to her, and she had just trampled on that by deciding on a more suitable guy. And I felt myself turn cold. Even at eighteen. Bitter and cold, and I never wanted to see her again.

She had turned on me, and I had been too immature to handle it. I had run, and used any excuse I could to go.

But now, seeing her, it brought back everything. The pop songs and the clichés were all correct: Love *is* a stranger. Love *is* a battlefield. Love *is* a four-letter word. Love *is* a miracle.

But I added a new cliché to the mix when I was eighteen:

Love is a prison, and the only way out is to open the door yourself, and walk away.

I glanced at her hand. I just stared at that sucker, and I wanted to touch it. I wanted to hold her hand. To listen to her for a while. I could not get the idea out of my mind that we should be in each other's arms, pressing together, melting against each other.

We talked old times, and laughed, and hesitated a little. She shut the store down, and I told her I'd walk her home.

Just as I had done as a teenager.

Outside, the snow continued.

3

The snow swirled and shivered as it fell beneath the street-lamps.

Pola would not look at me as we walked along Main Street with all its yellow and blue and red holiday lights strung along the stores. She still wore the large white apron, and it spread across her hips, tied tight around the back, accentuating her curves; her hair was pulled back severely, and an impish part of me wanted to pull at the bands holding it up and let it fall down around her shoulders.

She stopped. As if she could read my mind. The snow moved around her face as she stood beneath the lamplight at the end of the street. Her eyes seemed radiant to me. "Sometimes the past is stupid," she said. "Would you do things differently if you could go back?"

I nodded. "Pretty much everything."

She gave me a knowing look. "Well, me, too."

Her brief words, *me, too,* confused me.

I felt something I'd never quite experienced. It was like a small voice in my head that said: *You can spend your whole life not telling the truth about who you are inside. Life is easier that way.*

Or you can just 'fess up right now. Risk it. Throw it out there. Live up to it.

"I never stopped caring about you," I said, and I felt my face go red, and for perhaps the first time in a long time I felt it down to my toes. I felt my being. I felt as if this was the first time I'd ever stood up for myself in anything.

I expected her to laugh in my face, and I was willing to take it.

The look of astonishment that crossed her face soon turned into a slowly building smile and a damp sparkle to her eyes—a light glaze of tears. She wiped at the tears. "Don't say that."

"I know it may not matter now," I said. "I don't care. You may not care for me in the same way. I don't care." Joe Grogan's phrase came to me again, seeming completely accurate: *It's the damnedest thing.*

"Do you know I had to fight myself just to let you go?" she asked.

"What?"

She offered up a sad half-smile. "You would've died if you'd stayed here. You were too in love with me. And I was too immature. And I'd cheated on you, with my body and heart, and I did it because I knew you needed to leave. I couldn't fight my parents then. I couldn't fight anyone. And I let you go. I just let the best thing in my life go. I let it go for some stupid sense of what my parents wanted. And what everyone wanted except for me. And I didn't want you stuck here, with me."

A chill went through me when she said it. Something seemed to smash against my innards, and for a minute I thought I would be sick. Jumblies, indeed. But that feeling quickly passed as I stood there in the barest moment that seemed to be an hour. I stood and looked into her face, and something within me fought against what I was feeling in the pit of my stomach. It was an awful feeling of fluttering and slight dizziness, as if she'd caught me off-guard and had tripped me up.

Then she said, "If you knew that someone intentionally lied to you so that you would have a better life, even if that lie was the worst thing in the world, how would you feel?"

I thought for a moment and said, "If I understood the reason, it wouldn't bother me. A lot of people lie for no good reason. If the reason's good, it's understandable."

She closed her eyes, opened them again, and looked at me as if she had just said a prayer.

"It's the stupid past," I said. "Just like you said. Don't let it hurt you now. I'm here. I don't care about any of it. I'm here right now."

I was about to say something more, but I decided not to talk at all. I wanted to kiss her tears away. I leaned forward and kissed her eyelids, and then her nose, and then without even realizing where this might lead, my lips were over hers, and she opened her mouth gently. Her breath was sweet and felt like home as I inhaled it. I wrapped my arms around her, and drew her to me. Part of me was afraid she might pull away, but she embraced me before I had locked my arms behind her back.

"This is crazy," she murmured. She pressed her face against mine, and then under my chin, and then against my cheek.

"I know, I know," I said. I resumed kissing her as much as a woman could be kissed beneath a streetlamp. I reached up and drew out the twist of cloth that held up her hair, and it cascaded around her shoulders, and she opened her coat so I could put my arms inside it for warmth as I held her.

"We can't do this here," she whispered.

"The store," I said, glancing back at the darkness of Croder-Sharp-Callahan. "The lunch counter."

She laughed, looking up at me to see if I were teasing her. "You're serious?"

"Like when we first made love," I said, and my throat caught on those words: *made love*. It was the first time in my adult life I had ever said them. I had said all the other words that seemed more true in the past; I had used the profanity and the blunt language and the clinical talk, but not those words that had seemed both precious and mysterious.

"This is mad," she whispered, but her body betrayed a passionate urgency, and we held each other's hands like kids again and ran through the fresh snow, back to Croder-Sharp-Callahan.

4

Once inside, she locked the door behind us.

She kept the lights off, and we stumbled into stools and chairs and around the cash register. Somehow, our clothes fell away, although there was a good deal of tugging and unsnapping and unbuttoning and unzipping and boots that took a while to come off. I felt just as I had at seventeen, the fumbling numbskullery of a boy in love without a brain in his head, the explosion of the senses as we rolled together, and tasted and felt and burned against each other.

Somehow, from there, we went up to the empty apartment above the store, through the back stairs, half-dressed, the snow still spinning gently downward, giggling and passionate and me in my boxers and socks, bounding up the steps after her as she wrapped herself in her coat, but with nothing else underneath.

The apartment was one room, with a bathroom and a small kitchenette by the window. The window had a tattered and yellowed shade drawn down. An overhead light flickered. A mattress lay back against one wall. "It's clean, don't worry," she said. "We use it for naps at work."

I didn't care if it was dirty or newly washed. I leapt onto the mattress, and she came tumbling down on top of me.

I felt an energy within me, a renewal of forces stronger than personality or sustainable life. Something more than what I had been before that night. I wanted to give her so much, everything I had, every ounce of love and care and physical pleasure; I wanted to mold myself against her and her against me until you couldn't tell one from the other.

Afterward, I didn't even crave a cigarette.

5

"I've been wasting my life," I said, my lips against her hair, holding the scent of her for just a moment longer.

"You have not," Pola said.

"I have," I insisted. "I've wasted these years. I let go of my family. Of you. We could've been building a life together."

"You'd have been bored here. With me. It wasn't right, not then."

"I guess we had separate paths for a while," I said. And I knew it. Sorrow had held its sway over me for too long. The sorrow was not just my father's murder. It was a sorrow that had somehow crept its way into my soul and had burrowed there. It all seemed ridiculous now, in the arms of the woman I loved, on the island I had abandoned for no good or genuine reason.

"Maybe this was the way it was meant to be," she whispered, lazily and sweetly.

I held her longer than I had ever before held a woman in my arms. I felt her heartbeat against my chest. That peculiar and unfamiliar feeling of being bound to another human being in a way that breaks down all barriers and intimate territories. We made love with the energy of first-timers, and the sloppiness, too. She laughed when I tried to hold her in a way that made her leg cramp; and I began laughing when she took me inside her, not from silliness, but from a joy I hadn't even known could exist between two people, between a man and a woman in a secret of love that had been protected over several years. It was as if I had unlocked doors within me. She smiled afterward and told me that when we were in the throes of it, she enjoyed my laughter. "You sounded like the old Nemo. The one I fell in love with when we were children. The one who had joy." She kissed my lips, then my cheek, and neck. "Are you back, Nemo?" She looked into my eyes as if someone might be hiding somewhere in them.

Without realizing it, I had held my breath as she spoke. I had held on to a breath as if I were holding on to the years. I let out a sigh, the likes of which had not passed through my lungs or throat in all my life. "Yeah," I said, like some idiot, a gust of my breath escaping and taking with it a great burden. "Yes. I am back."

Outside the window, the wind howled, the beginnings of a storm, perhaps, but I didn't care. I felt safe, for once in my life. I felt safe with Pola.

I lay there with her, looking at the window, the snow, and for a brief second, I thought I saw a woman's face at the window.

I sat up, startled.

But it was gone.

It's in your mind.

"What is it?" Pola asked, looking from my face, back to the window. "Nemo?"

"Nothing," I said, settling back into the mattress with her, arms around her again.

6

"I want you to forgive me," I said a bit later.

"For what?"

"What I did to you back then."

"I didn't blame you," she said. "Like I don't need forgiveness myself."

"How I ever deserved even knowing someone like you . . ."

She held a finger to my lips. "Don't make me out to be a saint."

"But I was the one—"

"Don't. Leave the past where it belongs. All the bad things are in the past. We were barely more than children then."

"I don't even wanna talk," I said. "My dad used to tell me that the sun shines on a dog's ass now and again. And I just want to bask in the sunshine a little."

We kissed again, and lay there until we both knew it was time for her to go pick up her son at her ex-husband's. I didn't want to leave her side at all, but we parted, regardless. I told her that we'd have lunch the next day.

The separation of old lovers who discover a new love between them has got to be the most agonizing. You know what it's like, you know how much you want the other person, but you also know that things can get in the way of love. How I wished that two people in love could always be together, every minute, every hour, and never grow bored or tired or distracted—or worse, out of love by the familiarity of love. These were the crazy abstractions I thought about on my walk back to Hawthorn, down the snowy road at sometime after ten P.M.

And that's when I saw Carson McKinley in his truck, parked alongside the darkened storefronts, but beneath the red and blue of Christmas lights, masturbating.

7

Truth was, I didn't know if he was choking the chicken, but the truck vibrated, and I saw his sweaty face in the truck, so I assumed he was performing his favorite public pastime.

I never begrudged Carson his compulsion. Many a man has dreamt of doing just what Carson did in broad daylight or beneath the streetlamps, but few have the balls to follow through. As long as he was in his truck, the island sheep and horses were safe.

As I walked by the truck, I averted my gaze. The last thing I wanted to see after being with Pola, was a fifty-four-year-old with a beard and eyes like a crazed moron jacking off. But as I passed, he called out my name.

Now, with anyone else, I would've ordinarily turned to see who wanted to get my attention. But this was Carson McKinley.

"Hey, Nemo!" he called out again, his shout echoing slightly because of the cold and snow and emptiness of the street.

I turned. He looked out at me with his trollish face, half in darkness.

"Storm's comin'," he said.

"What?"

"I saw her. Storm's comin'."

The truck continued to vibrate.

Perhaps Carson McKinley might've somehow spied on Pola and me as we had our marathon of sex. I felt a disgust for all mankind. The memory of seeing my dad's porn collection didn't help. Women were right, most of the time we were dogs and pigs, and perhaps not even as good as anything that walked on four legs. Sure, there were men who did great things in the world, but in the ordinary things, we were completely the lowest of lows. Even my father, I thought—even Gordie Raglan, war hero, survivor of prison camps, who led the other prisoners to safety at great odds. Even his life came down to a stash of porn stuffed in the walls.

I didn't want life to be just this. Finding Pola again, not knowing if I could even feel that innocent love you get to feel as a kid, seemed like a miracle in need of protection. I stood there for a moment, judge and jury of Carson McKinley, who seemed the prototype of all that was dysfunctional of my gender. It was my puritan blood rising, I guess. Who was I to judge anyone else? I felt bad for Carson. I asked him if he was okay.

"She's a bad storm comin' down on us," he said. The truck began to bounce up and down. I turned away. He shouted after me, "SHE'S COMIN'! OH LORDY, SHE'S A-COMIN'!" This was followed by what I can only assume were orgasmic moans of McKinley pleasure.

"Merry Christmas to you, too," I said.

8

As I approached Hawthorn, feeling weary and frozen and in need of sleep like a drunk in need of the last drop from a bottle, I saw a light on in Brooke's room toward the back of the house. *You're up. You're always up. You need more life. You need more than Hawthorn, Brooke. You need to open some doors.*

Bruno's light was off, but this didn't mean much. I wasn't even sure if Bruno was in his bedroom asleep or across town with his boyfriend. *Well, good for him. At least he's got love. Hang on to it, Bruno, for as long as you can. It's a small miracle that needs protection. I didn't protect my miracle when I was a teenager, and I lost some years. Luckily, Pola protected it. Luckily, Pola loved me, too. So, Bruno, just make sure it's love and then hang on for dear life.*

I dropped onto my bed, and only then realized that I had left my boxer shorts in the apartment above Croder-Sharp-Callahan.

That night, I awoke to Brooke walking through my room at some ungodly hour. Unfortunately, I had that now-expected impression that it wasn't Brooke. I sat up and flicked on the light.

No one was there at all.

Both doors to my bedroom were shut.

9

The next morning, I discovered that Carson's fertility rite had indeed brought a storm.

We were buried under snow, not the most unusual oc-
currence for the island in December. By the time I'd trudged
downstairs to the kitchen to the smell of a rich dark roast of
coffee, Bruno and his boyfriend had already dug out most of
the driveway. Not that it mattered: The village plow, also
known as Johnny Sullivan, had yet to reach Hawthorn. There'd
be no driving that day.

Cary and Bruno started a snowball fight out front. As I
watched them from the kitchen window, it reminded me of
us all as kids. How we played all over the fields, how the
winters were rich with ice skating on the pond or snow forts
along the hill.

Afterward, the smell of coffee and a kind of rosy glow
seemed to permeate the house. I think it was just the way I
felt—I had this hope again, this sense that I'd come home for
a reason that was good. Not just because of my father's murder, but because I still had to find out if there was love for
me in the world—the only woman I had ever really loved.
Bruno noticed and commented that I looked a bit more chip-
per than usual; he asked where I'd left Dad's tool kit, and
then added, "You look the way I feel."

A bit later, I called up Pola. "You hanging in there?"

"Yep," she said. "Me and Zack are making hot cocoa. Want
to come over?"

"If I can walk a mile or two in the snow."

"Johnny'll be out soon."

"Well, then I definitely want some cocoa. With marsh-
mallows."

"We have a fire going. Zack and I are gonna go to Seabird
Hill and sled down it in a bit."

"You sure we're okay?"

"Nemo?"

"I mean, last night was . . ."

"I know," she said softly. "I wish we could've stayed together all night."

"Me, too."

"Why didn't we?"

"Don't want to spring it on Zack too quickly," I said. "How do you think he'll feel about . . . about this?"

"I don't know," she said. "Well, he's begging to go out and play. Come by when you get out from under it."

She hung up.

Part of me felt the phantom of girlfriends past in the hang-up. I felt the Jumblies in my stomach. *Would this work out? Were we just trying to recapture a past that couldn't last?* It was still all euphoria for me. All the goofy and no-good thoughts that run through you when you realize that love looms. I thought of every woman I had ever felt close with, how I had wanted to see if love was there within each relationship. But it hadn't been. Only Pola. It was crazy. Things like high school sweethearts weren't supposed to work out.

I spent the day either on the phone with Pola (the road didn't get plowed until nine o'clock that night), or going over my dad's papers. I found a notebook of his, and recognized his tiny scrawl that was so hard to read. My dad had kept track of everything that happened in his life, particularly in terms of the house. Here's one bit of it:

Stairway, back of house. Need repair on bannister. Call lumberyard. Call Bill. Make appointment with vet for Mab.

Bruno's baseball practice. 9 AM Sat. Take cooler. Brooke at 11, swim team.

Cheerios, milk, sugar, eggs, wheat bread, chicken breasts, case of Coke, case of Diet Coke, case of root beer. No Oreos for Bruno.

It made me laugh to flip through the spiral notebooks he kept, the closest thing to a diary he'd ever had. It reminded me more of him, of his way of organizing his life, than if he'd kept a more detailed record of his every whim and mood. I laughed, and then wept a little thinking about life's unfairness, that I'd never made things right with my father, that some insane person had murdered him and now there was nothing I could do to reach my father and tell him all the things you want to tell the dead.

As I sat there, I began to wonder about the past month's records. I flipped through the notebooks, but for the one marked that year, there were no strange entries at all.

I guess I wanted to believe that my father had noticed something. Had seen anything.

But again, my head ached, my stomach tightened, and I thought of him, lying in his own blood, sliced, someone standing over him with a curved blade in her hand.

Her.

I thought it: *Her.*

Why her? I closed my eyes. The sense of a woman.

Not Brooke.

Another woman.

As if the house itself had a woman hidden in it somewhere. *Hiding.*

10

That night, it must've been about three or four A.M., I awoke, sensing a presence in the room.

My heart began beating too fast, and I could taste something sour and dry in my throat. I wanted to get up, get some water, or at least flick on a light. But a half-sleepy fear kept me on the bed, trying not to move. *What was it?* I glanced to the bookshelf and the small desk by the window.

Then I saw her.

For a moment, I had a terrible feeling I didn't know who it was. I felt my heart beating within my chest, and a strange *shushing* sound that was like a pulse within me. I held my breath as if afraid that she would know I was awake and saw her.

For that slice of a moment, a terrible dread overtook me.

I had the sure feeling—the absolute conviction—that if there were such things as ghosts, this was one of them.

CHAPTER SIXTEEN

1

She stood near the white curtain of the window, the moon shining in her hair. I could not tell if she was looking out the window or looking from the window to me, for she was nearly all shadow.

It's Brooke, I thought. My heart still jackhammering. I felt clammy and cold, and didn't want to think this could be anything irrational. *It has to be Brooke.*

I was about to say something, but I didn't want to startle her. Brooke went from room to room at night, after all. Perhaps she had just stopped for a minute to look out across the woods, and think of our father.

The sensation of dread returned. Somehow, I felt that this was not Brooke at all. This was someone else. I only thought it was Brooke because it was a woman in the house, and Brooke was the only candidate. I began to believe (as you only can in those terrible early morning hours when the dark has not yet vanished) that this truly was a ghost. I felt like a child again, with a belief in anything that came my way.

It took courage for me to reach over and flick on the bed-side lamp. When I did, and the light flashed up in the room, it was Brooke. That nighttime imagination always did its worst with me.

She stood there, facing the window, her back to me, the reflection of her face in the mirror. She looked just like my mother at that moment. Just like her.

She wore one of her stretched-out sweaters and gray sweat-pants, her hair long and stringy as if she hadn't washed it for a few days.

"Brooke?"

She didn't respond.

"You okay?"

"I don't know what he wanted from me, not ever," she said, slowly, and in such a way that it gave me a chill. I realized a few seconds later that what scared me about her was that her voice didn't seem right. It seemed almost like Brooke's voice, but different.

"You probably should go to bed now," I said.

"He never loved me. Not the way he should have. Why couldn't he let me go? Why can't I leave? I don't understand any of this," she said. "That son of a bitch."

"Don't think about it now," I said.

"It's terrible what this island can do to you," she said, and she turned to look at me, but her eyes were nearly closed. For the barest second, she didn't look like herself at all. Was she sleepwalking? Her voice was calm and even, but something in her tone kept me on edge. "Not just him, but everyone. If you're an outsider, you're always one. Others knew, I think. They guessed. But no one stood up to him. Nobody protected me. Nobody wanted to know what was really happening. Not any of you. This place is a prison."

Then she went out through the doorway to the west, through the bathroom that adjoined my room with my father's old room. She closed the door behind her as she went on, presumably to the next room.

I left the lights on and could not sleep the rest of the night. I grabbed a book off the shelf called *The House on the Strand*, one of my favorites from my teen years, and sank back into a world of time travel and intrigue.

2

Nightmares grew within my head when I finally fell asleep at night, or in the early morning. Sometimes I got up in the middle of the night, just to avoid the bad dream. I'd go out and get a cord of pine from the pile just outside the front porch and make a fire in the living room and try to read, or flip TV channels in search of something to take my mind off the idea of sleep.

But I'd fall asleep eventually.

In my nightmares, I saw her. She wore blood as a gown. She had hair like a raven and skin as pale as snow. It was the Snow Queen. The Banshee. The Queen of Hell.

And I'd created her when I was a kid.

3

Soon enough, the regional news shows stopped running any-thing about the story of the murder, nor was it showing up in the papers, outside of the *Burnley Gazette*. Other tragedies and terrors took over the news in the world. Other families suffered and found reporters at their door; other good men and women were cut down by vicious killers; and my world sank back into a low throbbing pain at the back of my head.

I was beginning to feel trapped, but I had nowhere else to go. Oddly enough, I never asked Brooke about the details of our father's death, nor did I read the papers or watch the news. And none of us answered the phone.

"Writing any more books?" Brooke asked one evening. "I read *Igdarizilia*. Or whatever it's called. If it had been about something, it would've been a classic. But it was good."

"*Igdrasil*."

"Oh. Dad used to call it 'Godzilla.' I liked it. You needed more sex in it and maybe some more battles. That whole elf subplot bogged it down, and the names? You picked all the wrong Celtic names. Too hard to pronounce. You know it's rough when you need a glossary just to pronounce the names. Maybe you should write about real things this time," she said. Then she added, "I didn't like how you just threw all the dirty laundry in there."

"Huh?"

"Well, I don't doubt that the little nymph was me. You could've at least made her a little less slutty." She laughed, but with a bit of an edge. "Dad was in there. And Bruno. I'm surprised you didn't include the greyhounds."

I ignored her comments. It seemed to be a universal truth that the family of the writer never really wanted to appreciate the writing. "Dad didn't read it, did he?"

"Don't feel bad, he never read novels. I told him what was in it. He was proud. He said he didn't like the father character too much, but I told him it had nothing to do with him. You might not have wanted to make the father the ogre who tortures elves and abducts the Queen of Hell."

"It's fiction, Brooke. Fantasy. There's no reality about it."

"People want to read about real things, even in fantasy," she said. She thought a moment and her eyes became slits, as if she'd just been seized with some vague moment of genius. "You really should think about writing for children. The stuff you wrote when we were kids was good. I can still remember some of it." She meant everything she said to be kind and generous. I wasn't ever going to take offense at anything Brooke said, or anything Bruno might say. I didn't want to lose this bond we were creating in the wake of tragedy over something petty like my silly book.

I decided I needed to write again.

4

In my old room, I found some of my early stories, when I had just begun to learn to write.

I had dreamed of being a writer since I was nine years old. My father had gotten me a typewriter back in the days when it was the most advanced writing tool beyond a pen and paper. It was a secondhand beast from Croder-Sharp-Callahan general store, one that had sat on the shelf for nearly my entire life at that point. It was a thick, clunky Royal whose existence had begun sometime before even my father was born. But it served its purpose, and I learned to hunt and peck, for I'd had a bad year that year—it was the year my mother had left us, and this seemed to hit me hardest. My father asked me to write stories if it would help me, and I began writing them.

They were, at first, one-pagers, but soon I became adept at just writing and writing with no end in sight. I suspect I was obsessed with whatever story had gotten into my head. I wrote fantasies and stories of terror and happy stories of children who had wonderful mothers who hugged them and told them how important they were. In some respects, my ambition was never to be published, but to bring onto the page the nearly perfect, if dictatorial world of my imagination: the three-headed monsters, the perfect mother, and magical island, the boy who could fly—all the ways I wanted the world to be. In my mind, as a kid, I imagined all kinds of fantastic ways of living—of brushing the tops of trees with my feet as I flew, not like Peter Pan, but like a starling. Or animals that would speak to me in the stories. Or the kids I wanted to have like me, who did indeed enjoy my company. There were faraway lands based far too much on Hugh Lofting's Dr. Doolittle and Tolkien's Middle Earth, and creatures out of Edith Hamilton's books on mythology, which I began reading at eleven. Once I discovered Herman Hesse's *Demian*, I was done for; moving on to other covert reading (for none of these books were pressed upon me in school), I went to George Orwell and

H.G. Wells and Mary Shelley—and I was writing stories that mirrored my reading the whole way through. Writing stories—purely for myself, for I never showed these to anyone—was to not express myself, but to purge some of my imagination, get it out of my head, where it swirled and blocked me from living as a child. Brought it out into another dimension. There were times when I felt there were a thousand doors in my head, and I needed to open all of them to find the one important door. The one important key that would open it.

And whatever was behind that door would somehow illuminate what I didn't understand about my life.

In the meantime, I had to open those thousand doors and see what wonderful and dreadful beasts existed there, waiting for me.

I found the one story that probably meant the most to me from childhood. It was a complete rip-off of Hans Christian Andersen's "The Snow Queen," mixed with the Greek myth of Persephone. In the Andersen story, the Snow Queen's magic mirror is broken, and a shard of glass gets in Kay's heart. He is Gerda's brother, and he becomes a very bad boy from this. The myth of Persephone is the story of the daughter of Demeter's abduction into the Underworld by the king of that realm. I even noticed shades of Narnia and Alice in Wonderland in there. The story was called "The Ice Queen's Revenge." I suspect I called it this not because of the obvious derivation from Andersen's "Snow Queen," but because it was a little joke with Bruno. At four, when he wanted ice cream, it sounded like "ice queen," so I just made up the stories. At first, when I read some of them to him, he got scared, and stopped asking for "ice queen" at all.

5

Here is a bit of it, with typos and misspellings intact. I was ten at the time:

CHAPTER FIVE: THE ICE QUEEN RISES!

I SHALL COME FOR THE CHILDREN! the Ice Queen, the Queen of FROZEN CREAMY HELL, said, and she wrapped herself in the furs of bears and lions, and she had her Oomos, those filthy goblins of the Underland whose breath is so foul that people think its farts from a dead cow and whose hands are so grimey that they spread disease wherever they go, carry her to her Slay, made entirely of diamonds cut from the fingers of new brides. The Slay glowed and shined like millions of stars, and the Ice Queen, called by some Imyrmia, sat in it with her trusty demon servant, Chamelea, the lizard-faced and hog-bellied. The Slay was pulled by twin dragons, tortured in the Castle Fragonard that lies above the Lake of Glass and Fire at the very heart of Underland. The dragons were once kind-hearted beasts, but Imyrmia, in anger over their father's not wanting them to be slaves of her Relm, took them to her basement and turned them into zombi dragons doing only her bidding. She used bobbed wire to beat them onward as they flew up up up from the deep diamond and ruby caves of Underland.

When the Slay came all the way up into Earth,
lightning tore at the ground, opening it up for
Imyrmia's Slay. Blasts of fire and BELCHES OF FOUL
STENCH! blew up like a fart from an oger's butt. Even
the twin dragons hated the smell and coughed fire as
they rose into a blackened sky, their tails twisting
and smashing trees down as they went and setting entire forests ablaze with their coughs.

All the land knew of the Ice Queen's arrival, for
they had known her many years before. Once upon a
time, she was the Maiden of Snow, and she brought the
dancing elves and fairys of winter across the land.
She had made everyone have fun, and children through
the entire world could skate and ski and have snowball fights and make snow angels and snow people and
never go to school when the Maiden of Snow was there.
But then, she got picked up by the FEARFUL AND MIGHTY
ruler of Underland, a monster so dirty his skin was
crawling with germs. His hair was home to thousands
of cities of lice. His skin seemed alive with red
mites. When he walked, his feet never touched
ground, for rats and centipedes lifted the souls of
his feet up on their backs and did the walking for
him like roller skates. He is known as Dogrun the
Merciless. He wanted the Maiden of Snow in his kingdom because it was too hot and he needed better
weather. Underland was on fire most of the time. People there breathed the foulest stenches and drank
polluted water from the Twin Lakes of Rhea (which

were called Dya and Gonna, sisters enchanted and turned into lakes of brown lava full of wastes and chemical spills and oil spills.) Dogrun the Merciless needed a bride. So he grabbed the Maiden of Snow, Imyrmia, and she screamed, but she had to go into Underland with him. He forced her to marry him, and the heat of Underland melted her heart for him. But she herself made Dogrun's heart turn cold, and he could not be married to her anymore. She had turned Evil, and she ended up imprisoning him on the Dark Isle of Lost Devils, a place where those demons went who no longer had Evil Believers in the world above them. Dogrun was chained and kept inside a prison that had a high fence, painted all over with magical cymbals that clanged and smashed at him when he tried to escape. He lived out the rest of his eternal life there, eating the rats beneath his feet, the red mites on his body, and the lice in his hair.

And the Ice Queen ruled all in Underland.

And now, she was after the elf-children who knew her secrets.

They lived on Earth, and their names were Fearling, Burnt, and River.

6

Of course this was somehow about putting my little brother and sister and me inside the story—they were the only ones I read them to. Since Bruno's real name was Byrne, Burnt was close enough; and Brooke might be a "river," and my much-hated real name, Fergus, was close to Fearling in some way.

We'd have read it in secret, finding a room in the house where Dad would not find us. There was a wardrobe in his bedroom, and it was just large enough for the three of us to fit in. I had a flashlight, and I'd read to them. We pretended that we were somehow entering C. S. Lewis's *The Lion, the Witch, and the Wardrobe* right there, and Bruno, until he was six, would not venture to the back of the wardrobe even when we dared him for fear that another world opened up there.

The legends of Imyrmia, the Ice Queen, grew over the years, and she somehow transformed in my story to an even more powerful monster called, simply, Banshee, as I had begun discovering the Celtic myths when I was twelve, and felt that the Ice Queen needed a transformation and a new name. Both Bruno and Brooke still looked forward to the stories, and although we were all a bit taller and could just fit in the wardrobe without touching each other—with the occasional gas leak from Bruno, who seemed to delight in this—we'd climb in when I had finished writing another three- or five-page opus, and I'd have the best audience a writer could ever have.

As Banshee, the Ice Queen had changed. She was no longer the frosty beauty with blue skin and white hair. She had become more monstrous, denied the beauty creams and ointments and sorcery of Underland, which kept her eternally young and insanely beautiful. Banshee came out at twilight, surrounded by flies and mosquitoes, her heralds. She was ghoulish, and her skin was torn and leathered and dried against her bones. She had razors for teeth and fingers that scraped flesh, and she took the form of anyone she chose, anyone trusted, but as dark approached, she could not hide her true form, and when night fell, all was revealed. Alone with her hapless victim, she showed her true form.

In the Banshee stories, she became trapped on Earth, unable to go to her Dark Kingdom, and she wanted more than anything the souls of the three elves who had exiled her from her world.

Scared the shit out of Bruno when he was about six. I told him that Banshee was coming for him if he stepped out of bed after the light went out. This accounted for his bed-wetting, and yes, I feel ashamed that I put the thought in his mind. I tried to take it back, but once you've told a kid that kind of thing, it never completely erases from his memory.

7

I read through some of the stories, all of them bad, all of them somehow making me happy about my childhood again. My father had once had the ambition to be a writer, in his youth. He told me that he seemed to only be able to write the truth of things, and no one wanted to hear the truth. He'd hold up a novel from my bookshelf (*Treasure Island, From the Mixed-up Files of Mrs. Basil E. Frankweiler, Danny Dunn and the Anti-Gravity Paint*) and he'd say, "It's people who write lies like these who get published. Nobody wants the truth. They want lies spoon-fed to them." All right, he had a bit of the tyrant in him—perhaps all heroes do—and had never been able to read or enjoy fiction to save his life. I attributed this, again, to both a stern upbringing (his own father, the grandfather I never knew, disciplined with whips to the back, actual whips, in the smokehouse, the place of punishment), and to his two years in prison camps during his war. He nearly seemed vulnerable at those moments, when he was at his worst. I forgave him anything when I was a kid because I was so grateful that he hadn't left us as our mother had.

But those books on my shelf! To me they were worlds to explore. These were the seeds of my desire to write fiction, but I didn't think I'd ever be able to do it as an adult. Still, when I was twenty-five my first novel, a fantasy called *Igdrasil*, was published. (For those of you who don't know, Igdrasil is the Tree of All Existence in myth. My novel did it a disservice.) I could not make a living from writing, but I found that fantasy was what I could write best—high fantasy as it's called. And so this gave me the illusion that I could be a writer, but in fact, I had not been able to write another story or novel since selling that one.

It was a mental and physical constipation, my adult life to that point.

It was as if I genuinely was not meant to live outside of the island where I'd grown up—the world was too much. I needed the smallness of Burnley Island. The narrowness of the minds, the quietness of the winters, the serenity of the separation from the mainland.

Even Carson McKinley, spanking the monkey in his truck at the harbor.

But my dreams of happiness and writing fiction and loving life, all had been there, at home, waiting for me.

Sitting in my old bedroom, I pulled out that ancient typewriter—a Royal that had no business working, let alone with a ribbon of ink still in it that managed to smudge the odd "a" and "r."

THIS IS THE LAST STORY ABOUT BANSHEE

Now, before I tell you what I wrote, I have to tell you that whenever I write anything, I have to first write a page or two about things that are occupying my mind. It's a way of sweeping out the cobwebs, I guess, and is my version of therapy. I'm not sure if I believe in writer's block, but I do believe in general Brain Block, just as I believed in Brain Farts. Writing out the tangle from inside me seemed to get the creative juices going.

So I wrote:

My father is dead. Someone murdered him.

Who?

WHO?

Brooke is losing her mind. Bruno is picking apart the house. Brooke is painting. Bruno is playing the piano again. And here I am, writing.

It's as if we're just picking up where we left off years ago.

Brooke walks at night. Bruno has a boyfriend. I still love Pola. We have none of us figured out love right. Maybe Bruno has. Not me. Not Brooke. Our lives in shambles. Dad must have been the glue. Falling apart.

The Banshee is loose. The Banshee has taken us over.

At night, she watches us.

When I'd finished typing this sentence, I looked at it. I had no idea what it meant. Did I mean that Brooke watches us? The Banshee? Was this the beginning of a story, or was I still trying to clear my mind a bit? I wasn't even sure.

I typed:

```
At night she watches us, waiting.
```

Again, no idea what this meant, but it might be the beginning of a story I could write. It intrigued me.

Then:

```
Dad was murdered. At night. Not at night. Before
night.
     He wasn't killed at night. He was only found at
night. Killed earlier. Body cut. Torn. Sadistic.
Who? Who? WHO?
     It was the hour before dark.
     The magic hour.
     Why in God's name would someone want to kill my
father? War. His men? The enemy? His enemies? A psy-
cho?
     The Banshee?
```

I stopped, scratching my head, annoyed with the futility of this exercise.

I set the typewriter down at the foot of my bed.

8

Sometime around midnight, I was back in my bedroom again, exhausted from helping clear some of the debris that had piled up in rooms—Bruno and I made a go of sorting Dad's papers, and going through unopened boxes in the two rooms he had used for storage.

There was that old typewriter, just waiting for me to write a bit more.

I sat on the bed and plopped it on my lap.

Someone had used it.

Someone had typed beneath what I'd already pounded out:

```
Oranges and lemons say the bells of St. Clemens.
I am here.
I am here.
I am here.
I am here.
And I never left you.
Play it.
```

CHAPTER SEVENTEEN

1

The next morning, I told Bruno I knew he'd been the one to play with my typewriter, but he denied it.

But here's the thing: It's the kind of prank Bruno used to pull when he was a kid.

Sometimes I'd type part of a story out, and he'd type in two or three words after my last one (usually: stupid storie or Nemo lovs Pola Bear).

I didn't really believe it was him.

But I didn't want to believe that it might be something else.

That it might be Brooke, her mind wandering too much.

Her breakdown on its way.

2

Sometimes I could hear Brooke crying through the walls.

I worried a bit about what seemed to be a logical and terrible depression descending on all of us in the house, but most especially her. This made me sadder because she had somehow been a partner for my father—not incestuously, but in terms of being there at Hawthorn, living in the house, handling the financial matters, making sure that the roofer arrived on time, or that the pond got drained in the spring, and that nothing rusted, or that everything that broke got fixed. I suspected some part of her had wanted to be free of this life, but she must have felt guilt for the way her freedom had come. He was more of her life than he was of mine or Bruno's. Her loss was greater to some extent, and the fact that she had discovered the body made it an even greater burden.

We didn't get together to talk about Dad and how wonderful he was—yet. We saved our moans and cries and gnashing of teeth for the privacy of our rooms.

There had always been a barrier between me and my sister and my brother, and I was never sure where it had come from. We had gotten along famously when young, and had managed to share fairly equally among us. Despite my mother's taking off so wildly, I looked back on a lot of childhood as joyous, and some of it as full of hard lessons learned, but never with a sense that it was anything but the right childhood for me. When one of us was sick, the others would gather 'round the bedside and read aloud from books or bring soup and tales of the outside world. Yet, a barrier grew up between us, as if there were some unspoken crime we'd witnessed, or as if each of us had a disturbance within that seemed to intensify the more we were all three together. So we kept our mourning to ourselves and didn't share grief much.

When I thought of my father, how he was wrenched from us, alone in my old room, in my too-small bed, I cried, also. I tried writing a few more pages on the Royal, but it was as pointless as the first page I'd attempted.

In my head, I begged God for understanding, as if He lived there or had access to my brain. Minutes later, I'd question the idea of God at all given this kind of murder. Then I'd wonder if the pagans were right—if it weren't just a pantheon of spirits and forces and gods and goddesses all within mini-domains, ruling sections of this chaotic universe, with Nature itself the ultimate deity. Or if there was no God at all, God or gods, just the lives of animals on a rocky planet, all scrambling to survive, some of us built with an outrageous and unending hope that there was something more that existed between the words "live" and "die." Then I went back to God and the relationship between Heaven and mankind. I even had the gods of some ancient religion arguing with the God of Abraham. It got pretty silly the way my mind went. Suddenly, I was talking to my father in silence. I imagined him in Heaven, and then felt ridiculous for the fantasy. It was wishful thinking. I had no idea what happened when life ended. All my Catholic upbringing had brought me was a sense that I wasn't sure what to believe, for it all seemed like the wishes of men and women who didn't want to face the unknowable without a comfortable ending in mind. The altar boy in me felt guilty for thinking that.

These were nights of headaches. I'd look out my window over the slope of the hills and imagine I'd see the smokehouse out to the east.

The pictures of my father's final hours replayed in my head as if I'd been there, watching.

The battering of the door; the terrific storm; the way my father had heard some sound nearby; the dropping of the flashlight; and then, the shadow figure there, bringing the stinging blade into him.

Sawing.

3

All right, let me just get it all out of the way right now.

My father's murder was a cosmic fornication—a murder beyond what most people ever have to bear. Or dream about.

Someone got him from behind with a sharp blade. A curved blade. Under the arm, over the shoulder, in the back. They may have severed his spinal cord so that he had to lay there and take it. Or that may have come moments later. He may have volunteered to let them do it—there were no marks of restraints on his wrists or ankles, nor were there signs of struggle. At best, the fallen flashlight might've indicated he'd been knocked down first and was unconscious for most of the procedure. One can only hope.

Then they went at him. Cutting parts of him. Slicing. Curved blade carefully going in, cutting tendons. Cutting muscle. You had to assume the killer did this to keep him from escaping—but, in fact, there was no sign that my father had tried to leave the smokehouse, or even fight back at his attacker.

The worst of it was that my father might have been conscious for most of it.

All right, the worst of it was that each of us, my brother, sister, and I, had to now live with this without denial and without illusion.

No Brain Fart was going to rescue us with a weeklong fever of forgetfulness.

I could not think of my father after that without imagining the bloody room and his eyes looking up at the curved blade about to come down on another part of his body, and wonder what that must have been like.

The unimaginable began to haunt me. With it, the nightmares came, during daily catnaps and whenever sleep found me.

I could not get one image out of my head.

His eyes, looking up, as a shiny crescent blade came down.

In the nightmare, I felt as if I could see the misty face he had seen before he died.

She had long golden hair, and thin lips, and warm almond eyes.

It was Brooke.

When I awoke from the nightmare, Brooke stood over my bed.

In one hand, she cupped a small glass saucer, within which was a white votive candle, its flame small and blue-yellow.

In her other hand, a knife.

CHAPTER EIGHTEEN

1

"Brooke," I whispered.

The room had early morning light filtering through the white curtains—a blue-purple haze on the walls.

I reached over to the bedside table to flick on the lamp, but my hand trembled. I found the switch and turned it on. The glare of the lamp seemed like a noon sun.

"Brooke," I repeated.

"Nemo?" she said, in that same whispered delicacy with which she'd greeted me when I first arrived home. "It's you?"

A breath or two exhaled, she glanced at the knife she held in her hand. It was just a steak knife from the kitchen. "I heard noises."

She set the candle and knife on the table. Then she crouched down to pick up the small lamp that had turned over onto the floor. "I get scared at night," she said. She sat down on the floor beside my bed. "Dad doesn't have his guns anymore. The police took them. I don't know why. Don't ask me. Don't ask me. I'm going crazy here. I thought I heard someone in the house. I thought . . ." She glanced around the room. "I thought this was another room. I didn't think I was in your room."

"No one else is in the house. You, me, and Bruno. The doors are locked. Remember? I put all the locks in. If you want to see in the dark, just use a flashlight," I said, glancing at the candle. "You could trip on something and set it on fire. God, or stab yourself." It was an exaggeration, I guess, but I was tired of her nightly wanderings, which were freaking me out completely.

She ignored my comments. "The dogs are always the first to notice. They whimpered a little while ago. I had to close their kennels up."

"Probably they heard a possum outside."

"They were frightened. Nothing frightens them much."

"If you think someone might be here," I said, feeling as wide awake as I'd ever felt, my heart still beating like a jack-hammer, "you might want to let the dogs roam."

"I thought it might be my imagination," she said, her voice still barely more than a whisper. Her face turned glum and a bit stony. "I've heard it since before . . . well, before it happened. I kept thinking that someone was walking just ahead of me."

"It's the night," I said. I packed some pillows behind my back and sat up. The smell of the room came to me: It smelled like trash. I glanced at the small trash can by my old desk, wondering what I'd thrown in there. Banana peel? Half a sandwich? "I've stayed up 'til all hours sometimes, and I start imagining all kinds of things."

"I don't think it's that," she said. Then her voice rose. "Do you know that every night when I'm up—late—something in the house has moved?"

"Moved?"

"Small things. Things that no one would really notice. I notice them because I notice everything in this house."

"It could've been Bruno. Or me."

"No," she said. "Not things like that. Inconsequential things, things you wouldn't even touch."

"Like?"

"The thermostat. It goes up at night."

"That's Bruno," I said. "I'm sure it is."

"Even on the nights he's not here? It's up to ninety. But it's freezing anyway. Someone moves the dial on it up, but it still gets cold. I feel cold when I get up to check it. I feel something," she said. She leaned forward and brought her knees up just under her chin. As she put her arms around her knees, reminding me of a little girl, her sweater rolled back a bit. I tried to see marks from her bathtub mishap, but couldn't make anything out. "Some nights, there are windows open. In Dad's room. In the living room. I've checked to see if they're locked at four A.M. But then, by six, they're wide open."

"We've got storm windows," I said. "No one's getting in or out that way."

"That's the thing," she said. "The storm windows are still on the outside. No one broke in. No one left through a window. They just opened them. As if they wanted me to know they're here."

"It could be anything," I said. I grinned. "Dad's ghost." A joke. I felt grim for mentioning it. I just wanted someone to lighten up—her or me.

"No," she said, taking this suggestion far too seriously. "It happened before Dad was killed. It happened before Bruno came back. And the wardrobe. In Dad's room. It was moved."

"I can explain that," I said. "Bruno and I—"

"I don't mean recently," she said sharply, her mood changing. There was anger beneath her words, as if I were suggesting that she had somehow made something of nothing. "In October. Late October. Dad thought I did it. But I didn't. And then there were the noises."

"Brooke," I said. I reached out and tapped her knee lightly. "We're all suffering here. You probably more than anyone. You and Dad were so close."

"I think," she said, looking at my hand after it had briefly touched her knee. "I think that the killer is in the house. And has been. You know how Hawthorn was built. You know how it has those spaces."

"No one but a six-year-old could even get into those spaces," I said. "Look, you're stressed. It's normal. You were in the war zone. You sat with him. You saw what happened. It's normal that you're on edge. But for your own sake, you need to start working on ways to handle the stress."

I knew about the old, original structure of Hawthorn— how it had been one of those less-than-sturdy New England farmhouses that had little insulation and very little room at all. The present house, built in the nineteenth century, had engulfed it—the living room with its great fireplace and the two bedrooms beyond it were the only things left from it that showed. Otherwise, there was a hollow space behind the front stairs that had been part of the original "great room" and a one-foot-wide space between the old brick and the new insulation and the brick on the outside. It couldn't be reconciled with the later design, so it left this kind of thin wind tunnel that ran along the side front quarter of the house. When we'd been very little, Brooke and Bruno had been able to squeeze through it for as far as they could go—no more than a few feet in. By the time Bruno was seven, he could no longer fit, and Brooke couldn't fit by her ninth year.

"Someone could go through the walls," Brooke said, looking at me with an unflinching gaze. She had completely ignored everything I'd just said. "Someone could if they wanted it badly enough."

"Who?" I asked.

"The same someone I hear at night. I go from room to room, and I feel as if I can almost find him."

"Him?"

Her eyes widened. "I know it sounds ridiculous. But either it's a person or it's not. Who could it be, Nemo? If it's a ghost, what is it? Why is it here?"

"Want me to call Joe and have him bring some detectives through?"

"No," she said. Her eyes teared up. She raised her hands to her face and squished her flesh around as if it were clay. "God, I feel like I'm going crazy. Do you think I'm crazy?"

"Maybe we need to talk to someone," I said. "All of us. A shrink. Maybe we can go see Bruno's. He thinks she's God."

"Not bloody likely," she said, and then smiled through her sadness, for it was what our father had always said about psychiatrists. "It's my mind. It's unquiet. Do you know—" She stopped herself in midsentence. "No, nothing."

"What?"

"Nothing," she said. Then, "The night he died, I thought I heard someone downstairs."

I watched her. I had begun looking for signs of a breakdown. I really was worried that we had some kind of family insanity within us. Brooke, the contradiction: the most sturdy of us, also the most fragile.

"I didn't tell Joe. I don't think I should," she said.

"Did you see someone?"

She closed her eyes and rested the palm of her hand on her forehead, applying pressure there. "I can't seem to turn off my mind anymore, Nemo. I keep playing things back from that night again and again and again."

This time, her sweater slid farther down her arm, and I saw, along her forearm, gauze wrapped with white tape.

I leaned forward and touched the edge of her arm. "What's this?"

2

She looked up, then brought her arm down to her side.

Shrugged.

Tugged the arm of her sweater back down to her wrists.

"Accident. I fell asleep in the tub." She fumbled with words, as if trying to string together the right ones to make sense. "I . . . broke some glass . . . cut myself up . . . a bit."

"That's it?"

She nodded.

"What really happened?"

She nearly smiled—a sad half grin. It was part of how we'd interacted as children. Brooke never liked telling the truth when she was little, so she'd make something up first to make you feel better about bad news. After she'd given some convoluted explanation for something, I'd ask her: *What really happened?*

"I don't know if I was dreaming or not," she said, her slight smile returning to a flat line. "Bruno convinced me that I was. That I fell asleep in the tub and was dreaming, but I'm not sure. It was the night . . . the night of the storm. The night he died. There were voices that seemed to come from downstairs. I only really heard one of them. But it somehow made me sleepy to hear it, and in the dream I thought we were children again, playing the game."

Just hearing it made my brain go a little haywire—something within me rebelled at the idea of the game we'd played as children. I hated it, and was embarrassed by it. It was as if my mind squinted and cringed whenever the thought of the Dark Game arose.

"We were all playing it. You had the blindfold on, and Bruno was doing the counting, and I helped him with the reciting. And I was just there, somehow, not really in the Dark Game and not really outside it. I had glass in my hand. I was taking it and trying to cut at the rope around my wrists. But . . . but I wasn't doing it right, and the ropes became bright red ribbons floating around in the air. Bruno started laughing. So did I, but you told me to stop it. *Stop it!* you shouted, the way you used to when I was doing something wrong."

"Oh, Brooke," I said, my heart sinking a bit. I took her hand in mine. "Did you do this to yourself?"

"I didn't think I did," she said, her voice pure confusion. She glanced over at the knife on the table, and then at me. "I didn't want to kill myself. I really really didn't. I just . . . I just wanted to sleep. I wanted to be in the game again. But I felt like someone else was there. Someone else was with me. Inside me. Trying to get out."

3

Her face became all screwed up, wrinkling as if she were years older. "I woke up, not in the bathtub at all. I stood on the front porch. I didn't have anything on. Not a stitch. It was freezing. The storm that night—terrible. I was just . . . just . . . just standing there, with the door open. Rain coming down. Howling wind. Horrible night. The last thing I remembered before this was I had been in the tub. Somehow, I had gotten out of the tub when I was asleep, and walked through the rooms, down the stairs, and outside. That night. My arms were all torn up from the glass. Blood. Not as much as you'd think. The piece of glass was in my hand. I went back inside. I went back upstairs to the bathroom. When I turned on the light, I saw the glass on the floor. The water in the tub was all pink with blood. Only, something else was there."

"In the bathroom?" I asked, sitting up, drawing back a bit, crossing my legs in front of me. I almost didn't want to know what was there in her dream.

"In the tub. In all that pink, foamy water."

"What was it?"

She closed her eyes, her eyebrows pressing downward as if trying to force the memory from her mind. "It was me," she said. "I watched myself. I was dying. Blood was coming out of my arms slowing in gentle red ribbons. And then . . ."

I held my breath a moment. Denial was how I'd been raised. Deny anything even close to a bad mental state. Deny that life exerted any pressure on anyone. The voice of my father: "I was in the camps, and if I could survive that without cracking up, then anyone can survive anything if they just control their mind better."

But Brooke had been falling apart, even before our father's murder, even before sitting in his blood for hours.

And neither Bruno nor I had done anything to help her.

Bruno had found her wandering, naked, in the night.

I had seen her paintings.

Her mental state was a wreck, but we were ill-equipped to understand it.

4

"I was in the tub. All along I was in the tub," she said. "Looking up at what seemed like steam. But it wasn't steam. I thought for a second that it was the dream-me evaporating. In front of my eyes," she said. "I watched it for a minute as it went—it was just steam. The whole thing had been a dream. But . . . remember in the Dark Game? How we could go inside and outside ourselves?"

"Do I," I whispered, wishing that she had not mentioned it, wishing that Bruno had not mentioned it recently, wishing that I could forget we ever had played it. The source of her disturbed state.

The source of all our disturbances.

"It was like that," she said. "Just like it. Only, Nemo, there was something else. Someone else was there. It was like I had released someone from inside me, when I cut myself. It was as if I had never been alone before, and now I was—something had gotten out of me. It was just like the Dark Game. It was as if by bleeding, wanting to die—I did want to die—someone else came out of me. Like they'd been waiting a long time. Ever since we used to play it. Like they were waiting for me to open myself up and let them out."

5

Our father had taught the Dark Game to us.

Then, when we had been screaming in the smokehouse, he'd ended it.

He told us that he never wanted to catch us playing it again. He told us that when the game got to be too much, we should hit a wall and that it could get dangerous. "The mind is fragile, and you shouldn't play it so easily. It comes too easily for you. I shouldn't have taught it to you. I thought you were strong enough."

But the game wasn't so easy to give up, either.

Sometimes, we still played it—in the wardrobe or in one of our bedrooms. We stopped at some point—I think when I was about thirteen or so, I had stopped playing it completely. Something changed—perhaps puberty had eliminated the need for the drug of the game.

Or perhaps we had hit the wall in the game.

He told us that he had fine-tuned the Dark Game when he was a prisoner of war. It helped him escape where they had imprisoned him when he was a young man during a war that I knew very little about. He told us that you could make your mind do things if you isolated it and if you directed it. He said that when he was in solitary confinement, the game allowed him to forget the pain in his legs and shoulders, and he could travel outside of the well they'd left him in for a week or two—that he could stand on the ground and travel among them—all in his mind. "The human imagination has never been fully tested. It never will be. But I could swear that during those times, particularly in the hole, I could hear their conversation and wander about freely among them."

He told us not to play after dark because the game could ruin your mind if you let it. "Play it during the hour before dark, no matter what hour it is, it works best then, when the world is settling and your mind is calm," he had said.

"What happens at night?" I asked him.

"When I did it at night, it got hold of me," he said. "I couldn't get out of it on my own. Only when I hit that wall would I get thrown back into my waking consciousness, and it might be days before that happened. I'd be nearly starved, and so thirsty even my captors wondered at it. And my men . . ." He shook his head sadly. "They thought I was dead sometimes. In it. Sometimes it seemed as if I were dead."

We always thought he'd told us these stories to terrify us into not playing the Dark Game too much. After all, if it were such a deadly game, why even teach it to us? Why even train us to play it?

But the boredom of Hawthorn in the winter was too much. The cable might go out or the electricity, or our friends could not tromp from the village out to our place for a winter's day of games.

He used the Dark Game once for something that at the time made sense, but now seemed wrong: when Granny died. Brooke was inconsolable—she sobbed and screeched as if she would never be happy again. I was also bleating my tears out, for despite her harshness at times, I had loved the old woman who had read us stories and told us about Wales and Scotland as if she had been raised there herself.

So, our father, apparently at the end of his rope, had taken us into the smokehouse. We had thought it was to punish us for wailing so much, but he sat us down, and guided us through the Dark Game as a way to see Granny again. I barely remember it, other than feeling much better—closing my eyes on a summer afternoon in the cool smokehouse, feeling the bites of mosquitoes on my arms, and then moving in the dark of my self-imposed blindness into a different afternoon, and seeing Granny there, holding her hand out to Brooke and me, and the sweet, gentle voice of our father guiding us.

The Dark Game was simple: You closed your eyes, or you blindfolded yourself if you couldn't keep your eyes closed. One person, who put on his blindfold last, had to count to ten, and then began reciting a nursery rhyme.

It was a very particular nursery rhyme—our father's own Granny (my great-grandmother) had taught it to him, as she had been taught it as a child. He told me that the origins of the Dark Game went back further than even his two years in the prison camps. "It goes back before words were written down, and it's the rhythm of the rhyme that counts, not the words. The words just can be said. The rhythm gets inside you. My Granny told me that the Dark Game was used in dark times—when horrible things happened to people, and those who survived those things needed rest from it all. I took the Dark Game to the prison camps with me and modified it. I used what I learned there. It helps us escape in hard times. But it's not a toy. It is not to be abused."

The rhyme itself had to do with churches in England and a game that children once played while they recited it. It was a common enough nursery rhyme—I'd heard it since growing up. So it was not unique to the Dark Game. It simply was a way for the reciter to help the mind relax.

It began:

"Oranges and lemons, say the bells of St. Clemens.

You owe me five farthings, say the bells of St. Martins.

When will you pay me? say the bells of Old Bailey.

When I am rich, say the bells of Shoreditch.

When will that be? say the bells of Stepney.

I do not know, says the great bell at Bowe."

And it ended:

"Here comes a candle to light you to bed—

And here comes a chopper to chop off your head."

Then the reciter shut his eyes and began to guide the others—and we'd go in our minds where our guide took us, with no resistence. At some point, you'd be telling what you saw in your mind, over and over again, until you began really seeing the others there as well, with you. Where you went, what you were doing. You tried to rise outside of your body and just float there and watch yourself. Our father had told us it was a survival technique—and that it would help us understand how our minds worked. Looking back, I can understand now that we were probably too young to play the Game—because our imaginations were already strong as it was. But our father played it with us when we were all a little too rambunctious and bored at the same time, and the winter blizzards had come down on the island.

In the winter, we played the Dark Game a lot, and it was fairly innocent for a while. We could travel through time or to other countries or to places we made up. We could even see our mother—we would travel to where we thought we could find her. When she lived with us, we would travel to the store or to the kitchen and pretend we were near her. After she abandoned us, we pretended to travel to Brazil, to a beautiful home in the mountains.

But the last time we played it, something went wrong.

It was a flight of fantasy for us. It was our family secret— we didn't let other kids in on the Dark Game. I told Harry about it, but that was about it. Harry had been sad about his father's illness, and I wanted to help him escape. He was the only person who I believe knew about it outside of the three of us and our father.

At some point, something broke about the game, and we all just stopped playing it.

6

"You painted something about your dream," I told her.

She shook her head. "What do you mean?"

"In the greenhouse," I said. "I saw your painting. The one

of the dream you just told me. You, standing at the front door in the rain."

"I didn't paint any dreams," she said. "And who gave you permission to snoop?"

"You left them out. In the open."

"I did not," Brooke said.

7

We got into the kind of argument over this (whether or not she'd left her paintings out to be seen) that we'd had as kids. It almost felt good to spar a bit, and finally it ended as all our challenges had: We had to go downstairs to check it out for ourselves.

Brooke went ahead of me, key in hand.

Against my wishes, she had locked the upstairs hall door. She stood in front of me and turned the key in the lock, without apologizing for this lapse in judgment.

Then, down the backstairs in what we'd always called the sewing room (even though no one had ever sewn in it since Granny with her quilts and embroidery), through another set of doors until we came to the closest thing that could be called a hallway (five feet in length), and the door to the greenhouse.

Brooke went in, nearly as interested in the canvases as I had been. The one on the easel, and the one of our father she acknowledged.

But when she reached back to lift the third canvas, she nearly dropped it. "Shit!" she cried out. The dogs, upstairs in her bedroom, began barking at some noise. "Shit! Nemo! Is this a joke?" She turned to me, holding up the canvas.

CHAPTER NINETEEN

1

I saw the same painting I'd observed previously: a woman who looked very much like my sister, naked, her skin painted red, standing on the front porch of our house during a storm.

"It's your dream," I said, confused. "See? There you are on the porch."

"Did you do this?" she asked, and I heard tears and not a small amount of rage in her voice. "Did you bring this out?"

"No," I said.

"You did! You came back to do this kind of prank, the kinds of . . . of things you used to do. God, I thought you grew up! I guess I was wrong!" she spat, her rage like a gathering storm. Then she took the painting and held it up to my face as if she were going to hit me with it.

"Look at it. Look at it," she said. "Did you do this?"

I tried to focus on the canvas, but I couldn't. It was too close to my face.

"Brooke," I said, my voice rising, "look, what are you so mad about? It's your dream. You painted it. You."

I grabbed it from her hands, and when I did, I saw a kind of uncalled-for fury on her face. I took the canvas and set it down at my side. "What the hell is going on?"

"I want to know who's been getting into my paints and painting this kind of . . . obscene . . ."

"Brooke, it's you," I said. "It's the same kind of figures you did here." I pointed to the one on the easel, of the faceless children.

"It's not me!" she screamed. "I am not the one who painted that!" She pointed to the painting at my side. "How could I have? Christ, Nemo. How could I have? I did not do it!" Her shouts grew, and I had the strange feeling that something was vibrating nearby—something was shaking—I looked at her hands, clenched at her sides, trembling as she cried out.

And then, a sound as if a bomb exploded nearby.

2

The glass of the greenhouse seemed to bend slightly—I was overly tired, so I couldn't tell if this was right—but it was as if the glass of the wall behind Brooke rippled like water with something moving through it—something that moved snake-like along the surface of glass.

"Calm down, Brooke," I said. "Calm down, it's all right. It's all right."

"I am not losing my mind! I did not imagine this! This is a trick—you're trying to make me think I'm losing it, but I'm not!" she shouted.

"Brooke," I reached out and took her trembling fist, and held it in my hands. "It's all right. It's all right. Try and relax." I kept my eyes on the glass, for it continued its S-shaped ripples, and Brooke seemed to notice it as well—she looked up to the ceiling, the curved glass of it moving like a canopy in the breeze—just floating up slightly, and then resting back down again.

"I am . . . not . . . losing . . ." she said, and then went quiet.

She nearly fell, trembling into my arms. She was hot with fever as I held her, briefly. "Oh my God, did you see it, too?" she asked.

"I'm not sure," I said, but inside I knew this was a lie. "Yes. Yes. I saw it."

Her voice was a whisper. "Sometimes I see it at night. Something is in here. Something's in the house with us."

"We're stressed," I said. I let her go, and she wiped her hands across her face and smoothed out her hair.

"It's not just stress," she said. "Dear God, Nemo, I thought I was losing it. I've thought so since October. But you saw it?" Tears of what might have been relief—or even gratitude—flooded her eyes and streamed down her face.

3

I went to wake up Bruno. I got a bit of a shock going into his room—he lay there, the quilt pulled back, his naked back with a yin-yang tattoo near his lower spine. Next to him, slightly overlapping leg upon leg, snoring away, was Cary Conklin, the guy who had brought me over in the boat. Bruno's boyfriend.

I didn't really think to react—I had only just gotten used to Bruno being gay, so seeing his boyfriend in his old bed—far too small for the two of them, so they were draped over each other—made me feel a bit the way the three bears must've felt upon finding Goldilocks. I didn't want to wake Cary, so I tapped Bruno on his left foot. After a few taps, he snarfled awake and glanced back at me.

"Hey, Nemo."

"Bruno," I said. "Sorry to, um, wake you up so early. But something's up."

"Up as in 'important'?"

I nodded.

He sighed. "Okay," he whispered. "I'll be down in a few."

4

"You notice anything strange here?" I asked as soon as he bounded down the stairs, wearing a long T-shirt and red boxers. He had a harsh look in his eyes, as if he were furious for being dragged out of bed so early.

"Strange?" he asked.

"Things missing?"

Bruno shook his head.

"We were in the greenhouse a little while ago," I said, glancing at Brooke. "Something weird happened."

"Like?"

"Like the glass moved."

"Moved? Broke?"

"No," I said. "It was like . . ."

"Like quicksilver," Brooke said.

"What's quicksilver?"

"Like liquid," I said.

Bruno squinted and looked at Brooke. "You've been up all night." Then at me. "You don't exactly look all there, either."

"We saw it, tired or not," I said.

"Did you ask her?" Bruno turned to me.

"Ask me what?" Brooke raised an eyebrow at me.

"No," I replied. Then to her, "You walk up and down the house all night long."

"I know," she said.

"Why?" Bruno chirped.

"Why do you think? Our father was murdered. I can't sleep."

"No," Bruno said. He pointed a finger at her. "You were doing it before Dad died."

"No I wasn't."

Bruno half-grinned. "Come on. I saw you. I'd wake up and see you in my room. Just walking."

"I'm telling you," she said. She shot a glance at me. "I wasn't."

"You sure?"

"I don't lie," she said.

Bruno let out what I can only describe as a repressed breath, through his nostrils.

"I don't," she repeated.

"So the bathtub story is accurate," he said. "You fell asleep. You weren't trying to—"

"God!" Brooke closed her eyes. "*God*, I'm going to have a headache."

"Doesn't matter," I said to him. "I was there, too. I saw it. It was this rippling . . . thing."

"What time?"

I shrugged. "Six, maybe."

"Well," he said, spreading his hands out as if this solved everything. "No sleep, the light barely up outside. And you—" he nodded to Brooke. "Miss Xanax."

"I haven't taken one since the day after Dad was killed."

I closed my eyes, trying to figure out how this all could be. How could I have seen the same thing Brooke had seen: the glass of the greenhouse moving. "What about the painting?" I asked Brooke.

"I didn't paint it," she insisted.

"You did," I said. "It's the same as the others. And it's exactly what the dream was. The one you told me about."

"Let's not get into this again. Maybe we didn't see anything on the glass."

"Wait," I said. "You saw something on the glass?"

"You did, too," she said.

"No, I saw it move—like it was rippling or . . . I don't know . . . that's not what it was like . . . it was like it was blurring or something."

"I saw a woman's face," she said.

5

"Bruno's right. I'm exhausted," she added. "I've been up all night. It was a hallucination. You didn't see it?"

"I saw movement on the glass."

"Could've been clouds overhead," Bruno said. "It's foggy. In the greenhouse, it makes the walls look different."

"Who was it you saw in the glass?" I kept my gaze on my sister.

"Just a woman," Brooke said.

I watched her face—my beautiful, smart sister. The stress of what had happened had no doubt scrambled her mind a bit. Who wouldn't be a little shaken, a little traumatized, by finding her father dead, butchered? Bathed in blood. How could she not? How could she sleep? How could she function? That she could even speak to us about any of this was a bit of a miracle in and of itself.

"You need rest," I said. "We all do. And I think it's time we get some professional help."

"No shrinks," she said sharply.

"Then Dr. Connelly. Just a check up. We can all use one." I turned to Bruno for support.

"Sure," Bruno said.

"I guess I should talk to someone," Brooke said finally, a note of defeat in her voice. "And I can't exactly go to Father Ronnie anymore for counsel."

"Not since Dad told him to fuck off," Bruno said.

6

Bruno insisted on going to the greenhouse immediately after Brooke went back up to bed.

"I saw it, Bruno," I said. "The wall." I went over to the panes of glass and touched lightly against one of them. Tapped it. "It was as if it were made out of gel or something and just moved."

"How many hours of sleep did you get?"

"Five."

"You need to go back to bed, too," he said.

7

I went back to bed and woke up around one in the afternoon. The greenhouse seemed just as it had before. I sat in it, sipping my coffee, for a good half hour, wondering if I'd get that sensation again. The glass turning to rippling water. But it didn't. Wide awake, with the day well under way, I realized that perhaps I had, after all, been half asleep when Brooke and I had gone there at daybreak. Bruno, I figured, had been at least partially right. There had been a light fog that didn't burn off 'til three, and that might've accounted for at least some of what I'd seen—accompanied by my lack of sleep and my sister's rage. I went looking for the picture again, but it was gone. I assumed Brooke had taken it and put it somewhere else. I called Dr. Connelly's office and tried to schedule my sister in—even though it was a week or so 'til Christmas, his assistant knew, as the current local tragic celebrities, we might be able to cut in line. Called Pola, and wanted love to take me away from my fears about my sister.

8

And I thought about my father. He was never away from my mind. I thought about his face. His hands. His way of speaking that was a gentle twist of Yankee islander.

And I wondered why I had never really gotten along with him.

9

Got a strange phone call late one night. About two A.M.

When I picked it up, it was Paulette Doone. "You demons," she said. "You did it. You did it."

Then she hung up on me. I fell back to sleep, not really knowing what had possessed her.

In the morning I got a call from Joe, and he told me Ike Doone had shot himself in some cockamamie illegal hunting accident going after some wild turkeys he'd flushed out, and Paulette had begun telling everyone in the village, almost immediately, that the "Raglan curse" was upon them and that the Devil was all around our house.

Ike was not dead, just had a helluva wound on his left thigh.

"Try and ignore this kind of stuff," Joe said.

10

Pola and I went to dinner, for long walks—but my mind was too much on a murder and on my family.

Then, just before the weekend, Harry Withers found me.

CHAPTER TWENTY

1

The day was sunny and bright, and even though another snow had fallen recently, it felt warmer outside with the yellow sun and clear blue sky. When the winter's gray as in New England, you've got to get outdoors on those days that the sun finally shines.

On a dog's ass.

Stepping out the door, I was greeted with the bounding leaps and nips at my elbows of Madoc, the greyhound that seemed more like a skinny horse than a dog. He followed me a ways, and then, after a quarter mile or so, ran back for the house and his companion, Mab, who was barking down by the duck pond.

I wanted to enjoy a good walk on a lone country road.

Just as I was setting off, Harry Withers showed up.

2

Harry was impossibly dressed in a broad-brimmed hat and a duster jacket, and his square glasses, and a flop of thick brown hair nearly over his eyes. I laughed when I saw him.

"You look like the sheriff of Sagebrush," I said.

"I know, I know," Harry said. "Ridiculous, isn't it? I thought I looked like an Italian prelate."

"You found me."

"I gave you a little time," he said, somewhat sheepishly. "I heard you were in the pubs with Bruno, but I didn't come looking. Out of respect."

"Thanks," I said.

"Want to walk a bit?"

3

He hadn't changed much in the years since I'd been gone. He looked as if he were eighteen still, but with a bit of a paunch. His eyes had the kind of brightness to them that only someone who loves his life seems to have. His crooked smile was disarming, but painful for me to remember. It was some kind of muscle problem that he'd had since an accident when he was a baby.

He smiled at the worst times—always had.

His smile was some kind of permanent scar on his face. Happy or sad, he smiled. He told me he couldn't help it.

"They believe," he said, referring to the police, "that the

killer must have escaped right after the murder." He paused and added, "Is this going to upset you, hearing about it?"

"Not as much as it should."

He went off the road and bent down in the snow, practically squatting. He drew up a longish thick branch that had come down in the storm, broke off the weak branches from it, and said, "Instant walking stick." He took it with him and used it as a pointer.

"Over there, from the woods. That's what they think. Then, from there, to the harbor. Their own boat."

"Could be," I said.

Harry's smile intensified. Then it dropped to a straight line on his face. "I don't think so. In fact, it's basically not possible, but try telling that to Joe Grogan. First, I doubt one man did this. I suspect there were a few. And second, getting off the island during a Nor'easter is suicide. If they got in a boat that night, particularly some little motorboat, they'd have been lucky if they made it to the Vineyard. They're still here."

"Interesting," I said.

Harry pointed at the smokehouse, which lay back toward the house itself. He seemed about to say something, but stopped himself. Then he held the stick parallel to the ground and pressed it down. "They probably didn't tell you about the footprints."

"The killer's?"

"They've kept things quiet. Joe Grogan's seen to that. All the mainlander investigators have combed and questioned and pretty much turned over every rock. They even hauled Carson's butt in for questioning, and the poor guy could only weep and tell them that he thought he saw a demon that night. They almost took him away. If Joe hadn't stepped in, Carson McKinley would probably be in some state hospital in Boston getting drugged up every time he thought of sheep. Everyone on the island is scared."

"All six hundred?"

He shrugged. "Fewer this year. The McWhorters and the Carrs moved. When the propane delivery changed, the entire McHenry clan had to move back to Providence, and then one of the Women Whom God Forgot died. Sarah Hatchet was ninety-six. So we now have approximately, five hundred seventy-two. But then, you're back, and Bruno. Five hundred seventy-four."

I looked at him as if I had never known him. We'd had some bad stuff between us in the past. We'd had some good stuff as well. I had never been sure how much I really trusted Harry. "What do you want from me?"

He looked at me innocently enough. Like a puppy that just got slapped on the nose. " 'Want'?"

"Yep. Want. You and I don't speak for just about a decade, and now you want something. I can tell. I can sense it."

He chuckled. "Jesus, Nemo. You haven't changed much."

"Probably not." He was right. I really hadn't changed much in those intervening years. All my wounds were fairly fresh, at least now that I was back on the island. Maybe worse because of the murder.

"Okay, let me cut to the chase," he said. "I want to be a big-time reporter. I want to be on CNN someday. Or network news. I'm nearly thirty and on an island nobody cares about, writing up local gossip. I want something more. It's not an industry that wants middle-aged men joining it. It's an industry where you work up when you're young. And I'm not gonna get there from Burnley Island and a winter circulation of under a thousand—most of whom use the six-page newspaper to line their birdcages and paper train their puppies and wipe their asses—writing the occasional odd story about the octogenarian great-great grandmother who still knits sweaters from yaks that gets picked up by the AP wire because suddenly yaks are a hot topic."

Had to laugh at that last string of images.

"So you want a big murder story."

"Listen, I *got* a big murder story," he said. "But it's not enough. I need to *solve* a big murder story. I *need* to solve it. And I need whatever information I can get."

"Oh," I said. "You want to go in. The smokehouse."

"You got it," he said.

4

Harry went over the particulars of the murder. "There were no prints at all. No footprints. No handprints. No weapon found. There was enough blood there—pardon me, Nemo, I know this is hard to have to hear," he said. "But prints would've been made. One person or three or four. Someone. But the strangest part of all was what your father did."

I waited for whatever this was.

"He let it happen. He was alive for at least an hour. He was cut in places on his body, strategically, as if to keep him alive for the longest time, but he seems to have just lain down and let them slice off parts of his body after that," Harry said. "It wasn't just a murder. It was a surgical procedure."

5

"You haven't been over to it since it happened, have you?" Harry asked. He pointed again to the smokehouse with the stick.

"It's still off-limits," I said. "They might need to—"

He cut me off. "They went over that place for days. They didn't find a single fingerprint or footprint or anything other than your father's own prints. They came up with nothing. One of the top forensics experts in Boston came out for three days trying to collect something. It has them all baffled. You think you're going to get justice from anyone? Impossible. They can't come up with a case. The state attorney's gonna have to figure out where to point the finger, and each one of you has an alibi, except for Brooke, and no one thinks a woman of five-foot-four, even as sturdily built as Brooke, could do this and not leave a trace of herself behind. She took a direct route into that smokehouse and sat down on that bloody floor and went catatonic or something for a few hours before calling anyone. Only her prints show up, and they're known to have come long after the murder took place because of the way the blood had congealed. She is the only possible suspect, but they really don't think it's her, unless she went Lizzie Borden on his ass. And it would be nearly impossible for her to do it without some others helping, who again, would have left some trace of themselves in that room. It was a mess.

No one who did that would've gotten out. Grogan told some-one that your father might've even laid down and done it to himself. He drew a diagram of how it might've been done. But what I want to know is, how'd your dad chop his own head off?"

It was more than I was ready for. I nearly dropped into the wet ground and covered my face. I wanted to block out the images forming in my head.

To his credit, Harry crouched down beside me and wrapped an arm around my back. "I'm sorry, Nemo."

"Got a cigarette?"

"No. And you should quit," he said. "My dad died of emphysema. It's nasty. Smoked a pack a day and thought it wasn't much. Dead by fifty-three."

"My dad died by being chopped up, dead by fifty-eight," I said. The gallows humor was upon me. I really wanted a cigarette, but had left my pack in my other coat's pocket.

6

"Here's the thing," he said. "Brooke might've helped him do it. That's the only theory I've heard bandied about that might work. Brooke might've been in cahoots with your father on killing him."

"And you know how ridiculous that sounds?"

"Completely."

"If my sister were to help my father kill himself, there are easier ways. There's drowning in the pond. Smothering with a pillow. Gun at the back of the head," I said. More gallows humor. I couldn't help it. If you've ever gotten to such a point of confusion that it was almost as if you couldn't see out from your own eyes, then you know how I felt as I sat there on the ground.

"I know, and that's what Grogan told me, too, just about. But at some point—now, or a month from now, or a year from now, they may go after her. Unless someone figures this out. You know how the cops figured out the Manson murders?"

I shook my head.

"Right. They didn't. The reporters figured it out. Because investigators are looking at the small picture. But sometimes, it's the big obvious picture that spits in your face. I don't believe Brooke did it. I think a few people murdered your father. I have no idea what motive is involved. I have no idea who they are or where they went. But I think between the two of us, we can go in there and see if there's something the detectives missed. How many years has it been since Jon-Benet Ramsey was killed? Well, there's no actual suspect yet. No one can bring charges. This could be like that. But my fear is that Brooke is going to be the easy target, even if she's the wrong one. And yes, she'll be proven innocent, but that won't matter once she goes to court. It's a nasty system when it drags in a scapegoat. I don't want it to. I want it to drag in the killers. I want to be the guy to piece stuff together."

"You know what? I feel guilty for saying this, but I just want Dad to be buried and this to go away."

"Of course," he said. "But it won't go away. Not many murders out this way."

"I know." I sighed. "It's the worst in New England history. Or something."

"It's not that," he said. "There've been others that might be worse. A family was killed down on Outerbridge Island a couple of years back. They caught the boys involved, eventually. When Stonehaven, down in Connecticut, had that big mass murder back in the—what? Well, years ago, that was pretty damn bad. There've been murders all over the place. I think the Borden murders in Fall River still have the title of the bloodiest unsolved murders. But this one . . . well, it's ours. Burnley's. You know about your dad's business?"

I nodded. "If what you're asking is about his finances, yeah, I knew."

"He was a gambler. Not that he ever went down to Foxwoods or Atlantic City. I mean, he played the odds with his business instead of going the safe route. And money disappeared. Not a lot at any one time. Five hundred here, a thousand there. But if you look at the books, it comes to about 75,000 bucks over a twenty-year period. It wasn't in his bank account. Brooke doesn't have it," Harry said. "There's a lot of money unaccounted for. So maybe money was a motive. Maybe he had an old debt. Maybe it was a war buddy. Maybe it was your mom."

When he said this, I caught my breath. "As if she gave a damn. She'd have more money than God from my grandmother's will."

"She was disinherited," Harry said.

"Fuck," I said. "I feel like bones are being picked over."

"The estate never contacted her, she never contacted them. The detectives have been trying to locate her, too."

"Well, I'm pretty sure it wasn't my mother," I said, snorting. "Unless she came all the way up from Brazil to kill him and then take off again."

"When it comes to murder, you never know who it might be," Harry said. "Come on, let's go to the smokehouse."

7

Harry handed me the key. "I got it from Joe. He and his guys are so stymied, he gave me his blessing."

I looked at the key, which I had never seen in my child-hood. My father had kept it around his neck. What in God's name for?

I looked up at Harry. "Okay."

I unlocked the door.

CHAPTER TWENTY-ONE

1

To enter the smokehouse, we both had to lean forward, stooping a bit. The doorway was low, and the ceiling was not much higher. I felt a strange warmth, and half expected to remember all the hiding and the punishing and the secrecy that the smokehouse had been in my childhood, but not one bit of it came back to me. It seemed like an alien place. It would've seemed ordinary, but for the forensics work that had been done there.

2

In the smokehouse. Bloodstains. Chalk, fading. Fragrant, almost March-like smell of seedlings and freshly turned earth mixed with the coppery tang in the air and the smell of dead animal. *Dead man. Dead father.*

"Why do you think he came out here?" Harry asked.

"No idea. I really don't know."

"It's almost a ritual," Harry said. "He was laid out spread-eagle." He spread his arms and legs wide. "No ropes, no tethers. They suspect he was lifted up at one point, but then laid back down. Whoever did it let him go slowly. The major cuts didn't happen until near the end. Whoever did this wanted him alive for most of it. Whoever did this, he didn't fight them."

3

I caught my breath and held it. Then exhaled. "I feel like a little kid scared of the dark."

"You used to play that game in here," Harry said.

"Yep."

"I never understood it. I always wondered what was going on because when I tried to play it, I just didn't see what you saw."

"It was just imagination," I said.

"Sure," he said. "Like any other kid's make-believe game. You close your eyes and you start making a journey in your mind."

"Is that what you're interested in?" I asked. "The Dark Game?"

"Not really. But it happened here. Your father's murder. You played the game here, and you all had some strange stories to tell back then."

"We did?"

"You don't remember?"

"Done everything I could to not remember. And then some. I just seem to remember creating a fantasy world."

"An escape hatch," Harry said. "That's what your dad called it. I heard him yelling at you one time because he found some rags we'd used as blindfolds. And he told you not to keep using an escape hatch, that it was only for truly bad times."

I looked up and around the walls. Harry shone his flashlight into the corners of the stone walls.

"Awful," I whispered through gritted teeth.

The blood had begun to turn brown on the stone. The ceiling of the smokehouse was too dark to see. Harry's flashlight spun around; he went to the walls and carefully looked at things that I had no desire to see, let alone know about. I just caught a glimpse of the markings on the floor where my father's body had been found, a jigsaw puzzle of a body, cut in several places. I got the feeling that someone else was there, in some dark recess of the place. I began to feel the small hairs on my arms stand up. I felt the way I would've waking up from a nightmare that had seemed all too real.

The temperature inside the smokehouse dropped several degrees, and I felt something on my earlobe, as if an insect were crawling along it, tickling.

I felt light-headed, and the room seemed to spin. I tried saying something to Harry—*I think I'm fainting,* I wanted to say, but words wouldn't come out of my mouth.

"Holy shit!" Harry gasped as he turned toward me, and I felt the beam of the flashlight on my face like an exploded

sun—it blinded me for an instant, and when my vision returned, I felt as if I were looking out from someone else's eyes.

4

The world seemed to prolapse in on itself, in to a black hole
of darkness as a wave of nausea went through me and my
knees buckled. I knew I would fall, or was in the process of
falling, but suddenly, it all went dark.

5

When I woke up, I was outside, looking up into the empty
sky, feeling a coldness at the back of my neck and the worst
headache of my life pressing against my skull.

"Nemo?" Harry asked. He crouched beside me; I felt his
arm under the back of my neck, supporting me.

I tried to speak, but my mouth felt dry and raw, and I
could feel the beginnings of a sore throat.

Harry's face was white. He had scratches all along his
cheeks. His lower lip was cut and bloody, and he had the
purplish beginnings of a black left eye. "Jesus H. Christ,
Nemo, what in God's name was that all about?"

I coughed out, "I don't know." Felt like razor blades in
my throat.

"Is that you in there, or do I need to hit you again?" Harry
asked.

I felt pressure from his arm across my neck.

He was afraid I was going to lunge at him.

CHAPTER TWENTY-TWO

1

"You nearly beat the crap out of me," Harry said. His face bore thin red marking around the eyes and nose. He sweated profusely. "I thought it was a seizure. At first. It was like trying to help a grizzly."

"Sorry," I said, feeling awkward apologizing for something that I wasn't even sure had come from me. "I can't believe it."

2

I felt as if something had been torn out of me against my will. I felt raped in some awful way.

Cold and torn and used by something that had pressed its way into my body.

It was a feeling of insanity.

Was I going crazy? Was this a sign? Was it stress?

I tried to remember the stories that my father had told of Granny and how she'd had her spells when she'd start talking to people who weren't there; or when my grandfather had tried to set a hearthfire in the gas oven and nearly blown up Hawthorn altogether but for the quick thinking on my father's part.

But those were old-age diseases—those were dementias that came after seventy.

They weren't this.

Part of me genuinely could not believe it.

Part of me even harbored a damning hope that Harry had made it up and would tell me in a moment that it was a big joke. That he'd scraped up his own face, punched himself with the back of the flashlight, and was having a good one at my expense so soon after my father's murder.

"Let's get back to the house," he said, easing up on my neck and chest. He stood up and offered me his hand. "I don't know what the hell just happened, but you look like you should lie down on something other than mud."

3

Once I felt well enough to stand, I decided that I wasn't going to go back to the house.

Not just yet.

I had grown a bit worried about Brooke's nocturnal ramblings through the rooms of the house, and I didn't want to add yet another disturbance to her life if I could help it.

Harry offered to drive me to his digs in the village—he'd

inherited both the *Burnley Gazette* office and the house in which it existed. He had a big fat Jeep Grand Cherokee that was about seven years old and seemed like it had the crap kicked out of it in dents and nicks—the roof itself had a dent that made it seem as if an elephant had fallen on it. "I got it cheap. One of the rich guys got in a wreck up island two summers ago," he told me. Then he laughed. "Christ, I can't believe I'm talking about this car. All I'm thinking about is what just happened."

4

When we got to his office, the first thing he did was get a bottle of aged Scotch from the middle file drawer by his desk.

"None for me," I said.

"You sure?"

"Okay. Okay. Maybe just a little."

"It's for me, Christ almighty," he said. He filled a tumbler with the brown liquid and drank half of it back before coming up for air. Then he filled a mug about half full and brought it over to me.

The warm fire of the Scotch was a nice antidote to the ice I'd been feeling in my flesh.

"How bad was it?" I asked.

He pointed to the scratches on his face and around his throat. A dark bruise on his wrist where I'd apparently tried to tear his arm off. "And you tried to bite me," he said. "You practically knocked the wind out of me, Nemo. I'm not sure how, but you did."

"Shit."

"Any idea why?"

"No."

"You said you'd get all of us," he said. "And then you knocked the flashlight out of my hand." He made a motion with his arm as if he were physically trying to remember what I had done. He moved his arms slowly and cocked his head to the side. "Then you . . . you reached up and tore my glasses off. Somewhere in there, your fingernails went into my face. Not sure when you hit my lip. And you socked me a good one right here." He tapped a finger just below his left eye. The skin around it had grown darker.

"Jesus. I'm sorry. Jesus."

"Ever have seizures?"

"None that I know of."

"Ever have a scan done? MRI?"

"No."

"When was the last time you had a physical?"

I shrugged. "College. Junior year."

"Any accidents?"

"Like what?"

"Anything that would cause trauma to your head?"

"Nothing. Accident free. I guess I fell on the sidewalk once down in Virginia. It was muddy. I slipped and hit my knee and elbow. Hard. That's the only thing I can think of."

"Didn't you get hurt on the ice once?"

"Oh, yeah. You mean when we were fourteen? Yeah, I fell and cracked my head open."

"But you were checked after that."

"Nothing beyond some stitches."

He took another swig of Scotch. "You didn't even sound like you."

"Who'd I sound like?"

"No idea. Someone different." As, an afterthought, Harry Withers added, "A woman."

5

He went over it again:

"So, I'm looking around. I was crouching down, and I hear this noise. Well, maybe not much of a noise. It's like a high-pitched sound. I smell smoke, but I'm not sure why. Except it's an old smokehouse and it's winter, and you know how sometimes those old stone houses can reek of smoke if they've ever had it. Only you say something right at that moment, and I'm ignoring you—you say something I don't quite understand. Now that I think of it, it was as if your tongue was heavy in your mouth, like you'd been shot up with novacaine. I turn my head back, Nemo, and you're standing over me. The freaky thing about it is that not a second before, you were across the room. I know it's a small room, but I would've heard you. But it was as if you suddenly were just standing over me.

"I'm not one to get startled over nothing, but I have to admit, my mouth went dry when I saw you, and I felt something in the air, as if the weather had changed outside, or as if there were static electricity. Maybe the feeling you're supposed to get when lightning is about to hit where you're standing. That's what it felt like. And I look up at you. I can't quite see your face. It's not so dark with you right there that I can't see your face at all. But you seem funny, and I'm a little freaked, and I hold the flashlight up, and that's when you knock it out of my hand. But I see your face for a second, and Nemo, it ain't your face, buddy. It's someone else, it's like you took off a mask. I don't know what was so different, but you looked angry, and your lips seemed different.

"And then I stood up, and you were whispering something over and over again. I said, 'Nemo?' and you started in on all that stuff, and it's just not you, Nemo. I know you too well, and it's not you at all. You clawed at my face and my glasses went flying, and I had to shove you as hard as I could, which is why your head probably hurts a little, since you hit the wall and went down.

"It was like . . ." he said, finishing with a last sip of Scotch.

"Like?"

He smacked his lips. Shook his head. He nearly grinned when he said it. "It's gonna sound crazy. But it was like you were possessed."

I thought for half a second he had said "obsessed." Then I remembered that Harry had been the superstitious one. He had always believed there were ghosts on the island—at least as a boy. I had figured he had outgrown this, but based on mentioning possession, I assumed he still believed that there were ghosts. And that they got inside people.

As if reading my mind, he said, "It's probably just stress. Anxiety. All the crap you've been going through since you got back."

I nodded.

He leaned forward slightly, staring at me with an intensity that made him seem a bit maniacal. "We gotta go back there, bud. This time with a tape recorder."

CHAPTER TWENTY-THREE

1

I agreed to go back to the smokehouse with Harry.

I didn't want to go in there again.

I didn't want to feel it.

Not a terrible feeling, or a fear of being out of control.

I had been turned on in the smokehouse. I had felt an arousal the likes of which I can only call sexual, but which seemed more encompassing than that.

It had been like some kind of high within my bloodstream, and when I finally tried to figure it out, I realized:

I had felt like a kid again, on the cusp of pleasure and a rare, nearly erotic feeling that all my burdens in life had been lifted.

It was like taking a hit of a really powerful drug that made

the user feel euphoria, excitement, and a liberation from gravity itself.

2

Harry and I trudged up one late afternoon, about three or so,
with flashlights, and a digital voice recorder that Harry usually
used when interviewing some old salt or corporate CEO who
vacationed up island. "Just talk normally. It'll pick up all kinds
of sounds. It's a sensitive bit of machinery," he said.

Unlocking the door to the smokehouse, he made an "after
you" gesture with his hands.

3

I stepped inside, and nothing happened. I stood in the smokehouse, closed my eyes for a second or two because I did feel
anxious just being there.

I guess it was during those few seconds that something
did indeed happen, because when I opened my eyes—it was
little more than a blink—my watch—and Harry—told me that
twenty minutes had gone by.

And it was all on tape.

4

"It's fantastic!" he said, with the glee of a boy. "Oh my God,
is this ever amazing! It gave me goosebumps, standing there.
It was absolutely chilling!"

"Harry?" I asked.

He pressed the PLAY button on the small cylindrical machine.

"Who are you?" Harry's voice on the tape.

Silence. I glanced at Harry, but he kept his eyes on the recorder.

Five minutes or more passed. I tried to block out all other sounds in the room, and any from outside the window. I was sure I could hear the whirr of the tape itself. I leaned slightly forward as if I might miss whatever it was that he was so keen on. I imagined myself standing there, eyes closed, in some kind of trance.

And then something changed on the tape. Like a small mouse scurrying in a corner. Just a whisper of a noise.

I tried to focus all attention on that small sound.

And then it exploded.

"LET ME OUT!" The scream was so loud it was nearly distorted on the tape. "LET ME OUT! PLEASE! OH GOD! LET ME OUT! DON'T DO THIS TO ME! PLEASE! OH GOD! LET ME GO! PLEASE SOMEBODY LET ME OUT! GOD HELP ME! GOD HELP ME!"

PART THREE

"You owe me five farthings,
Say the bells of St. Martin's . . . "
—*traditional*

CHAPTER TWENTY-FOUR

1

The voice kept screaming until Harry shut off the machine. He held it in his hand, looked down at it, then up at me.

"Worst part is," Harry said, "I've heard this voice before."

2

Harry said, "I interviewed a psychic once—a medium. She and her husband rented the Houghs' place up on Grotto Road for the summer four years ago. My dad still ran the paper, and I was trying to do those pieces about local color and the tourists, and she had just gotten on some TV show about reaching the other side or something, so she was a near-celeb. She told me that she'd channel to show me what it was like. I may be wrong, but it was that voice. I've got the tape somewhere back in the files." He said this as if he were just thinking it aloud for the first time. "Either you're possessed," he added, "or you're insane. You choose your adventure."

"Insane," I said, and looked at the small tape machine and wished it didn't exist.

"Ever had any problems of this sort before?"

"This is ridiculous," I said.

"Ever had any problems of this sort before?" he repeated.

"No."

"That you know of," he said.

"Harry," I said. "Give me a break."

"Can I get your permission to do something in that smoke-house?" Harry asked.

"Depends," I said.

"You want to find out who murdered your father?"

"Of course."

"I think the police missed something." He wiped his face with his hands. "I have to ask you this, but it's insane enough as it is. Do you believe in ghosts?"

"No," I said immediately.

"Good," Harry sighed, half grinning. "I was afraid this was fraud, and you were trying to create some bizarre defense."

"Why the hell would I do that?"

"In case Brooke gets arrested."

"She won't."

"She shouldn't. She might. She did sit in there for hours before calling Joe Grogan. Her prints are the only ones there."

"She didn't do it," I said. "And I wouldn't suddenly start . . .

acting out . . . or something . . . Who would the ghost be? My grandmother? My dad?"

His face became unreadable. "I don't know. I don't know. It . . . sounds . . . like a woman. Don't you think?"

"I don't know. It sounds like me with a fucked-up voice."

"Not like you at all," he said.

"You believe in ghosts?" I asked.

He shook his head. "No. Not *believe*. Open-minded skepticism. Look, let me find the other tape. We can go over this. You might want to hear it. Maybe it'll mean something to you."

3

That evening, we sat in Harry's uncomfortable living room, and he played the tape. It was on an old reel-to-reel that his father had used for interviews. The psychic, named Mary Manley, had written two books on the subjects of life after death. One had been called *Where Angels Fear* and the other, *Talking to the Lost*. Harry pointed to the books up high on his dusty bookshelf, next to the fireplace, in which he'd built a comfortable, rosy fire. We picked at our white cartons of noodles and chicken with the chopsticks, although I ended up going for a fork. Harry told me about her books.

"She mainly went where she said the spirits took her. She investigated the Gisslers' Bed and Breakfast up in Cullen Town, Vermont, after it was said that the disturbed spirit of a dead man kept yelling at the guests. She claimed it was a fake, something put on by the owner's oldest son, who out of sheer vindictiveness wanted his parents to sell the house and get out of the business. She's a great detector of fraud in the world of spiritualists and mediums. She also exorcised the spirit of a little girl who haunted a playground in Vancouver, and that's what got her on the television shows, because the mother of the dead girl claimed that there were reasons why it had to be her dead daughter. Her books are moderately level-headed, although she had theories that sound a little silly if you think about them. But one that makes sense is that if there are ghosts, they're not literally the person made invisible. They're the energy of that person, trapped for some reason. Unreleased energy. She used the metaphor of gas trapped in rock. Manley says it's like that. Or carbonation in a soda bottle—you shake it up over and over again, and pretty soon it explodes. It's not a human being per se, but a force. Well, let's listen," he said, and got up to turn on the enormous tape machine.

"What preparations do you make?" Harry's voice seemed a bit nervous on the tape.

"Well, it's not religion. It's basic practicality. Some spirits are bad energy, and I have to protect myself. So, first, I spend a day or two in purification. I meditate. I do some yoga. I try to put myself in some relaxing place. I don't fast—I eat quite a bit during that time because I'll need the strength. I take time to talk to whomever I need to in order to settle past disputes. That's part of purification, settling the past. It's not a simple fix, but if I can make the first step, whether it's an apology to a friend or business associate, or a long letter I write to my dead father and mother in order to show gratitude for what they gave me and how they cared for me. Basically, whatever is clouding my mind needs to be dealt with beforehand. Then I just go to the place of disturbance and open myself to it. You may think this is some pristine pure thing, but in fact, its feels sexual. That's not politically correct to say, but I get an erotic and sexual feeling from it. That's why my mind needs to be clear and my body strong. I am going to be invaded by another presence, and I have to open my arms and wrap myself around it. If not, it will be rape. The presence will rape me. That's the danger of this. If I have not given myself to it completely and willingly, I will not remember anything, and it will have power over me, and it will destroy me in some way. Psychically."

"So, you're here. It's midsummer's night on Burnley Island. We're sitting up on Lookout Rock at seven at night. It's fairly quiet. Do you sense anything?"

"Not yet. Perhaps there's nothing."

"You told me eariler—"

"Yes. I felt something here. Like a gravitational pull. Not just all who had died here. Every place on earth has had death and violence and bones buried. But when the spirits linger, it's because they're trapped. Most are not trapped. Here, something is trapped and is waiting. Not here, not on this boulder. But somewhere here."

Harry switched the tape recorder off.

"We went all over the island that night. It seemed like a colossal waste of time, Nemo. 'Til we got to your place." He switched on the machine again, fast forwarded, listened for a word or two, then fast forwarded the tape some more. Then:

"Here."

"Here?"

"It's strong here," she said.

A cut in the tape, and then a strange sound like a strong wind.

"I edited the tape. Badly," Harry told me.

Then, "Here. Right here," the woman said. She whispered, "I can feel it. It wants to come into me. I'm inviting it, but it doesn't want to. Shhh . . . It's all right. It's all right. No, no."

"What's happening?" Harry asked on the tape.

A silence.

Then a different woman's voice. "OPEN THE DOOR! LET ME OUT! LET ME OUT! PLEASE! GOD HELP ME! I WANT TO LEAVE! I WANT TO GET OUT!"

4

Then nothing.

Harry stopped the tape.

"Holy shit," I said.

"Oh yeah," Harry nodded. "I dropped the tape recorder after that. She grabbed me, and her eyes went white, rolling up into her head. I practically had to throw her down. Ever see documentary footage of voodoo ceremonies? It was like that. It was like something had taken her over. When it was through, she was exhausted. She slept for two days. After that, she refused to come back. Hell, she refused to talk to me again. She left the island a few weeks later and wouldn't take my calls. Her husband told me that if I bothered them again, he'd call the cops. I had been calling a lot. I wanted to know what had gone on. And then I got a letter from her. No return address. All she wrote to me was: *Don't ever go in that place again. Something terrible happened there. Some ritual. Some awful, powerful ritual.* And that was it."

"It was at Hawthorn," I said.

"We were outside the smokehouse," Harry said.

5

"Why the smokehouse?" I asked. Rephrased it: "Why did you take *her* to the smokehouse?"

Harry shrugged. "Someone died there, maybe. Maybe a hundred years ago. Or who knows. She didn't exactly stick around and tell me. I mean, if you buy this. Do you buy it?"

"Not really. It's . . . fucked up. But . . . it was because of the Brain Fart," I said, nearly impulsively.

He wagged a finger at me. "Don't make me go there."

6

But it was too late: The moving image of the past had already begun showing in my brain. Me and Brooke and Bruno, sitting on the big plush blue sofa in the living room, after we had our Brain Fart.

Harry Withers, all of nine years old, sitting beside me with a big gold watch and a chain—his father would've killed him if he had known Harry had taken it. Waving it back and forth, saying, "Look at the watch, how shiny it is." He had learned it on TV and in some books, when he saw some hypnotist put an entire studio audience to sleep. Harry had always been up for hypnotisms, seances with an old ratty Ouija board he had (which he called a Weejun board, not understanding the difference between Ouija and Bass Weejun shoes). None of us was up for being hypnotized, but eventually we did fall asleep—out of exhaustion and boredom.

7

"It was the Brain Fart. We had it, and it was at the smokehouse, and you tried to hypnotize us back then," I said, vaguely wishing for some of Harry's Scotch to help dull my senses a bit.

"What's that smokehouse mean to you?"

"It's an old smokehouse."

"Tell me about it. Its history."

"Well, far as I know, the current one was built sometime around 1850. I'm not up on its history. They used to smoke meat out there."

"What else?"

"It hasn't been used since maybe. I don't know. My grandfather never used it. It's just been sitting."

"Funny. It's been my experience that somehow everything is used for something. Even if it's not apparent at first."

"Profound," I said.

"It's true. At least, I've found it to be true."

"I never knew about it if it were ever used when I lived here. Dad might've stored stuff there. At one time. But he usually used the cabin for his tools."

"That's not true," Harry said. "You told me yourself when we were kids. You called it 'the place of punishment.' "

"Oh. Yeah. It was. That's what we called it. Before I was

THE HOUR BEFORE DARK

nine or ten, that's where Dad would haul me or Brooke off to spank us."

"Just spank?"

"Well, with a belt a couple of times. Nothing too horrible. It stopped at a certain point." I remembered more: "And my grandfather used to take him out there, too, when he was a kid. And my uncle. There was a post in the middle of the floor—well, in the dirt. Dad put the wood-slats of the floor down long after that. There was a post and Grandpa would tie one or more sons to it. Dad said it was stuff that people get arrested for now, but in his childhood, that's how it was. Whippings. Birchings. I asked him why he didn't tell anybody, and he said back then, there were about 100 people on the island, and most of them just looked the other way. Most of them thought whippings protected boys from growing up bad. Dad had horrible stories about it. My grandfather seemed really sweet, but my dad said he sometimes got whipped so hard that his back stuck to the sheets at night because of the blood. He hated that old man. He was practically happy when he died so that Dad could take care of Granny." I paused a moment. "Harry, there's no ghost. Unless it's my great-grandma."

"Forget the word 'ghost,' " Harry said. "It's a phenomenon. Belief in the after-life doesn't need to come into this. A phenomenon. That's all it is. Right now. In the meantime, I want you to ask Brooke if she experienced anything there."

"Brooke?"

"Sure," he said. "She was in the smokehouse for a couple of hours."

"So were cops."

"But the cops didn't experience any phenomena. You did. Brooke might've," he said.

Grabbing my cup of hot tea from his newspaper-stacked coffee table, I asked, "Do you believe in ghosts, Harry?"

He smiled. "You and me were altar boys, Nemo. I believe that a man's body and blood can come from wine and a wafer. I believe that a woman who is a virgin can give birth. I believe that God decided to come to the world in human form a couple thousand years ago. Do I really believe in all that? Yes and no. Part of me wants it to be true. Part of me thinks it's a way of re-imagining existence, and our relationship with whatever created the world. Maybe virginity means purity. Maybe wine and water mean acceptance of a transcendant idea—that water can be wine. Maybe there was this guy who aligned himself so well with the truth of all existence that it was as if he were the son of God. But you know what? I don't know. It might literally be water into wine, and a man who was God. I want to know, but I don't. I'm not smart enough." He leaned back in his leather chair and swiveled it around. He pointed to the tape machine. "If people die and remain where they died, that seems a bit easier to swallow, doesn't it? Not that I do. I mean, ghosts? Not really. I've experienced this twice now. With you. With Mary Manley. If it had only happened once, I could forget about it. But twice?"

"Well, it's weird. I'll give you that." Then I let out a kind of hyena laugh of relief.

"What was that about?" he asked.

"You used to hold seances."

"Oh, please. It was just a Ouija board."

"You do believe in ghosts, don't you?" I asked.

Harry didn't answer immediately.

Then he told me the story about seeing something once, when he was twelve years old. "One time, I was sleeping over at your place. And I sat in the love seat. You sat in some kind of spindly chair. We were up late. Everyone had gone to bed. And I brought my father's pocketwatch out."

"And you tried to put me under," I said. "Like you tried to do with all three of us before. Only you didn't."

"I did put you under," he said.

8

"You were surprisingly easy. It was as if you'd been hypnotized before. I just never told you about it. I was . . . well, I was too scared. At first, I did stuff I'd read in this book on hypnosis. I put some ammonia from the kitchen under your nose. You inhaled it as if it were nothing. Then I pinched your arm so hard it left a red mark. Not a squeak out of you. Then I had you say something silly, something humiliating to a twelve-year-old. I'm not sure what it was, but I can guarantee it made me laugh. And then, when I asked you to recite a nursery rhyme, you began this long one. This one with fruit in it and bells."

"Oranges and lemons," I said. "Christ."

"Whatever it was, it gave me chills the way you said it. You said it like it was a ritual. I even thought you might've been doing it on purpose and perhaps weren't hypnotized at all. But at the end of it, you said something to me that I will never forget, Nemo. Your eyes popped open, suddenly— quickly enough that I nearly jumped out of my skin—and you said, 'Your father's dying. He'll be dead soon enough.' I stared at you for ten minutes after that before I brought you out of it. I made sure you wouldn't remember even being hypnotized. But it scared me, what you said. And the thing is, we didn't know my father was already dying. He was. You had told me something in that trance that was absolutely true. So I did it again."

"Again?"

"Hypnotized you," he said. "A few months later, I had to see if you really had said that. If you could tell me things."

"I would've known if you'd hypnotized me."

"I don't think so," he said. "I did it a couple times. You didn't know. I had a control phrase. If you heard it, you'd go under. You were extremely suggestible, Nemo. It was as if you'd been hypnotized by someone for years."

"That's an awful thing you did," I said. "You really did it?"

"Sure. It *was* awful. It was like some kind of big secret I had. But I couldn't help myself. Not after you'd told me about my father's upcoming death. And you told me other things. I didn't want to find out much. I'd just ask you about things I wanted to know about. You knew things that a boy your age could not possibly have known. You had this wealth of knowledge. I could ask you nearly anything. . . ."

"What are you getting at?"

"I asked you something, when we were eighteen, hanging out by the Triumph Theater, smoking our cigarettes."

"What?"

"I asked you if your mother was ever going to come back. And you know what you said? Under? You said that she had never left. You started wailing. It sounded like you were a two-year-old. I couldn't bring you out of it. Nemo, you don't have any memory of it, do you?"

I shook my head. "Jesus, Harry. Christ. You did that to me?"

"I'm sorry," he said. "But when you told me about my father . . . and it turned out to be true . . . I just couldn't . . . I couldn't stop. You *knew* things Nemo—only it wasn't like it was you. How could you know the things I asked about?"

"You didn't tape record any of that, did you?" I asked.

He shook his head. "I wish I had. And don't look like that—I didn't do it all the time. Only a few times. But it scared me each time. I just wanted to figure you out."

"Figure me out? Why?"

He took a deep breath. "There was always something wrong with you. No—not just with you. Something at your house. It was like something I couldn't figure out. Like there was a cloud there. Or some unspoken thing. And I guess maybe I wanted to find out more. Maybe it was the reporter in me. That sounds goofy, but you were writing your stories back then, so that was no more goofy than me wanting to investigate things. I found . . . everything about you and your family fascinating. But I wanted to figure out what it was that kept me—I don't know—*confused* about you."

I stared at him long and hard, thoughts spinning around in my head as if I was equally confused by Harry Withers. "Okay, how'd you do it? What was the control phrase?"

"If I say it, you might go under again."

I laughed. "After all these years?"

"Would you consider going under again?"

I didn't know what to say. But I was curious and annoyed

at the same time. I had so many chunks of my childhood that felt as if they'd been removed without my knowing, like a perverse operation.

I was determined to prove him wrong. "All right. Let's do it. See if you can put me under."

Then he said something to me, but I couldn't remember what it was ten seconds later; and the next thing I knew, I blinked.

9

He no longer sat behind his desk.

Instead, he stood over me.

"Nothing," he said. "I thought I put you under, and maybe I did for a minute. But nothing."

"Nothing on tape?"

He glanced at the digital recorder in his hand. He had begun sweating, but I didn't feel particularly warm in the room. "Nothing. You said nothing. You just seemed asleep."

"Well, so much for that," I said, somewhat pleased that I wasn't just some guinea pig waiting to be exploited.

He walked back behind his desk, glancing around his bookshelf, touching the spines of various volumes. "It's here somewhere. Oh, here," he said, drawing a tall, slim paperback from the shelf. He turned and held it out to me. "Take it."

I went over to his desk and took the book from him. *Talking to the Lost* by Mary Manley. I looked at him, shaking my head. "Harry . . ."

"She's not like other kooks who do this. Just skim it a

little, when you get the chance," he said. "There's a section about childhood rituals you might want to look at."

10

Even on the way out the door, he began ranting about mysteries and ghosts and strange, weird, wacko things. But everything in my being fought the idea of a ghost or any supernatural phenomena at all. It was all make believe. *It's like the Dark Game,* I told myself. *It's like pretending so hard that it seems real. But that's all it is. Maybe it's the stress. Maybe the psychic's moment outside the smokehouse was like the Oracles at Delphi—there's some kind of underground gasses released at the spot, and it causes some sort of seizure.*

Even that seemed stupid.

Admittedly, everything I thought of to counteract the idea that it was "a ghost," which is how Harry described it (gullible believer in all that he had always been), all my arguments both within my head and outside in the world that I could see around me—it all meant nothing. Something inside me felt as if this voice coming from me in the smokehouse did have some significance and meaning. I just could not decipher what any of it meant.

It reminded me of the Dark Game far too much.

In the Dark Game, we would pretend that we were talking to the dead sometimes. We would pretend that Granny was still there, and that she was with us. The Dark Game allowed us to open our eyes within our minds and draw back what our father had called "the illusion of reality."

As children, this had been powerful for us. It was as if we had a childhood imagination to the nth degree. It became a place for incredible creativity—after we'd played for long periods of time, I'd go in my room and knock out a story about the Underland, or Brooke would start drawing on pages and pages of paper, as if she couldn't stop—as if she had some inner vision and wanted to get it all down.

I suppose it's where Brooke got her talent in art—something she had tried to hide, but was now coming out in those paintings—and where Bruno got his wild musical talent that allowed him to compose some interesting melodies from out of nowhere. And in my own modest way, it was probably where my ability to make up stories had appeared, not that it had brought me anything other than anxiety.

But the Dark Game was a creativity firecracker that we each had within us, even as adults.

CHAPTER TWENTY-FIVE

1

I clung to the possibility that Harry's and my adventure in the smokehouse was somehow less than it seemed. Maybe the Dark Game that we'd played to pass the endless winter days had some detrimental effect on each of us, on our subconscious minds, the way a hypnotic suggestion might. Maybe we were all susceptible to hypnotic suggestion because the Dark Game was its own powerful form of self-hypnosis.

Well, of course it was, I reasoned as I trudged in the snow-swept street. *Of course, the Dark Game was just hypnosis in the form of a game. That's why Harry could hypnotize me so easily. That's why I spouted silly things to him when I was a kid. Our father had taught it to us, but he had learned it from his granny and modified it in the war to survive. It was a bit abusive for him to teach it to us as a method of momentary escape, but what could you do? Childhood was like that—full of pulls and pushes from grown-ups who had no conception of what they were doing half the time to fuck up their kids.*

I felt heavy from the weather and the burden of destiny that had already been loaded on my shoulders. My father's memory didn't need more irrationality.

I left Harry's place, book under my arm. I wondered if perhaps I was going insane—just the post-traumatic stress kind of thing. After all, my dad had been butchered. I had gone into the very place where it had happened. His blood was still on the walls. It might not be a stretch for a guy to break down and start babbling. Since Harry had been a kid who really believed in far too many things, and since Harry had been stuck on the island his entire life, I figured that maybe he'd gotten into island lore a little too much. He had spent part of the evening talking about the ghosts of the Native American dead who had been seen up on the white cliffs at The Oaks in a terrible fog; or the ghost of the infamous pirate Johann Redd, who supposedly still protected his buried treasure on the islands up and down the coastline, unable to remember where he'd buried it, so he went from island to island in search of the doubloons. I had known these stories since childhood, and even if they'd fascinated me as a kid, I'd never met anyone who had actually seen one of these ghosts.

2

Walking along the slippery sidewalk on Main Street, I drew out my cell phone and tried to call Pola, but the phone wasn't working. *It's a Dead Area. The whole damn island's got to be a*

Dead Area for making calls most of the time. I ended up calling her from the pay phone at Hanley's Mobil station. She immediately picked up.

"I knew it was you," she said. "I thought you were mad for me. Then you drop off the face of the earth."

"Can I come over?" I asked, a plaintive whine in my voice that I could not knock out.

"Something's wrong?"

"Not really," I said. "I just want to see you."

"Ready to meet Zack?"

3

Pola's house had once belonged to a man I knew as a kid—his name was Fisher, and he paid me a lot of money to mow his lawn in the summer and keep his driveway clear in the winter. He'd sold it to Pola and her husband four years before, and then, when they'd gotten divorced, Pola had kept the house while, according to Pola, "he kept just about everyting else."

It was a small, cozy Cape Cod, just two bedrooms, a living room that seemed no longer than one of the bedrooms. I adored it on sight—Pola was everywhere in it, in the pastel of the walls and the stencils near the ceiling of her son's room, to the old captain's trunk in the living room that served as both coffee table and footrest. The living room was decked out in full Christmas regalia—and it made me painfully aware of how, since our father's death, my own family had not bothered with cheer or decorations. Her tree was small but heavy with homemade touches, cranberry and popcorn strings, what looked like eggs decorated with beads and ribbons, no doubt a school project for Zack; and along the edges of her windows, small, blinking, colorful lights. At the fireplace, a long red stocking with Zack's name on it. Presents nestled beneath the tree.

"Zack!" Pola said, calling her son down from the attic. She turned to check my expression. "You sure you're ready to meet him?"

"Of course," I said. "Why'd you lock him in the attic?"

"He's going to be an inventor," she said. I heard the clip-clop of his shoes as he came down the narrow stairs that went to the top of the house. "It's barely a crawlspace up there, but he has his inventions. It's his mad scientist laboratory. You know how kids are. It's where he and his friends can play games and have a little privacy."

A lanky boy of nine came running, his white sweatshirt covered with what might've been axle grease. He had a mis-chievous look on his face, and he had his mother's eyes and smile.

"Is it supper yet?" he asked.

He looked at me just as curiously as I looked at him. "He looks like you," I said.

"Some people think so," she said. "I can't really tell. He looks like himself." She said this exuberantly, and as he came down to the bottom step, she went and grabbed him around the neck and shoulders in a swinging hug. "Zack, this is an old friend of mine."

"Hello!" Zack shouted, as if I wouldn't be able to hear him. Then he shrugged off his mother's arms and walked rather formally toward me. He put his hand out, and I shook it. His grip was firm. "Good to meet you, sir."

"Zack, this is Nemo Raglan."

"That's a funny name," Zack said. "Nemo Ragman."

"Zack," his mother said. *"Raglan."*

"Oh," Zack said, as if he suddenly understood. He grew more serious. "You're the one whose dad got killed."

4

Zack explained to me that he was sad about his dad, too, because his dad had left and found another mom two years before, and Zack didn't really like the other mom that well because she wasn't the real thing.

Supper consisted of homemade chili that was the most delicious I'd ever had; Zack talked nonstop through supper, and wanted to know all about things that had nothing to do with the island. What was Washington like? Boston? Had I ever been to Chicago and seen the Sears Tower? Had I ever seen the World Trade Center before the bad guys knocked it down? What was my favorite hockey team? He liked Wayne Gretzky but only because he thought the name was funny. His favorite band was the Bare Naked Ladies, although I suspected that it was because of the group's name and not because of the music. Ditto for his second favorite: Alien Ant Farm. He asked if I had ever played lacrosse, or if I had ice skated like he did out at Hanley's Pond. He said his best friend, Mike, had taught him how to cross-country ski, but he'd only done it once. He told me that he wished he had met Albert Einstein, and he wondered if I had. When I told him no, I did tell him my favorite Albert Einstein quote. (It goes: "There are only two ways to live your life. One is that nothing is a miracle. The other is as though everything is a miracle." He thought this quote was cool.) He asked me if I'd ever read anything by J. K. Rowling. Then he proceeded to regale me with why he thought the Harry Potter books were the best books ever written, why he believed there might really be a Hogwarts School, and why I should make sure to go read the books even if I'd seen the movie.

Pola got up at one point and came back to the table with a copy of my novel, *Igdrasil*. I felt my face flush. I wanted to rub dirt all over myself. It felt more than slightly embarrassing to know she'd read my only published novel.

As if to ward off any criticism, I immediately said, "I really wish it hadn't been published." It was a lie, but I just didn't want to face that book, the failure of my dream.

"I love this book," Pola said. She flipped the pages. "Look how dog-eared it is. I re-read it all the time. It's just like having you here to talk to."

Zack looked at me with wonder after that and told me that I should think about writing books the way J. K. Rowling did, "the kind where every kid wants to read them."

After supper, it was nearly his bedtime. Pola went upstairs for a while to make sure he got into his pajamas, brushed his teeth, and was ready for a little late night reading. It was utterly charming. He did the reading (from a book called *Great Inventors Through the Ages*), and she sat in a chair by the bed, and listened. She invited me to read some, too.

I asked Zack what his favorite book was, and told him that

I'd read a few pages to him. He asked me to read some of my novel.

"You may not like it," I said.

"I will love it," he said. "I will think it's the best book if you read it to me."

Such was his enthusiasm that I read the passage from my novel about the hero when he was a boy, and how he had learned the language of the wind and rain. Zack smiled the whole time.

When he closed his eyes and yawned a bit too much, I flicked off his bedside lamp and joined Pola, who had been in the doorway while I read.

Pola and I stood outside his door, just watching him in the shadows.

"He likes you," she whispered.

"I'm guessing a kid that great likes everybody he meets," I said.

"Poor little guy," she said softly. "He's got his troubles like anyone else." She didn't elaborate, but I figured it had to do with the divorce. I remembered how abandoned I'd felt when my mother had run off. I doubted a wound like that ever would heal, but would always remain a bit of a scar no matter how many years passed.

Even for Zack.

It was the closest I had ever come to having my own family, that moment. Standing with Pola, leaning against the doorframe, watching her son in bed, all covered up, drifting off to sleep.

I think it was nearly like being part of a normal family. A family that seemed at peace.

Sure, I knew it was fake. I wasn't Zack's dad; Pola and I still had the past to contend with, and would have to deal with it one day; the scene was all make believe.

But it was a moment taken out of time for me.

It was like lingering at the edge of a wonderful dream I had always wanted to have.

Loitering with intent.

5

I'd like to say that we did the mature thing and went downstairs, sat in the living room, and just held hands.

But the truth was, I couldn't keep my mitts off her. It was a sacred love turned remarkably profane: The feeling of being part of her life again was just a complete turn on. I felt horny the way I had at sixteen with her, and I had this urge to merge. I wanted to touch her and feel her warmth, just be as close to her as I possibly could get, our lips touching, our bodies wrapped around each other.

But that was in my head. We mainly kissed and cuddled, and the intensity of her warmth went right down to my toes.

After a bit of making out, she drew back.

"Something wrong?"

"Nothing," she said. "But you sounded bad on the phone. Want to talk about it?" I didn't respond at first, still in a sort of passion-driven state, the aroused, animal moment that needed to simmer down a bit.

"Is it meeting Zack?"

"No, of course not," I said. "No, it's not anything like that. I hate even bringing anything up."

"You don't have to," she said. "We don't have to talk."

We began kissing again, and after a few minutes, she drew back from me again. This time she sat back up and moved to the end of the sofa. "Something's up. I can tell."

"It's crazy," I said, wondering at her powers of observation. *Could she read me that easily?*

"It's probably not crazy," she said.

And then I just let it out. I felt as if the largest burden of my entire life released in one fell swoop, and I began jabbering about it all—about feeling something in the greenhouse, about Brooke and her painting, about the money in the wardrobe, and finally, about what had happened with Harry Withers in the smokehouse.

The voice.

6

"Do you believe in supernatural crap?" I asked. It was the only way I could put it without laughing at myself. It sounded ridiculous.

"I'm not sure belief is an issue," she said thoughtfully. "Nemo, are you sure it wasn't your voice?"

"Positive."

"You don't think Harry did some kind of trick?"

I shook my head. "No. He believes it's a supernatural phenomenon. He thinks there's a ghost."

She grinned, and then said, "Really? A ghost?"

"I know. I don't believe in them, either."

She looked at me with an unsettling concern in her face.

She reached over and took my hand in hers. "You've been through hell since he died."

"True."

"I can't even imagine what it was like. I used to see your father every day, at his store. It's left all of us feeling unsafe and worried, but most of all, I can't imagine what it's like for you. And now, this other stuff. Do you really need it?"

She was a smart woman. Smarter than I had remembered. "Stress?" I asked.

"I don't know. But it sounds unhealthy. I don't want you to get hurt. Who knows what it is? Maybe there are such things as ghosts. Maybe there aren't. But there's something bad in that smokehouse, and there's something you need to avoid for now."

Strangely, her words had the opposite effect on me than they probably should have. I held her hand as she spoke, and I thought: *What am I afraid of? There are no ghosts. This is something else. This is my mind cracking a bit, trying to make sense of everything. It's coming back here, it's reopening old wounds, it's feeling love and feeling abandoned all over again. It's living in Hawthorn. It's the house. It's everything that comes up from it. What am I afraid of? What is there to fear?*

"You're not listening to me," Pola said.

"Yes, I am."

She smiled. "No you aren't. What are you thinking? Just tell me."

"I guess I'm thinking that maybe I've just been afraid of things. My whole life. Avoiding what's hard to look at or figure out. That maybe I left here because I was afraid of what I didn't understand. Something in me is resisting the idea that something's wrong at home, with Brooke. Something in me doesn't want to face it. But I think I have to. I think I have to stop leaving things behind and start looking into them," I said. It felt like a huge relief to say it. "I've been afraid of home. All my life. I've been afraid of it."

7

I spent the night with her. I woke up early, and not wanting to wake Pola, crept into her kitchen to make some coffee for myself with a minimum of banging around. Harry's book, *Talking to the Lost* by Mary Manley, was where I'd left it on the counter. I picked it up, sat down at the small table in the breakfast nook, and began flipping pages.

It looked ridiculous and dull—I read a sentence or two. ". . . the prophecies at the Windward House were followed by rappings on the wall . . ." and ". . . I saw an aura that screamed, dark and terrible, around the woman, and I knew that she was possessed by the child . . ." It all made me think that Harry's childhood obsessions with aliens and hypnotism had never quite matured.

As I skimmed parts of the book, mainly glancing at the pictures, I realized I should just look through the index. I flipped to the back, scanned down the page, and saw the words "games: children, p. 123"—and flipped to that page.

8

Mary Manley had written:

I've found in my studies of gifted children that when they've been raised in what I'd term an extreme situation, they often create rituals to help them cope with the trauma. To some extent, all children do this, but the ones I've studied, who seem to possess a level of telepathy, have had heightened trauma in their lives. Witnessing the loss of parents in a car crash, as one subject in the California study had, drove the subject to develop a unique religion that had a hierarchy of gods and goddesses and a language that could be perfectly translated, with nearly 600 words in it. The child was only five years old. Similarly, the man I call Eric B also had developed a stylized ritual in order to escape an extremely abusive childhood, in which he was tormented endlessly by his mother, who kept him locked in the house until he was nearly fifteen, at which point she died. When he was discovered, he did not believe anyone could see him. He had so convinced himself he was invisible that it took nearly six years for him to learn the magical system he'd created in his head did not correspond to the real world.

Yet, he could prophesy disasters and predict, with some accuracy, the outcome of football games at his local school. His gift of prophecy seemed to be directly related to both the trauma he had suffered, as well as the ritual he had created to keep himself safe and sane during those years in the dark.

We've seen soldiers in prison camps do this as well. Who in the world can forget Micah Rollins, a private in World War II captured by the Nazis, who manifested burns on his face from believing—in his ritual—that he had flown so fast through the air he had begun to burst into flames upon entering the Earth's atmosphere? Correspondingly, Rollins's ritual had begun not in the prison camp, but as a child in his Kansas home. At the age of six, he'd been running with his mother through a summer thunderstorm, when both of them had been struck by lightning. His mother had died, but Rollins survived. I have no doubt that the rituals he created as a child were what allowed him to survive in the German camps as a POW.

The result of these games and rituals that children of extreme trauma have created seems to be a manifestation of some inner reality. With a woman named Willa Trent in Barstow, California, the depth of what she'd experienced as a child became the very thing that nearly drove her to suicide when she was forty-two years old. She had created such an inner world since childhood that she could no longer cope with the outer one. The attending psychiatrists and clinicians, who studied her as if she would show them about the inner workings of the human mind in a way that no one ever could, all came away with the notion that Willa was a fraud. Yet, in her forties, having tried to take her own life, it was found that she could levitate at will. She had done this since childhood, but had never really believed that it was real, only that it was part of a complicated game process she'd created that was part hopscotch, part prayer, and part witchcraft. (It will be noted that Willa did not believe she was a Wiccan or a Pagan at all. She firmly maintained that she based her witchcraft on cartoons and fairy tales.) I was able to witness one of Willa's levitations (before she went into seclusion, refusing to see either doctors or the press ever again), and while it was less remarkable than the word "levitation" might suggest, I saw that Willa had taken what was once called "mass hysteria" to a new level. She had not developed the power to fly. What she had done was develop a powerful telepathic power that was beyond language. She did not speak within people's minds. She created images in them. She had somehow made herself able to project images into many people's minds. Interestingly, it was primarily the medical profession that swore to having seen her rise off the ground. I did not. But I learned that, in fact, Willa Trent had developed a powerful will, and a creative form of telepathy I had never before witnessed.

9

I set the book down and closed it.

I sipped coffee and stared at the back of the book, at Mary Manley's photograph.

Then I went back to the pages I'd just been reading, and skimmed a few:

. . . what the psychologists and the psychiatrists seem to have missed in the cases of Willa Trent and Micah Rollins was that they had simply done what all children do. To the nth degree. Most children have difficulties in their lives. Most don't understand the world adults foist upon them. How many children are sexually abused each year? How many witness murder? How many are beaten? How many are outcasts? Those children may ritualize their differentness. They may create their own ways of dealing with the continual abuse or affront to their own nature. But if you multiply that abuse by ten, or one hundred, how much more powerful will those rituals be on the minds of the children? We know so little about the developing mind of a child—and when that mind has been crushed in some way, a strong child may create a ritual for compensating for the boot on his back. A strong child may create a sense of security with an imaginary friend, a game, a ritual, a religion. Because without it, perhaps, reality is too terrifying to face at a young age. But it is in adulthood that these children need to slough off the old skin of these rituals. No doubt, many do. But there are those who do not—like Willa Trent. Like Micah Rollins. Like Eric B.

Each of them faced a trauma in adulthood that forced them back into the childhood ritual for survival.

And the manifestations from their minds became more powerful as a result.

CHAPTER TWENTY-SIX

1

I thought about the Dark Game, and how its ritual had somehow messed with our minds. I didn't see our childhood as
particularly harrowing. Perhaps our mother leaving had been
the extreme moment that Manley wrote about. Perhaps it even
explained my having taken on a voice, a distinct personality,
inside the smokehouse, but that wouldn't explain why Mary
Manley herself had also been "possessed" (using her own ter-
minology) there. *Ghosts. Games. Rituals.*

Murder.

I just wanted some ordinariness to creep back into my life.

As I sat in Pola's kitchen, I felt an urgency to get back
home.

I was going to take off and write a brief note to Pola, but
I waited.

Nothing's wrong there.
This is all just messing with your head.
You'll get Brooke to the doctor in a day or two.
And then maybe you'll get a check-up, too.

2

When Pola and Zack got up, I invited them to Hawthorn just to hang out a while.

The three of us drove through the village in the early morning just as the sun was coming up through a haze of cloud and mist. The road, finally plowed out to Hawthorn, had its requisite potholes and ice patches intact, and Zack laughed each time his mother's car hit one or the other.

I felt a little hope in my gut, which seemed to be a new kind of feeling.

3

Brooke was, of course, still asleep, and I didn't bother going off in search of Bruno. I set Zack to work in the kitchen with me to make eggs and bacon for breakfast, while Pola sat on a nearby stool and watched us try to coordinate the various pans and plates.

It was chilly in the house, and Zack decided that someone needed to make a fire in the fireplace in the living room.

After a relaxing morning, talking old times and letting Zack tell me the history of his life as a young inventor, I went out the front door again to get some wood from the pile by the front porch.

4

It was still misty out, as it sometimes was even on the coldest of days on the island. The smells of cleanness that snow and ice brought with them lifted my spirits as I went. As I trudged through the crusty snow by the porch, I lifted some of the wood—the top layer was wet, and so I dug down deeper in the pile. I thought I heard a noise—as if someone were nearby and had perhaps called my name, only indistinctly.

When I glanced up, I saw a woman standing at the open door of the smokehouse.

CHAPTER TWENTY-SEVEN

1

I set the wood back down on the pile.

My heart began to beat rapidly. I don't know why. There was nothing frightening about the woman. She stood in front of the door to the smokehouse, with fog all around her, and I was nearly positive it was Brooke. But I didn't call out to her or wave. My mouth went dry, and I squinted to see her better, but each time I tried to focus on her, she seemed to blur more. I felt a strange prickly heat along my back and felt feverish at the back of my scalp and along my forehead.

Brooke just stood there, and then she went inside the building.

My breathing was rapid, as if I'd run a mile, but in fact I had remained perfectly still for a minute or two. My heart rate felt as if it were increasing, and I suddenly thought of the one or two news stories I'd seen of men my age or even younger who suddenly dropped dead of heart attacks. It was pure fear within me, and I could not for the life of me understand why the idea of Brooke being inside the smokehouse would have such an effect on me.

It's not Brooke, some voice within me intoned. *It's her. It's the Banshee. It's the ghost that Harry Withers believes is there. It's whatever killed Dad. It's something evil. Some malevolence that exists. Some awful spirit of darkness that you conjured up.*

Yes, you. Don't deny it. You three, playing your games, playing your Dark Game after dark. Using the game to conjure devils.

Using the Dark Game to bring something into existence.

Some force.

I would never before have entertained such an irrational thought. I did not believe in these things. I did not believe in the spirit world. In evil entities. In conjuring ghosts.

But the child that still lived within me, the boy who had kept his eyes closed and been with Brooke and Bruno as we played that game, as we took it to heights that our father would never have dreamed we would, that we remained long after dark, sneaking out of the house to go into the smokehouse, that awful little icy building and conjure the Banshee.

Bring her forth.

It has to be your imagination. It can't be real. You're under stress. It's anxiety. It's normal under current conditions. Your life is all Jumblies. Your world is upside down. You have love and hate confused in your family. Your father whipped you when you were a boy. Your mother left you and never contacted any of you. You grew your imagination with your brother and sister in a game that was too powerful for young minds. Young minds that could create within themselves something hideously evil. Something dark.

The Dark Game wasn't supposed to be played at night.

The Dark Game wasn't supposed to go on like it did.

And one night, it got out of hand.

One night, the night when the Brain Fart began, it went too long. You almost died. You came to in the woods with blood on you; Brooke was found out in the field, shivering from cold; Bruno was soaked with fever-sweat. You three had done something terrible with the Dark Game.

Or it had done something terrible with you.

Your father knew.

He knew that it had gotten the better of you.

He knew that you were no match for the Dark Game.

He knew that whatever was in the smokehouse was evil.

He knew about the Banshee.

2

With all that burning in my brain, you'd think I would've not walked across the road and down the slight hill, crunching through snow, to find out who was inside the smokehouse.

But I had to. I could no longer take the sense that something in the world was so skewed that I might just be losing my mind, even as I was beginning to feel the hope of a renewal with Pola. The hope that something wonderful could be salvaged from the waste of my life and the nastiness of my father's death.

When I reached the smokehouse, I saw that the lock had been torn off. Ripped away.

I glanced back at the main house. I imagined Pola and Zack pulling out the Scrabble board or flipping through the stack of magazines Brooke kept by the coffee table.

From within the smokehouse:

The smell that came at me was like the stench of a dead animal, its stomach ripped open.

I had a flash of an image in my head:

My father, lying on the floor.

I entered that place regardless of fear and inner turmoil.

The place of punishment.

3

Some part of me had been hoping she would have vanished, this phantom, this Brain Fart of some kind. Or even that Brooke would be standing there, in a somnabulistic trance.

But instead, I saw her clearly.

She stood at the center of the smokehouse as the morning light entered, and even the light touched her skin. She had a corporeal presence. It was not Brooke, nor was it some other woman of the village. I felt a terrible hunger from her—the look in her eyes, the tortured grimace of her lips pulled back across her teeth, the sense I had that she was somehow a smudge of darkness, as if I could see her aura. I felt immediately that this was the woman I had sensed when I closed my eyes at night. This was the woman I had feared when Brooke went from room to room in the house. I felt electric waves of fury emanating from her—the only way I can describe it, for it did feel like a power surge in the air.

Then the door to the smokehouse slammed shut behind me.

I felt a series of electrical shocks along my arms and up my spine. It was as if I had begun short-circuiting. I was barely aware of the blood that dripped from my nose, as it had when I'd been a boy and the air was too dry in winter.

I thought that I was dying right then.

Right there.

Darkness descended within the smokehouse, like a candle just snuffed, with only the diffuse glow from the door's window allowing me to see one square of light.

It fixed upon her face.

CHAPTER TWENTY-EIGHT

I thought this was a vision that I'd see at the moment of death.

My bones seemed to pain me, as if they wished to break free from my flesh.

I could not take a breath as I watched her.

Her face, seething. Her visage cruel.

Her eyes staring as if she could not see me, as if I were the ghost.

My mother.

CHAPTER TWENTY-NINE

1

I lost focus as soon as I saw her face.

It was as if my tear ducts had suddenly released a gusher, and it all went blurry. *My mother?* I stood there, motionless, frozen, numb on the outside, in the pinpricks along my arms and legs and deep down in my groin, my balls feeling as if they wanted to curl up inside my body never to descend again. In that moment, I felt as if my body were something alien, and my mind, what intelligence I possessed, was separate and hovering, still connected by nerves and the whoosh of blood (which I seemed to hear within my ear canals), but an entirely separate entity that had acknowledged that the flesh and bones surrounding it were of some other being, and that being was scared shitless. I didn't piss my Levis, but I had one of the few nosebleeds I'd had in my lifetime.

Did I mention the awful word: insane? Not the big version of the word, not INSANE as in irredeemable over the chasm, but the lowercase *insane*, the insane that was just a wriggling little worm in my head. It could not be my mother. I could not see her clearly anymore, anyway. My vision was going bonkers, and my body seemed to be crapping out on me—and still, I felt it was her.

Do people do this? I wondered. *Do people whose loved one has been slaughtered begin to break down and see things? Like the serpent shimmer of the greenhouse glass, and my sister's visions. Was I succumbing to it? Temporary, mild hallucinatory visions?* I felt the cold of the world. Not the winter and its snow and ice. The cold of the world—all that was ugly and fruitless and unloved and irredeemable. The shrugged. The sloughed.

And then the blurry image of the woman whom I knew to be my mother was gone. My vision returned, albeit with a generous hosing of tears—or so it seemed to be at the time—and I saw the wall again.

In my mind, the awful thought: *She has come home. She has returned. From Brazil. Brazil. Brazil.*

And another, awful part of me began chattering, a looking-glass world jabbering:

It's your mind. It's only you. You let it get to you. Let it all get inside you. You were insane as a little boy, and you're crazy now, all the Raglans are crazy, you're inbred Yankees, what killed your father was some evil people, some sadistic narcissistic killers who enjoyed the slaughter, and this vision is your mind melting down. It's your own personal China syndrome. It's your fucked-up nature finally imploding and fucking you up even more.

Yet, I experienced a split, even as these words ran through my head. I was not insane. *I know I am not. I am perfectly sane in a normal everyday sanity, the kind that might crack at some future point, but not now. Not healthy and twenty-eight and knowing that there are no radio signals coming into my head from another planet or that the government has some conspiracy going that directly involves something I know, or that the Devil is trying to find out what I'm thinking.* I was not insane—to even think it, I knew that I could not be. To even question my sanity, I must be sane. I must be.

I was alone in the smokehouse with a bloody nose and a revulsion in my body, as if I had been carrying around in my vital organs, my whole life, some devouring parasite that had begun fighting against its host.

And then something touched my hand.

Something that sent a ripple of disgust and revulsion through me, beginning at the palm of my hand. A terrible, nearly sexual feeling, that touch, that invisible feeling of something warm and moist pressing itself into my hand, a woman clutching my fingers, squeezing them, an unseen woman who was there in that dreadful place with me. In the second it happened, I felt like a child again and opened my mouth to cry out, only my throat was too dry; I tasted the blood from my nose as it dribbled onto my tongue. It was not the metallic taste I'd expected, but a sweet, sugary spike; *stop squeezing my hand,* I thought, *let go, you're hurting me.*

The pressure on my fingers continued, and I stared at my hand and watched the skin ripple as if some magnet were pulling at nails beneath it, and the nails moved the flesh—

and the tickling continued—and I felt the pressure of finger-nails along my wrist, and saw the skin press in like a sponge—and then a sharp pain came, and a small droplet of blood appeared on the surface of my skin. I thought it was from the nosebleed, but it bubbled up from my wrist, and a cut in the skin grew slightly—

cutting into me.

Stop it.

Stop it!

I brought my other hand down and tugged at the wrist that was held so tightly. It seemed ridiculous—I kept looking at the place where the blood and pressure were, but it was nothing, nothing.

I pulled at my arm with all the power I could muster and tripped, falling backward.

I realized that my head would hit the stone wall of the smokehouse, and sure enough, when I landed, I felt as if my brains had just been smashed against some enormous boulder.

I lay on the wood-slatted floor of the smokehouse, the back of my head throbbing and banging. I looked into the darkness, and again found the square of light that came through the window, the hazy light of morning.

And in that light, I saw a face from Hell.

Not my mother at all.

Perhaps not even a woman.

Stringy, matted hair hung over the blood-soaked face.

The mouth, open, had small nubs of what must have been broken teeth.

The eyes were empty, their sockets drawn back, as if it had not been enough to tear the eyes out, but someone had gone further and dug the holes deep, scraping back the flesh.

I saw pinpoints of light—not from the square of the window, but from the pain in my head. I knew I was passing out, and I was somewhat relieved that whatever I was seeing would pass—or kill me.

I heard a metallic sound, as of a knife being sharpened against stone, only it seemed to be louder and nearly like a bell.

I blacked out.

2

The Dark Game came to me—I dreamed it or remembered it in whatever corridors my brain still had working. I knew I dreamed, and I knew I was the grown-up Nemo, but I was somehow hovering and watching myself at the age of nine, as I stood there with a blindfold on, holding hands with my sister, a sullen eight-year-old, and Bruno, an impossibly small four and a half.

"Here comes a candle to light you to bed," we all three recited, "and here comes a chopper to chop off your head." Three or four times we said it, and Bruno seemed to be crying beneath his ragged blindfold, which looked as if it had been made from one of my mother's old pantyhose.

Then young Nemo said, "We'll go there again. We'll find out why she went there, and we'll see if we can bring her back."

"Daddy said not to," Brooke said, her voice like the chirp of a sparrow.

"I'm the Master of the Dark Game tonight," Nemo said.

"It's nighttime," Bruno whined. "I'm scared."

"Don't be. It only works now. We'll stop by dark, I promise. It's still light out. But the power happens now. Let's go find her," Nemo said below me. "She'll come back. We can make her come back where she is, and then none of it happened."

"I'm scared, too," Brooke whispered. She nearly broke contact with Nemo's hand, but he held on to her fingers.

"Don't break the circle," he said. "Follow me."

"Where?" Brook asked.

And then, the Nemo-of-nine said, "We're going there, we're going back before that night. We're going back to the house, and we're going to do it different, and we're going to make sure that none of it ever happens again. We can find her, and we can bring her back."

But his face had begun to perspire, and I could feel his heat—and the heat of the other two—they were burning with fever, even in the freezing cold, they were frying themselves, they were pushing their minds too hard.

3

I opened my eyes.

I was still inside the smokehouse, on the floor, with a gargantuan ache at the back of my head, and an intense feeling of exhaustion. I sat up, my muscles sore as if I'd been running for miles, my body covered with sweat, a shivering throughout.

I could barely bring myself to look at the square of light.

Nothing.

No one.

4

It felt as if my mind were flashing on and off.

As if lightning played within my head.

I closed my eyes to remember the Dark Game.

5

Holding hands with Bruno and Brooke, in a circle, peeking beneath my blindfold to make sure they weren't peeking at me.

Reciting the nursery rhyme, and then feeling as if we were soaring—all three of us—into a darkness.

And there she was, waiting for us.

Our mother.

Not quite our mother.

Our mother somehow rebuilt inside our imaginations.

Our mother crossed with the Ice Queen.

The Maiden of Snow.

The Banshee.

A hybrid of our idea of some monstrous woman and our beautiful mother, with her honey-gold hair turned white, and her eyes yellow-red and fixed with a cruel but cold, snakelike gaze.

Somehow, somehow . . . we had created her.

In our ritual.

CHAPTER THIRTY

1

I must have stumbled out of the smokehouse, but I barely remember it. When I came to, Pola and Zack were calling to me from the porch of the house.

When I glanced their way, I thought I felt a pull. A gravitational pull, trying to draw me back into the smokehouse. Like invisible fingers, tugging at me.

The sky was heavy with the smoky clouds that generally meant more bad weather—the predictions had been for yet another storm, as we always got on the island in December.

I had the odd sensation that I was dead. Dead and crawling across the ground, but not feeling it. Trying to resist the pull, that force, that magnet, which wanted my body back in the smokehouse.

I heard Pola's cries, and then a sound like the giant wings of a bird flapping close to my ear—

My breath was labored.

I felt as if my lungs were frozen.

I felt hands upon me.

With some effort, I turned slightly to see who had their hands on my shoulders.

As if I saw her at the end of a long dark tunnel, Pola knelt there beside me.

Her lips moved, but I couldn't hear her.

Next to her, standing over the two of us was her son, Zack.

His eyes were wide, as if he were seeing something awful, and he wasn't looking at me. I knew who he saw. I knew he must see her as well.

Not Pola, but the other one.

Then I heard Pola's voice. "Nemo? Nemo, are you all right? Nemo?"

I watched, unable to move or speak, feeling a chilling paralysis in my bones, and saw Zack move away.

As if someone were calling him, and he alone could hear the voice.

2

Sound returned, and then more clear vision; finally, after a minute or so, I felt the pinpricks along my legs and arms and the soles of my feet. I could sit up, and felt wet in the snow.

Pola was nearly in tears, but she fought to keep them back. "Oh, my God," she said. "You frightened me. Are you all right?"

I said the only thing that came to my mind. "Where's Zack?"

I wiped my eyes, for they stung. And then, with Pola's help, I got up.

"Zack?" Pola glanced around. "Zack?"

Her son stood at the entrance to the smokehouse.

Zack looked back at us.

"I thought I saw something," he said, but then bounded back over to us.

I still felt shaky, and somehow coated with shame, as if the haywire nature of my brain was its own kind of humiliation. I might be losing my mind, the way that Brooke felt she had been losing hers. I might be suffering some nasty post-traumatic bullshit that would require years of medical attention.

But I felt sane. If you can feel sane, and still feel the sputtering of the circuits of your brain, then I knew I was sane.

3

"Why would I see my mother?" I asked.

I sat on the living room sofa and watched as Zack swung a poker around the logs in the fireplace. Pola struck a match and lit the fire, then came back to sit with me.

"You've been through too much," she said.

"No," I said. "I want to get Harry out here again." I reached for the phone. "You might want to go home."

"Why?"

"I just feel weird about it. I don't want you to worry about anything, and Harry is . . ." I held up the phone and began tapping out Harry's number.

"I'm staying here," Pola said. "If you and Harry want to go out there again, you're free to. You're crazy to want to, if it affects you this much. But Zack and I can just stay here by the fire."

"We can't go home now," Zack said, pointing to the window. "It's snowing again."

It was an understatement on Zack's part: Outside the window, the storm clouds were growing, and what came down was less snow than sleet.

Harry picked up the phone on his end, and I said, "Harry, can you come out here? Now?"

4

After I got off the phone with Harry, I went to go wake up Brooke. Pola offered to come with me, but I asked her to stay in the living room. I had a feeling, something I didn't like having to admit, and it was simply that I didn't want Pola and her son to know about the Dark Game or about what I feared might be all of us cracking up in the wake of our father's death.

I jogged up the front staircase. Unlocking the door to the first room upstairs (locked, just as I had warned Brooke away from doing), I opened it upon a mess. The room I entered, the room that we'd thought of as the sun room, looked like a whirlwind had gone through it. A chair and table had been turned upside down, and papers were scattered all over the floor. As I went from room to room, it was as if someone had been on a tirade, tossing pillows and papers and kicking over trash and pulling drawers completely out of the dressers.

Brooke was not in her bed, but the sheet was half torn off. All the votive candles were left sitting on their shelves, upright, still lit. There were some on the floor.

I called out to Brooke, to Bruno, but got no response.

Then I thought I heard a woman crying. Was it in my head? Was it in the house? It was the most pitiable sound.

I ran in its direction, regardless. Doors opened and closed, and I felt as if I were running through rooms in someone else's memory, for I saw flashes—moments of my father in a room as he had been when I was a child, or of Bruno as a little boy sitting in his red wagon in the rumpus room, or my mother, writing letters at her desk—it was as if my memories were jumping out at me. *Close 'em off. Close 'em off.*

I found Brooke in the greenhouse, sitting on the cold floor, surrounded by her paintings.

5

"The dogs are gone," she said, looking up at me. "They ran off. They haven't come back. Bruno's after them, but I think they're gone for good. I let them out, but they won't come back."

I stood over her, glancing out through the green glass to the snowy fields and woods. "They run sometimes. Don't worry."

"No," she said. "They've been gone all night."

As she told me of her efforts to find them, nearly freezing to death as she went through the woods with a flashlight, calling for them, I looked at the canvases that were spread out around her.

Each of paintings was of our father, dead, bleeding, looking up at someone.

6

I put Brooke to bed, wrapping her in quilts and comforters to still her chattering.

There was condensation on her window, but no words fingerpainted there.

Outside, snow mixed with sleet continued falling.

Then I went to my own room.

My typewriter was on the floor by my bed, as if someone picked it up off my desk and dropped it there.

I retrieved it from the floor, and when I did, I noticed the papers just under the bed. I reached for them, drawing them out.

Someone had been typing.

YOU CAN'T KEEP ME TRAPPED HERE. I AM GOING TO DESTROY YOU.

PLAY THE GAME FOR ME.

PLAY IT.

PLAY IT OR SHE WILL DIE.

JUST LIKE HE DID.

CHAPTER THIRTY-ONE

1

Bruno arrived, having chased the greyhounds all the way to the other side of the woods. "Something spooked them last night, I guess," he said, dragging them in, all of them soaked from the outdoors. We got towels, dried off the dogs, and put them in their kennels.

Then he told me what he'd discovered.

2

While I'd been at Pola's house, Bruno and his boyfriend had been tearing apart the ceiling of the dining room. It had begun to bow and bend a bit, heavy with drippy plumbing from a leak Bruno hadn't been able to identify, although he had assumed it was from our father's bathroom. He had already recaulked the tub and tiles upstairs, but the water damage had increased in the ceiling below it.

He had a stepladder set up, and Cary passed him tools while he pulled at the ceiling. It burst all over him as he sat at the top of the ladder.

Mosquitoes and tiny gnatlike flies swarmed down from the damp open hole that was left behind. He was amazed that mosquitoes could be living in the gaps in the ceiling and walls in the dead of winter. "But the water was warm, so I guess they just kept breeding," he said.

3

He led the three of us into the dining room and pointed to a suitcase on the rug, by the table. "I already opened it, but maybe you should take a look."

I got down on the floor and turned the suitcase on its side. Popped it open.

As I did this, Bruno said, "He must've put it in there when he put in the new tub upstairs."

"A long time ago," I said.

Inside the suitcase, wrapped in plastic and old newspapers, was more money.

4

"Wow!" Zack said. "You're rich!"

Pola drew him back from bounding forward to pick up some of it. "What's all that from?"

"It's like there's another house underneath this one," Bruno said. "Dad's buried treasure."

"Look at all this," I said. I unwrapped the plastic off one pile of bills. "Did you count it?"

"Barely touched it. I crapped out and then had to go hunting those dogs down. For all I know . . ." But he didn't finish the thought.

"Hell, Bruno, it looks like ten—maybe twelve thousand dollars here."

We spent an hour counting it. Some of it was in neat stacks, others had been thrown loosely into the plastic wrap and newsprint. Zack helped out by counting the stray bills that had fallen loose. "Fifteen thousand," I said when I'd finished the final count.

Bruno looked tense.

"Fifteen thousand," I repeated.

"Well, now we know where he stashed it," Bruno said.

5

Bruno began pacing after that. "He hid stuff in the house. He did it. He did the repair on the tub. Shit, he did a repair on the front stairs. What do you bet there's something behind there?"

"The crawlspace?" I asked.

6

I tried to talk him out of it, but Bruno got a crowbar and a drill. I followed behind him, trying to reason with him, then shouted at him to stop, but by the time I grabbed him by the shoulder, he had already smashed the crowbar into the wall behind the front staircase, leaving a huge hole in the thin wall.

He opened up the wall, and reached into the dark opening.

But there was nothing. Just the empty space that ran along the front quarter of the house, behind the stairs.

"I bet I can squeeze back there," he said.

"I can do it!" Zack volunteered, leaping up, raising his hand as if he were in school.

"You're too big," Pola said.

"I can do it," Zack said.

"Nobody is going in there," I said.

"Remember how he kept repairing things?" Bruno asked. "How he'd always be working on something—the pipes, the walls. What if he put money back there? What if there's more?"

"That's crazy."

"No, it's not," Bruno said. "He never trusted the bank. He never liked anyone knowing what he made. He and Brooke used to fight about the store because he never kept up with the books."

In a moment of silence, Zack whispered in awe: "I bet there's pirate treasure back there."

I stared at the wall by the staircase, and the raw tear he'd just made in it. "Don't do it! This is crazy!"

"Let's find out," he said, without waiting for any approval from me. He smashed the crowbar into the drywall. It went through. "He had a hand-axe somewhere. He always kept it. Go find it."

"You're going to destroy the house," I said.

Bruno's face looked as if it burned with fever. "I think this house is sick. I think it needs some destroying."

7

When he'd opened the wall up with an axe, a crowbar, and some reckless hammering, we saw what we both wished we had never had to see.

It was our mother's suitcase.

Her red dress.

Her beige shoes. The ones she wore often. The ones that she left the house in.

Even her rosary and a small statue of the Virgin Mary that she had taken with her.

To Brazil.

Not to Brazil at all.

The only foreign country we knew was Hawthorn itself.

CHAPTER THIRTY-TWO

1

By the time Harry showed up, I had asked Pola to take Zack home—it would not be the kind of day I'd anticipated. The only problem was, roads had worsened. Harry said even his SUV had been skidding on the road, and the only reasonable way to get back was to walk. I sat down with Pola in the den.

"Here's the thing," I told her. "There's something wrong with us. Maybe it's some kind of stress from the murder. Maybe it's something inside me. Inside Brooke, too. But I don't understand it. And my fear is that there might be . . . well, some kind of danger here. I have to be sensitive to Brooke's feelings in this, but I think she may be cracking up under all the pressure. And I may be also."

"Let's all go," she said. She took my hand in hers. "Let's

all of us just go. We can walk to town. We can walk in the snow. It might take half an hour at the most. You don't need to be here." She didn't say it with any hyperserious gaze in her eyes; she sounded perfectly practical.

And it was true, we didn't need to be there. I didn't need to be at Hawthorn.

But I could not leave my sister there in that condition.

Nor could I ignore something that had been building since I'd arrived.

I had felt the pull of the Dark Game.

I had left the island to avoid its pull. To get away from what was bad inside me.

But the hallucination of my mother—she had seemed like flesh and blood—she had seemed there.

The words from the typewriter.

Brooke's paintings.

Pola looked at me as clear-eyed as I had ever seen anyone. "Do you know that you did this to me when we were young? That you shut me out of your life even then? That you closed ranks with your brother and sister and father as if I didn't matter?"

I didn't detect anger in her voice.

Just the truth.

The absolute truth.

"I know."

She offered a weak smile. "Do what you need to do. We're going to stay here. By the fire. But if I'm going to be part of your life again, I don't want to be shut out. Ever."

2

Pola and Zack remained in the house; we let Brooke sleep.

Harry, Bruno, and I went to the smokehouse.

3

We skipped the blindfolds. Bruno and I faced each other. Closed our eyes. Harry, with his small recorder out, sat on the wood-slat floor.

I have to admit, I began laughing at first, and then Bruno did as well, as we took each other's hands.

"Want me to hypnotize you? Would that make it easier?" Harry asked.

I opened my eyes and looked at Bruno, who kept his eyes closed. "I think we need the blindfolds."

"All right, then," Harry said. He took his jacket off, then his shirt, and drew his undershirt over his head. He ripped it up into a few strips, passed them to each of us, and then put his shirt and jacket back on.

"I just feel silly," Bruno said, looking at the rag in his hand.

"Feel silly, then," Harry told him. "Did you feel silly when we were kids and you did this?"

"No," he said. "It was serious then."

"It's serious now," Harry said. "Do you want to know how serious? Let me play something for you." He held up the digital recorder. "Nemo, in my office. I put you under."

"And nothing happened," I said.

"I lied," he said. "You did say things. Only I didn't want to face them. But I need to know if what you told me when you were under is going to come to pass."

He pressed the PLAY button of the recorder.

My voice.

"Harry Withers, you're going to die. Soon. You don't want to make it happen. Not again. You don't want to. You will die. Slowly. Painfully."

Clicked it off.

He shrugged. "Maybe it's bullshit. Maybe not. You used to predict things when you were under," Harry said. "You knew that my father would die of emphysema. You knew other things. This doesn't seem silly to me. I want to know everything that you know."

We began the ritual.

4

I didn't imagine anything, but recited the poem about the bells, and then chanted, "Here comes a candle to light you to bed, and here comes a chopper to chop off your head," repeating these lines again and again. I slipped back into them easily—as if I felt better about myself for saying them.

As if I'd wanted to say them, in the smokehouse, the way I wanted a cigarette or the way I might want a drink.

It felt like an hour went by. We stood there. We held our hands together.

Nothing.

And then it came.

5

In my mind's eye. Bruno was there with me, watching. Aloud, I described what we were both seeing:

My mother.

She was naked, her womb ripped open, and her eyes ran with blood all around them. My father held her, his skin soaked with her blood as it pulsed from the thousand cuts he'd made in her.

And again, he raised the shiny crescent.

Crescent moon?

What was it?

It flashed and came down against my mother's skin.

A small, curved blade.

The blade of a scythe.

CHAPTER THIRTY-THREE

1

One of us let go of the other's hands. I wasn't sure which. I nearly fell backward, with the force of being let loose from the game.

I had forgotten its power.

"He killed her," Bruno said, tearing off the blindfold.

2

"He may not have," Harry said.

"Bruno, it's a game. It's some mindfuck. It may not be real," I said.

"Her clothes are still here. Her things. He used the Dark Game to survive the POW camps, Nemo. He used it with us to control our minds."

I felt as if a gun had gone off right next to my ear. It was as if the words exploded something, and for a few seconds, the world went silent.

"He used to hurt her," Bruno said. "You may not remember it, Nemo. But I do. He probably hurt her that night."

"Right here," Harry said. I'd nearly forgotten that he was in the smokehouse with us.

It only took us a few minutes to decide what to do next. We really had no choice.

3

It was so cold outside that I felt as if my ears were going to burn off, and the snow was heavy, and the wind had begun blasting from the north. This time, I was covered from head to foot in a thick down jacket, a wool cap, with a thick wool scarf wrapped around my neck. Bruno was less concerned with the cold and wore his trademark brown leather jacket and jeans, with a baseball cap scrunched down on his head.

He carried the shovels, I carried the axe and crowbar. The flashlights were stuffed in the four pockets of my coat.

Harry had remained in the smokehouse and was speaking into his recorder. Ever the reporter.

4

Inside the smokehouse, we set up flashlights around the floor.

They lit the place decently.

The smell of blood was not quite as strong as I had experienced that morning.

I crouched down and touched the slats of the floor. "He put them in the year she left." My father's blood had dried and frozen the wood.

"Yep," Bruno said.

We began smashing the floor and pulling the wood up as it broke. I piled it in a corner.

We took turns with the shovels, for there were only two of them, a long- and a short-handled.

Bruno cracked the hard surface of the dirt below.

It took an hour to get to it, but we found it.

A canvas tarp, wrapped around the remains of a human body.

Harry crouched down and drew something from it.

"What's this?"

It was a crescent-shaped object. Rusted.

"It's what I always imagined her having. A crescent moon," I said, feeling blood draining from my face.

"He murdered her with it," Bruno said.

We stared at it, and then at each other, for a long time.

I said nothing. I could not comprehend what we'd found. I could not understand it logically.

Our mother had been murdered.

Our mother had been murdered by our father.

He had buried her there, in the place where we had played, when we weren't being punished in the same spot.

Then he had created the Dark Game so that he could stop up our memories.

He fucked each one of us up with that ritual. I wonder if he even knew the power it had for us. The way it had been an addiction for us, going to the smokehouse, or even in the wardrobe in his bedroom, or down by the duck pond.

How our lives had been empty without it.

I felt that now.

Playing it again.

I felt its pull.

It wanted to be played.

It had created a hunger, carved out a place for us.

Made a home within our minds.

5

"She was furious—telling him that she'd never cared for him and that she hadn't wanted children at all. I sat out on the stairs and listened and saw what I could from the bannister. He was practically on his knees," I said, remembering the look on my poor father's face as my mother, seeming more wicked than she had ever been to any of us before, told him how he had destroyed anything he'd ever touched and how if he loved the children so much, he could take care of them, but she was going to South America, she was going for love, and she was not going to spend another minute in the hellhole known as Hawthorn or the awful place called Burnley Island.

Even as I said it, it sounded false. I hadn't drawn that memory up in years, and this time, it didn't sound right. It sounded too perfect.

"Like it's from a movie," Bruno said. "Or made up. Like he made it up. Like he made you think that had happened. Face it, he murdered her. He killed her. Here."

"The place of punishment," I said.

"I want more," Bruno said, a silly look coming over his

face. He took deep breaths, and leaned over, resting his hands on his knees. "That wasn't enough."

"Bruno?" I said. "You okay?"

He looked at me wild-eyed, nodding. "We need Brooke. I want more of it. I want to go back to that night. In the Dark Game. Harry, don't you think she should be here? We just got a glimpse. Harry, you can be part of it. You played it once."

"Nothing happened. I didn't see anything."

Bruno glanced over at me. "All of us. Pola, too."

"No," I said. "Not Harry, either."

"Then Brooke," Bruno said, nearly panting as if he'd been running a few miles. "He fucked us over for life, Nemo. We need to go back there. We need to play it like we used to play it. Only not by his rules."

6

Brooke was in no condition for any of this.

She looked at him as if she could not quite focus. "I'm so tired, Bruno. Bruno, Nemo, let me sleep. I'm so tired."

"Get up," Bruno said. A roughness had come over him; and I also felt it. It was the hunger for the game. We wanted to be back in it. It gave us something, no matter how awful it seemed afterward, it gave us something. And when it was over, it took it away. "Come on. Let's go out there again. Let's play the Dark Game there. Now."

Brooke protested, and I told him it could wait, but he was enraged. "We are going to play it!" he shouted, and somehow, I knew that I had wanted to play the Dark Game again, ever since I'd returned.

The nightmares had been waiting for me.

The doors had been locked in my mind.

I let Bruno vent all the repressed fury he'd held inside, and I was afraid he was going to hit Brooke; I lunged at him, and drew him back from her bed. "Stop it!"

Then, I told her about what we'd found in the smoke-house.

7

In the smokehouse again, with Harry standing away from our circle, we began. Brooke had taken some tranquilizers and was fuzzy with the rhyme, but she accepted the blindfold. Her hands, and mine, trembled.

Harry glanced at his watch. "It's not quite dark yet," he said. "It will be soon."

"Perfect," I said. "The hour before dark you start. And if you keep going, it becomes real."

8

"Oranges and lemons, say the bells of St. Clemens." We all said the rhyme. Bruno, the most enthusiastically. I felt the shivering of Brooke's hand in mine and kept a firm grip on her. It was cruel to do this. It was perhaps even evil, for her mind was fragile enough at this point. But the hunger was in me. Just as it had been as a boy. I was merely a conduit, a channel for the Dark Game.

"You owe me five farthings, say the bells of St. Martin's," we said, and it continued until the line "And here comes a chopper to chop off your head." As silly as it was, it gave me strength, and I felt more connected to my brother and sister than I had in years. It had been the missing piece to my existence. It had been the surge of power I'd regretted ever leaving behind.

We were one.

We were one in the Dark Game.

And then, with one voice, we began speaking, as if our minds had merged, and the words themselves took us into another darkness.

CHAPTER THIRTY-FOUR

1

It was the night our mother left.

2

"No, Daddy!" I cried out, but I could not stop him from beating at her with his fists.

"You goddamn whore! You have done this for the last time!" he shouted. He barely looked like my father at all. His face was contorted, and his eyes wild and angry. He grabbed my mother by her long golden hair and pulled so hard that, as she screamed, long strands of blood-tipped hair came out in his fist.

She tried to fight him, but he kept punching her. I jumped

on him and beat my fists against his back, but he shook me off and kicked at my face.

"You goddamn whore!" he yelled at her again. Brooke and Bruno stood in the doorway crying.

"I'm going to punish you, you bitch! You kids, get out to the smokehouse. You're going to see how whores get treated!"

And then it was as if we were floating, all of us, and I could go in and out of my father's mind at will, and I heard the voices he had within him. I felt the tortures that had been inflicted upon him, the whippings his father had given him, and the muddy hole he'd been kept in for months at a time while he played the Dark Game himself—and something else was there in his mind; something else lurked within him.

Something created by the Dark Game itself.

A monster.

Not a human being turned monstrous.

But a creature that had knives for teeth, in circular, lampreylike rows, going down its throat. Something was loose within him, something he could not control.

Banshee.

3

Next, we watched as he held our mother up in front of us— she was barely conscious—and he tore her blouse from her, and then her bra, her pantyhose around her ankles, her pale white skin bruised.

We saw three children—they were us—tied with hands behind our backs.

"NONE OF YOU DESERVES TO LIVE!" my father screamed. "NONE OF YOU! YOU ARE ALL BASTARDS AND FOR ALL I KNOW I'M NOT EVEN YOUR FATHER! I AM THE FATHER AND WHAT I SAY GOES! NOT ONE OF YOU IS EVER GOING TO BREAK MY RULES, YOU UNDERSTAND ME?"

"Please," my mother said. "Please, God, please, oh God, please."

For a lightning-flash of a moment, I saw her not as a woman, but as a lamb about to be slaughtered beneath a farmer's axe.

My father's booming voice caused the children to tremble.

They had duct tape on their mouths.

He was going to hurt them, as well.

"YOU ARE ALL BAD! YOU ARE ALL EVIL!" my father yelled, and then his voice softened, and he kissed the edge of my mother's lips. "You're making me do this. You have evil in you. It needs to be cleansed. It needs to be wiped free."

The broken handle of the scythe was in the corner.

The blade was in my father's hands.

The children's eyes went wide as the blade came down into my mother's throat.

4

And then we were all crying, digging in the dirt.

My father was digging also, burying my mother's body.

"None of you should be alive. None of you. She was a good woman, but she went bad. You each are going bad. I can see it coming," he said, and Bruno began moaning the loudest.

My father ripped the tape from his mouth and grabbed Bruno around the waist, hugging him.

My father wept.

"Don't kill me, Daddy," Bruno sobbed.

Again, I had that strange sensation. I could move into my father's mind, and I felt the monster there, and when I tried to picture it, the word *banshee* came up. Inside my father. Growing. Struggling against him. I felt the killings he'd done in the war, some justified by battle, others, darker, for he had been playing the game. The monster had grown within him like a tumor. A dark blotch of cancer in his mind, taking him over, but retreating, in remission.

"I love you, baby," he said to my brother, and began sobbing himself. He released Bruno, and pressed his hands to his forehead. "Get out of me!" he shouted. "Get out of me!"

In his mind, I felt it, some kind of change, some shift of his blood.

He replaced the duct tape over Bruno's lips.

Little Brooke was gone. Her eyes glazed over. It had been too much for her. I moved through her mind and heard:

"Daddy is not doing it. It didn't happen. She went away. She went away. Somewhere else. Another place called Brazil. She went away. Daddy did not do it. Daddy did not tie her up. Daddy did not punish her. Daddy did not punish her and make her hurt. DADDY WOULD NEVER HURT US! DADDY LOVES US! HE'S ONLY PUNISHING MOMMY! BUT IT'S NOT REAL! IT'S THE DARK GAME! SHE RAN AWAY FROM US BECAUSE SHE DOESN'T LOVE US!"

I felt as if I were shot back out of Brooke's mind.

When I looked at my own nine-year-old self, I wasn't exactly all there either. My eyes had the same glassy look as did Brooke's, and it was the saddest thing I'd ever seen.

Who could blame these children?

Witnessing this.

Seeing it happen.

I went inside my own mind, to get a sense of what I could be thinking, and all I felt was darkness there—so much that it stung for me to stay inside my childhood self.

I drew back and watched.

My father filled in my mother's grave, and then sat with us all day.

All night.

Then, against my will, I was sucked into my childhood self, and I felt intense pain, as if my skull were about to explode, and something eel-like swam through my skin, making me feel uncomfortable in my own flesh.

In that little boy's mind he was in a small boat on the sea. In the sky, an enormous silver crescent moon, but it was barely dark yet.

My father was turned with his back to me. He had a fishing line out in the water. When I looked in the bottom of the boat, near my bare feet, it seemed alive with wriggling fat eels and freshwater trout, their tails flipping as they tried to get out of the boat.

He turned to face me, and his eyes were no longer there, but blood poured from the empty holes.

(*Someone cried near me. Bruno?*)

"Don't be afraid," my father said. "Just close your eyes. Don't touch anything."

I glanced down at the eels in the boat. The eels were in the child's imagination. He wasn't in a boat. He wasn't near the water. But he wanted to remake the world so that it made sense to him. "Them?" he asked, looking at the eels.

"Just stay still here. Keep your eyes closed. Don't lean. No talking. Ignore the noise," he said. "Listen to what I'm about to say. Listen very carefully. Each word I say is important. Each word is like a key to a door. I want you to imagine a small red light, so small you can barely see it. Everything about it is completely pitch dark, but the light is red like a tiny tiny fire. I want you to follow me with that fire, follow me as I take you somewhere else."

I watched an eel with a mouth like a python as it devoured one of the fish. I nodded, not wanting to say anything to him.

"She went away," my father said, returning his gaze to the ever-growing moon as the seagull's shriek became a scream. "But someday, she'll be back. Nemo, you saw her on the stairs. In her red dress. You cried and you tried to grab her, but she was mean to you. She didn't love any of you. She didn't love me. A man waited for her outside. They were leaving you. Abandoning you. You three slept in my bed that night, you slept there and we all wept together that she didn't love any of us anymore. . . ."

I was expelled from my childhood mind and floated again, watching as my father used what can only be described as brainwashing techniques, combined with the Dark Game itself. Hours passed in seconds, and the children remained in that smokehouse for days, being fed, peeing and shitting in their clothes, while my father kept them prisoner.

And the Dark Game began to take them over.

5

Beneath the blindfold, aware again of being in the smokehouse NOW with Bruno and Brooke.

Brooke whimpered and seemed to be forming words as if she were just learning to speak.

Bruno whispered, "The Brain Fart."

6

I was a bird flying in the air, looking down as each of us left the smokehouse as children. My father carried Brooke in his arms, for she seemed sick and feverish. Bruno held my hand, and fell on the snow (it was December then as well). At the house, the little boy named Nemo began to panic—you could see it in his eyes, and his skin turned pale—he let go of his little brother's hand and ran down, away from the house and his father.

Ran down through the fields. We felt the sucking hunger of his mind, as if it had been carved up in that Brain Fart, and something instinctive made him run away.

Down to the woods the little boy went, and when he got there, he began biting his own arms, just above the wrist.

Even drawing blood.

But a man came there and took him to the stream to wash the blood.

It was his father.

The monster within him was gone.

The father took his son in his arms and carried him home.

7

Aloud, NOW, in the smokehouse, I said, "Bruno, Brooke, do you feel it?"

After a moment, Brooke whispered, "What is it?"

"I don't know," I said.

But whatever it was, it went through the three of us like a current.

I was convinced that there were four *people holding hands in that circle.*

We were not there without something else also being there.

Holding our hands, holding them tightly, not wanting any of us to break the circle.

8

"It's Mom," Bruno said. "It's Mom, I can feel her. It's . . . it's . . ."

"Oh God, do you feel it, Nemo?" Brooke asked, her voice suddenly full of energy, where it had sounded drained and exhausted moments before.

And I did feel it.

An electrical current flowing through us.

We saw her.

Our mother.

But not as we wanted her to be.

9

We watched as our father, just two weeks before, stepped into the smokehouse.

CHAPTER THIRTY-FIVE

Cordie Raglan sniffed at the air, and we smelled it as well: a powerful odor.

Dead animal.

He crouched down and touched the floor.

What was he thinking? I couldn't sense anything from his mind. I didn't seem to possess the power to move through him any longer.

And then something grabbed him.

I expected to see a ghost.

To see our mother there, with blade in hand.

But instead, it was Brooke.

She attacked with the ferocity of a wild animal.

The first slice came down on his shoulder.

The blade went in and out, and my sister engulfed him.

CHAPTER THIRTY-SIX

1

Suddenly, I felt my mind explode, and for minutes I began to see a strobelike white light flashing in darkness.

We'd let go of each other's hands.

2

"It wasn't me!" Brooke cried out.

I tore the blindfold from my face.

The flashlights on the ground cast eerie shadows around us.

"I didn't do that," she said. "I didn't. It could not have been me."

"I know," I said. "It was something else. It was the Banshee. In the game."

There was a terrible smell in the smokehouse as we three stood there.

"I want to keep playing," Bruno said, and his voice was curiously like that of a child.

The odor grew stronger, and I began to feel sick.

"Harry," I said, turning around.

What greeted me then was something I could not have imagined. Not have wished upon my worst enemy.

Or my best friend.

3

First, I have to tell you that the Dark Game was within each of us now—and all of us at once. It had been waiting there, waiting to open those doors, and close others, within our minds, just as the doors in Hawthorn had opened and closed on us, just as life had opened and closed on us.

I felt different. I remembered the high that I'd felt as a boy, as if I had no problems whatsoever, as if I could do or be anything, and how we'd play the Dark Game and soar like birds, or swim beneath the sea like eels wriggling into the fathomless depths. I breathed more clearly. I felt stronger. Sweeter.

And when I saw what had become of Harry, it terrified me, but that switch had been flicked inside me and I wasn't sure if it was the Dark Game scaring me, or the sight of him.

He lay crumpled on the ground.

There was a look in his eyes as if he'd seen something too terrifying to live through. A kind of awe and astonishment, and he nearly seemed alive to me. As Joe Grogan might say, it was the damnedest thing.

I knelt down and held him. He was gone. Tears came to my eyes. I didn't understand this. I wanted to know what he'd seen, why he had to die.

Why I even let him be there with us.

Why the Dark Game had to feed off him like that.

4

Bruno was the first to notice. "Look, it's dark out. We played past twilight. It's real now. That's what happens. It's real." He spoke as if drunk, with both a lazy slurring of words and a nearly hyperactive physicality.

Brooke began shuddering. "I didn't do it. I just could not. I didn't."

"What happened that night?" Bruno asks. "Why did you sit there for hours?"

"I don't know!"

"You do know! You know, you're just not saying!"

Something within Brooke seemed to break. "I was playing it. By myself. I closed my eyes. I went into the darkness. I couldn't help it. I couldn't."

I went to her and put my hands around her, but felt cold inside toward her.

Toward myself.

The Dark Game had won.

It had been lurking and biding its time.

The Banshee, the only thing I can call the creature I felt stirring in my brain now, with the face of our mother crossed with the Ice Queen, crossed with the lamprey-monster of nightmares, had remained a small parasite in our brains, but the Dark Game had brought it out. Fed it. Let it grow.

"The night he was killed," I whispered in Brooke's ear, "you tried to kill yourself. You played the Dark Game. By yourself. Your blood spilled. And it came back to you."

She drew back from me, her eyes wide with horror.

Then she pushed me back; I nearly fell over, her strength had increased so much from the game. Her eyes seemed wild, but not with fear. Something else. Something that reminded me too much of the Banshee.

She crouched down by our mother's remains and plucked something from them.

The scythe. She glanced back at me like a wild animal, as if she didn't even recognize me at all.

Then she ran for the door, flung it open, and ran out into the snow.

Bruno grabbed me by my shoulders and snarled, "Let her go! You brought this back! You and your friend!" Then he let go of me and grabbed the sides of his head. "Get it out of me! I don't want it in me! It's burning me!"

I felt it too, a slight rise in my body temperature, and we both saw the other one, standing there between us.

The Banshee, with her eyes harsh and unforgiving.

Our mother.

Our monster.

The ultimate Mistress of the Dark Game.

And then the howling of the wind, as the creature before us became a shadow and swept out the door, across the dark night.

I ran out, and shielding my eyes, followed the shadow as it moved toward Hawthorn itself.

5

The front door to Hawthorn was open wide.

Inside, silence.

"Pola?" I called. "Zack?"

Behind me, Bruno, and what had become a blizzard.

6

Inside the house, the living room was silent.

The fire continued to burn in the hearth.

"Pola?"

From upstairs, a single, muffled scream.

7

I ran up the stairs as quickly as I could; the first door was locked.

Smoke came out from beneath it.

Inside my head the words:

Here comes a candle to light you to bed.

8

I turned to Bruno, who had followed me up. The game was in him too much—his eyes—his heavy breathing as if he were consuming oxygen like beer.

"Your keys," I said. "Do you have them?"

"Let's play it again," he said, licking his lips.

"Give me your keys," I said.

9

By the time I'd opened the door, I could already smell smoke. My heart raced as I bounded from room to room, and as I opened each door into the next room, the gray smoke began to come my way.

"Brooke! Pola!" I shouted as I went, and when I finally got to Brooke's bedroom, it was locked.

"Brooke!" I pounded on the door.

"It's all right!" Brooke shouted from the other side of the door. "It's all right, Nemo! I'm going to go into the Dark Game! The fire won't hurt me!"

"Unlock the door! Brooke!" I rammed the door with my shoulder, and it gave slightly. "Brooke! It wasn't you! It was that thing. It's inside all of us. It was in the smokehouse. It was in the game. You don't have to do this. You didn't kill him!"

"It's all right," she said, and her voice became sing-song as she recited the Dark Game rhyme. "Here comes a candle to light you to bed, and here comes a chopper to chop off your head!"

I busted the door down, my shoulder feeling as if it were nearly dislocated from the effort.

The candles were overturned, and the curtains had caught fire.

I saw something that I will never in my life forget.

Brooke stood near the bedroom window as the flames rose on either side of her, and even seemed to be under her feet.

She began to rise, just imperceptibly, so little that I thought I imagined it.

And then she levitated higher.

The whites of her eyes went into her head, and her face became contorted in the same rage I'd seen in the phantom of my mother at the smokehouse that morning.

"HERE COMES A CANDLE TO LIGHT YOU TO BED!" she screeched, waving the crescent blade in her hand and slashing at the fire itself. "AND HERE COMES A CHOPPER! HERE IT COMES, NEMO! A CHOPPER TO CHOP OFF YOUR HEAD! TO CHOP YOU INTO PIECES WHILE YOU WATCH! WHILE YOU LIVE UNTIL THE LAST SLICE HAS GONE IN!"

Behind her, the window burst open—the storm windows as well exploded around her. The blast sent her body forward.

She began to glide on a current of air toward me.

It's the Dark Game. It's nothing more. It twists what you see. It fucks with you.

I gasped as I felt a whoosh of air being sucked out of my lungs.

Things seemed to move slowly; time had changed subtly; the fire itself moved in slow motion.

It's the Dark Game. Play it. Play it as the master of it.

I grabbed Bruno by the wrists. "We have to go there now. Right now!"

Bruno looked at me as if I had just told him we were going

on a roller coaster. He grinned, nodding, and closed his eyes.

I closed mine, terrified that I'd open them again to find the scythe coming down on my neck.

Let's go there, let's go. We'll find you, Brooke. We'll find you there, and we'll bring you out. Come on.

I felt Bruno's mind slip into mine, easily, like a hand in a glove.

Calm, as well.

In the darkness, I saw Brooke, her blindfold on.

In the darkness, I reached over and pulled the blindfold back. Tore it from her face.

I saw her eyes look up at mine.

My little sister.

I opened my eyes again and let go of Bruno's hands.

Brooke was nearly next to me, but she was on the floor; the fire spread near her dresser.

"You watched him torture me! You let him kill me!" she shouted with the voice of our mother. She swung the scythe up and seemed to bring it down to Bruno's arm, but he moved at just the last second, and it sliced, instead, into his leg. I grabbed her by the wrist and shook her. I felt a jolt of electricity go through us, and that awful sweet feeling of the game.

She dropped the blade. It slid across the floor. She twisted her arm out from my hand and lunged at me, her teeth nearly going to my throat. It was like fending off a mad dog.

I threw her back with all my strength; she landed on the bed, its sheets catching fire as if she were the fire herself.

The howling wind outside the broken window—

The booming of doors being slammed shut in the house, one after the other.

Brooke began biting her arms, reopening the cuts on them, blood on her lips. The flesh curling back as the wounds spread wide.

"Yes! Yes! Hold my hands," she said. "Hold my hands. We don't have to be here. We can go there. Into the dark. We can be with her. With Mother."

I rushed to her and yanked her up from the burning bed; the skin along her neck had begun bubbling from the burn, and her hair had caught fire. I wrapped her in the quilt, snuffing out the flames along her scalp, and lifted her up.

She pressed her lips to my neck as I carried her, licking. It was the nastiest thing I'd ever felt. I didn't care. She would survive this. We all would.

It's not her. It's not. It's not a ghost. It's something we created in that game. It's something that exists in it. We don't play it. It plays us.

I carried her out of her bedroom, opening one door after another to get out of the house; she clawed at me the whole way, scraping my neck and tearing at my coat like it was made of paper.

"Bruno, come on!" I shouted.

10

The fire had its own power—that same surge we'd felt—and it spread too fast on the upper floor. Flames shot out of the windows.

I lay Brooke down in the snow on the quilt.

"Watch her!" I said.

I went back in for Pola and Zack, but as I raced through

the rooms on the ground floor, I saw shapes of things—of children—of us, the three of us, children in the house, as if I were seeing quick flashes of moments from my childhood. Part of me wondered whether I was still in the smokehouse.

Still in the Dark Game.

My brain was flashing on and off, as if it had a struggle to make sense of everything that had gone on that night.

At the other end of the house, in the greenhouse, the door leading outside was wide open.

I saw light down by the woods. A flashlight's beam.

I cupped my hands around my mouth and shouted Pola's name.

I heard a call back up from the woods.

Pola's voice.

They were safe.

II

I stood outside and watched Hawthorn burn, as it probably should've burned years before. The greyhounds were on leashes—when we'd been in the smokehouse, Pola and her son had taken the dogs out through the back of the house, and they'd run off again. Pola and Zack went out in the storm, leashes in hand, to get them back. And come back they did; perhaps, those dogs even saved the lives of the woman and boy who chased them down.

Bruno took Brooke up to Harry's SUV, and we sent Zack running across the road to go ask Paulette and Ike Doone to call the fire department if they hadn't already.

I was hoping that the place would just burn.

None of us could ever live there again.

None of us would want to sleep in that house, or even in its general vicinity.

12

"I don't think life has meaning," I said to Pola. "I just don't. Not after this."

Pola took my hand, squeezing it lightly. It was like some Morse code between us, and I felt some meaning in her touch. *No Dark Game there.* "Don't die twice," she said.

I glanced at her. Her face, beautiful and undisturbed. She was a survivor of things. She was someone I wanted to understand better.

"There's plenty of time for what will come. You and I will grow old. We'll be haunted by the past. But it's just the past," she said. "I'm not sure there are answers here. In this world. It's just mystery here. I think all we're supposed to do is ask the questions. The answers are for later."

I had nothing to say to this. I had no defense. I felt an enormous burning within myself, even as the last of the house went, and with it, some screams in my head that I suppose had not stopped since I'd been a little boy and had watched my mother die at the hands of my father.

There we were: Pola, her scarf tied around her hair, her beige jacket wrapped around her body; and me, standing on the gravel of the roadside, watching the fire consume the night.

In the darkening sky, the ashes floated gray and white, upward, like snowflakes turning from the earth back to the heavens.

I had no words left. I reached for her, clung to her, held her, and I wanted life more than anything else in the world.

CHAPTER THIRTY-SEVEN

1

The murder of my father was never officially solved. There were no fingerprints. There was no evidence beyond pictures in our minds. Bruno and I knew it hadn't really been Brooke. We knew it had been something else. An energy there, brought from darkness.

A power, fueled by a children's game.

Fueled by fear and anger and terror.

And by something we would probably never be able to fully understand.

Perhaps, a psychic spark against a flint of human madness.

Not our mother.

But the Banshee that three children had conjured once upon a time.

2

I suppose if Harry hadn't been diagnosed as having a heart attack, Joe Grogan would've believed our stories about apparitions and possession and a game that drove you mad and turned you into some kind of psychic generator. We didn't mention Brooke. "He had a heart murmur," Joe told me. "It could've happened at any time."

I knew better. Even Joe had seen the way Harry's face looked. It had contorted not in pain, but in fear.

But I let it go. No good would be served by protesting about what no one—least of all a policeman with an orderly and skeptical mind—would not believe unless he had been there to experience it.

My mother's remains were positively identified from dental records, and we buried her in the Raglan cemetery down beyond the woods, but not 'til spring. I insisted that she not be buried near where my father was finally laid to rest, but at the opposite end, near Granny Pree, whom my mother had loved so much.

Brooke left the island; Bruno and I remained; Pola and I took in the greyhounds, both of whom wreaked havoc on Pola's small house, but Zack adored them.

I adored them as well, for they had saved two people I loved very much, just by being out of control.

3

We three decided to sell off parcels of land, once summer came around. We all could use the money, and Bruno expressed an ambition to build a small place on the other side of the woods, far away from where Hawthorn had stood. So, we'd keep a few acres, and sell the rest as buyers became interested. Bruno and I wanted Brooke to have the lion's share of any sale, but she insisted that whatever sale MontiLee Stormer could get, the proceeds would be divided three ways.

I still had to overcome my fear of the place.

I went there in March and wandered the ruins of the house. I couldn't bring myself to go near the smokehouse, and frankly, congratulated myself on that wisdom. No use opening that door, ever again.

As I walked around the property, with the winter chill and that whistling wind still biting at my neck, I felt a peace I'd never experienced there before.

It was gone.

Whatever had been there that was bad.

It had left.

Burnt itself out.

4

We had a reunion of sorts in June at Hawthorn—Midsummer's Eve, to be exact. The longest day of the year, which also meant the longest twilight.

The weather was delightful, the mosquitoes were a bit heavy, and Pola and I spent an afternoon cooking and preparing, with Zack running errands to make sure there were enough potatoes for the German potato salad, and for last-minute runs to Croder-Sharp-Callahan for paper plates.

Zack invited his friends, Mike and Mike's sister, Jenny,

whose parents were going off on a sailboat with another couple that evening. It was nearly like having a big family in tow, but I loved every minute.

Bruno and Cary met us in the village. We drove from there out to the property.

5

All that was left of the house was its foundation and what I'd best call "scraps"—broken glass, burnt out frames of windows, some brick rubble—the leftovers of a house burning. Wild-flowers, brightly colored in lavender and yellow, had sprung up around the foundation, and we settled on the southern edge of the foundation for our picnic. Cary had a huge quilt, which he spread out, and it fit nearly all of us, with our feet hanging over the edge in the fresh green grass. The kids went off to play games down by the duck pond.

"How's the book?" Cary asked.

"Crap," I said. "But what the hell. I'm putting everything I have in me into it. It'll probably never get published."

"It'll get published," he said. "And I'll even read it. What's it called?"

I didn't want to tell the title at first, but I couldn't very well keep it a secret too long. "*The Dark Game*," I said.

"Ah." Bruno nodded. "And it's about?"

"Innocence and evil," I said. I didn't want to talk much about it. The story for the book was pretty much writing itself, and I'd discovered that the less said about a writing project, the more urgent it seemed to me to write it. "How's the business?"

"Same as yesterday," he said, grinning. "Same as tomorrow."

"MontiLee sell this place yet?"

"Three offers, but she said we should turn 'em down. She said give it another three weeks of summer, and we'll get the real offers."

"Regular entrepreneurs we are," I said. "Brooke probably wishes we'd just take an offer soon."

"Brooke never responded," he said.

"She'll show."

"I'm not sure if she's coming," Bruno said.

"She'll be here," I said.

I knew my sister well enough to know that she'd somehow find a way back here for this one gathering. She had, after all, been the center of the family in ways that neither Bruno nor I ever could be. Yet, he and I had chosen to remain on Burnley, despite the past. Brooke had moved on, going first to the Cape, and then up to Maine, getting work in an art shop there.

I suppose she also had reason to never come back.

But the three of us had found some peace together; some middle ground of friendship that seemed to surpass the bad memories.

Since Bruno and I saw each other fairly regularly in the village, we just talked about the weather and the onslaught of summer tourists.

I followed Zack and his friends down to the duck pond to show them how to skip rocks.

"You choose a good flat one," I said. "Like this." I angled it and threw it in the pond, but it sunk without a skip. "Been too many years," I said.

Zack laughed, picked up any old rock he found, and tossed it—the damn thing skipped three times before sinking.

"You've been practicing," I told him.

Pretty soon, Jenny and Mike were pretty much just throwing pebbles into the duck pond, and the ducks, wisely, either flew away or skedaddled to the side of the pond farthest from us.

Jenny found what looked like the torn remnants of an old sheet, with light green flowers on it. She held it up. "Somebody lost their bed," she said.

"Must be a squatter's," I said.

"What's that?" Zack asked.

Jenny made pouty sounds as her brother tugged the sheet away from her.

"Someone who camps out someplace where nobody notices. They squat," I said. Zack gave me a funny look. "It's not a precise definition," I added.

"Give it back!" Jenny protested.

"It's dirty!" Mike said, flinging the sheet back to his sister. "Take your ol' dirty sheet."

"It's pretty," little Jenny said, wrapping it up in her arms. "I'm gonna take it home and wash it and cut a dress out of it."

Mike and Zack rolled their eyes, and Jenny ignored them, rolling the sheet up as if it were some great treasure.

Zack grabbed my hand and wanted me to lean down so he could whisper something to me.

"What?" I asked.

"She's here."

When he said it, I felt that terrible bonechill again, and I looked at him as if he were some kind of evil child—for just a second. In my head: *the memory of the Banshee, her fury, her absolute cold hatred for us, for any who were at Hawthorn.*

But then I looked in the direction he pointed, and it was Brooke, up on the road. She had gotten a lift from Joe Grogan, who waved to us as he drove away.

I left the kids to play and trudged up the hillside.

6

"You made it!" I shouted as I reached my sister, and she had a smile the likes of which I'd never seen her reveal before. It was so wide that it seemed to want to break away from her face.

She was probably healthier than I'd ever seen her also— her face was no longer pale, but had a rosy glow to it. She wore some heavy silver bracelets on each wrist, no doubt her method of hiding the thin white marks left by the cuts. "Guess what?" she said, and before I could say another word, she said, "I'm pregnant."

"Holy crap," I said. I grabbed her and hugged her, and felt as we had as kids. The good part of kid-dom. Bruno huddled nearby with Pola and Cary, and he shouted out, "And you look it! You must've put on ten pounds!"

"At least," she said.

We sat around, chewing on fried chicken and drinking Coke from the can, and at about six o'clock Bruno began telling the kids the history of the Raglan family—and Brooke and I tuned it out.

We went walking a bit.

"Who is he?" I asked. "This guy."

"A total wastrel," she said. "He's a poet who also works on boats up in Camden. He does a good business. And he's a really good poet."

"Marriage in the picture?"

"Does it matter?"

"It's up to the two of you, I guess," I said.

"He wants to. He's proposed. I don't know. It happened so fast. When I got out of the hospital in February, well, you know."

"Sure," I said. "You just wanted to get away."

"As far as possible. But I couldn't get out of New England. It's a Raglan curse. I met him in March. He told me it was love at first sight for him. I guess I love him. I mean, I feel like I do. But I don't trust it."

"The feeling?"

"I just don't. I don't know how many years it'll take to undo all this . . . well, *damage*. Is that the word for it?"

"Sounds right to me."

"He told me he'd wait."

"He know about the baby?"

"Not yet. I just found out two days ago for sure. Nemo, I'd never talk about this with anyone else, but I feel comfortable asking you. Do you think I could ever be a mother?"

"What do you mean? Of course you could. You will be."

"I'm not sure," she said. "What if it's some kind of mental illness? What if what happened to us is . . ."

"In our blood?"

She heaved a sigh, an enormous weight from within.

"Come on, Brooke."

"I'm more worried about the game," she said. "I'm still not sure what it was."

"The game is over. He taught it to us to control us."

"No," she said. "I've thought about it a lot. It controlled us. It may have controlled him, too."

I sighed. I just wanted to move on. "What our father and mother were has nothing to do with you now."

She let out a mocking laugh. "Of course it does. Of course it does. Nemo. It has a lot to do with me—and you and Bruno—now."

I realized how dumb I'd been sounding. How we'd always talked around each other. How all three of us had to stop it if we were going to reach out into our own lives into new families and protect them and ourselves. "You're right. It had a profound effect on us. You look like Mom. I look like Dad. You paint like Mom. Bruno plays music like Mom. I'm as stubborn as Dad was. But what happened at this house was not about that. It was about human evil. And maybe about what that leaves behind. But it's gone. It got burned out. None of us gets a fucked-up-free life, Brooke. Nobody. Even Pola and Cary—maybe nobody went nuts like Dad did, but everybody gets slammed into the ground by life in one way or another. And I guess the choice is what we do with it. You can wallow in that past. You can let this wonderful guy go, this guy who adores you and writes poetry and fixes boats and puts you and your child first and who believes in love at first sight. You can even lose the baby. You can get it removed, and tell yourself that it's for the best, that someone like you shouldn't bring a child into the world. Or you can make the choice that you will overcome this. Just like we overcame it in childhood. I was thinking about the Brain Fart, Brooke. I was thinking about it, and why it was there, and the only thing I can come up with is: We are meant to forget. We are meant to put aside childhood. We are meant to say goodbye to the families we came from, particularly if they're bad for us. We are meant to move on and create our own families. That's what none of us had done. We are meant to have a Brain Fart so that all the bad things don't keep us from what life offers. And for you, life is offering what you wanted: a family. Dad couldn't provide it, not the way it's supposed to be. He was a murderer, plain and simple. He butchered our mother. Maybe we can blame the prison camp he was in. Maybe we can blame the way his father whipped him. Maybe it was just madness. Something happened here that was terrible. Something continued to remain here afterward. But it's gone now. It doesn't have to be in *here*," I said, and I placed my hand near her heart. "It doesn't have to live here. Don't make room for it."

She glanced at me a bit archly. "You've been to a shrink?"

"What, and you haven't?" I laughed. "Oh yeah. Big time. After all this, probably for the rest of my natural born days. You want to know what helped?" I twisted around and pointed back to Pola and Zack. "Those two. And even the good things we had as kids."

"There were good things?"

"We three had each other. No matter what storm was out there, we had each other," I said. "And we still do. Now, tell me, you want this baby?"

Her eyes glazed over with tears. "Yes. I want this baby.

I've wanted a baby for years. And I want him, too. I love him. I'm afraid to love him. But I do."

"You need to tell him," I said.

"Nemo?"

"Yeah?"

"I don't know if I'm out of the woods yet," she said, a slight tremble to her voice.

"I suspect it's all woods," I said. "And nobody's out of 'em."

7

I walked with my beautiful sister back to my beautiful wife (yes, we had the small ceremony in the early spring, just the two of us with Zack as both ring bearer and best man, and a justice of the peace), my brilliant stepson and his friends, and my fabulous brother and his handsome lover, and for a moment, at twilight, I thought, *This is pretty damn good. Life is great. The world is good. The universe has some benevolence to it. We live our lives in the hour before dark. The dark itself will come— but there's no need to rush. When that hour passes, perhaps the real game begins.*

We broke up the picnic after nine. The sun was on its way down at last. The woods were a haze of green; the smell of night sea in the air. I watched Bruno dance with Pola and Jenny as Zack and Mike fought over the job of deejay with the boombox he'd brought; or Jenny, running along the fields, with her newly found sheet trailing behind her like she was a princess in a make-believe world, while Zack and Mike used sticks as swords for knightly duels, while Pola shouted at them that they'd poke an eye out; Cary went around looking in the rubble of the foundation, now and then calling out that he'd found some widget or other that was still useful; and Brooke and I sat and talked about what kind of name her baby should have, what name would be a good Raglan name even if the kid wasn't going to be a Raglan.

Albert Einstein once said, "There are only two ways to live your life. One is that nothing is a miracle. The other is as though everything is a miracle."

I tried to convey this to my sister as we sat there, half on the grass, bitten by mosquitoes, half on the quilt, with the last of the longest day of the year passing over us like a warm presence.

The door was hers to open.

8

As it grew dark, Zack and crew had gone off to play with their sticks and sheets, but when Pola called after him, there was no answer.

"He's probably running around the woods," I said.

"He'd answer," she said. She glanced at me with a brief look of panic.

"Don't worry," I said. "He's around."

Pola and Bruno and Cary went off to the woods to round up the kids, and I started walking up to the roadside, carrying the now-trash-filled cooler with me.

The way the darkness comes in summer on the island is like a tinge of blackness shimmering at the edge of the tree-lined sky.

The smells of summer were at their height: honeysuckle and lavender and lilac.

"Zack!" I called, and heard the name echoed down below in the woods, as the others called to him. "Mike! Jenny!"

And then I saw that the door to the smokehouse was open slightly, and I felt as if my heart were about to stop.

I went over to it, opening the door wide.

Stepped inside.

They stood in a ring at its center.

Around their eyes, blindfolds—torn from the sheet that Jenny had picked up at the duck pond.

Zack had just finished reciting the nursery rhyme—I heard the last line of it.

Here comes a chopper to chop off your head.

I stared at them in silence. I looked around at the stone walls and out into the night as darkness swung low around the slopes and trees beyond the property.

Then back at these children.

I watched Zack. This little boy whose world had been disrupted: his mother and father divorced, a new man in the house, the memories of that awful night in December still no doubt immense in his mind.

A world that he didn't choose himself.

Who had taught him?

The Dark Game was an addiction. It wasn't something that could be stopped just by wanting it to be stopped.

Knowing it was there, it got in your blood.

Children were going to play it.

They had begun playing it before dark, and now, with full night around us, it would take them over. They must have heard about it. Zack would know about it, just from listening in on conversations. Children did that sometimes, and adults never really thought they were listening so carefully.

Zack looked the way I must've looked at his age. Blindfold on, saying what seemed like unintelligible words.

For the barest second, I thought that perhaps this was wholly innocent. That it was my own experience, and my own perception that colored my intense negative reaction to watching children play the Dark Game. That we three—Bruno, Brooke, and I—and perhaps even our father—had twisted it with the terrible trauma we'd gone through together. With watching our mother be brutally tortured and murdered. With whatever my father had experienced in those POW camps when he'd been in his twenties.

It was us. No one else. Not other children. Surely.

"Zack?" I finally said, still reeling inside from the initial shock. "Zack?" I took a step forward, and then another.

The hairs on the back of my neck stood up. My throat went dry.

I felt a crackle of static electricity in the air.

When I reached him, I crouched down and put my hand on his shoulder. The other children's breathing seemed labored and heavy.

As gently as I could, I tried to wake him.

To bring him out of the game.

But in his mind, he'd already gone elsewhere.